# WATCHING YOU FALL

## ALSO BY DREDA SAY MITCHELL & RYAN CARTER

*Gone*

*Girl, Missing*

*Believe Me*

*Say Her Name*

*Trap Door*

*Spare Room*

*One False Move* (Quick Reads)

*Death Trap*

*Snatched* (Kindle Single)

*Vendetta*

*Killer Tune*

### The Gangland Girls Trilogy

*Geezer Girls*

*Gangster Girl*

*Hit Girls*

## Flesh and Blood series

*Blood Sister*

*Blood Mother*

*Blood Daughter*

*Blood Secrets*

## Big Mo Suspense Series

*Dirty Tricks*

*Fight Dirty*

# WATCHING YOU FALL

DREDA SAY MITCHELL & RYAN CARTER

This is a work of fiction. Names, characters, organizations, places, events, and incidents are either products of the author's imagination or are used fictitiously. Any resemblance to actual persons, living or dead, or actual events is purely coincidental.



Published by Thomas & Mercer, Seattle

www.apub.com



EU Product Safety Contact:
Amazon Media EU S.à r.l.
38, avenue John F. Kennedy, L-1855 Luxembourg
amazonpublishing-gpsr@amazon.com

ISBN-13: 9781662535734
eISBN: 9781662535741

Cover design by Emma Rogers
Cover image:© Josep Curto / Shutterstock; © Douglas Sacha / Getty Images

Printed in the United States of America

# WATCHING YOU FALL

# Prologue

The house is in complete darkness apart from the fire burning in the grate in our living room. The flames throw just enough light to show the dead body lying on the sofa. There's someone else here too, the one who knows why all this happened. The destruction of my home, my family and my soul. He knows why but he doesn't want to tell me. I already know the what, the where, the when, and everything else except the why. And if it costs me my life, I'm going to find out what lies behind the devastation of everything and everyone I love.

And I'm willing to do whatever it takes.

# Chapter 1

My dining room table is groaning under the weight of presents and cards. It took two trips to bring them all home. There are posh chocolates, household gifts and flowers, lots and lots of flowers. There's a rare orchid in a pot, and you catch the scent of it as you walk by. I pick up one of the cards. It's from a brother and sister and says that I'm the best. Another is from a lawyer couple, and they offer their deepest gratitude for all I've done for their child. Some of the cards are handmade by the children and a lot of time and care has gone into them. Others are intricate 3D cards that come from grateful parents. There's even a card from the head of the school where I serve as her deputy.

'Many thanks for all the work you've done this year, Josie, you've been a breath of fresh air.'

Many teachers get gifts from parents and children at the end of term but I'm more than fortunate in that respect. Not all the parents at my school come from wealthy backgrounds but many do. It's highly likely that they're competing with one another in their generosity, or perhaps they think I'll remember them when I'm marking their children's tests. I pick up another card, this one from Albert, one of our special needs students. He's drawn a picture on the front of the two of us smiling. Inside he's written a simple message. 'Thanks Miss Thomas! You're so kind!'

Deep in my belly, I feel an urgent need to tear the card up and throw it in the bin.

My husband Trevor drifts past but stops to stare at the table. He puts one hand on my waist and picks up a box of Belgian chocolates with the other and examines it. He looks at the other gifts and sighs. 'That's the diet gone out of the window then.' He reads Albert's card and is impressed. 'They really love you at that school, don't they? I wish my colleagues and customers loved me.'

'Albert's not a customer, he's a student.'

Trevor shrugs. 'In a way he is though.'

He looks into my face with sympathy. 'Are you all right?'

'Of course.'

He doesn't believe me but knows to leave it at that.

Out in the back garden, my own children are playing bat and ball in the shade of the trees. The last of the day's sunshine is coming through the leaves and they are dappled in golden light as they run around. The garden itself has nearly as many flowers as our dining room table. Trevor's the gardener and treats his various blooms as a firework display with all the different colours rising and falling through the summer. The warm breeze carries their scent to whichever corner of the garden you sit in. When the children see me slip on to a bench to watch them play, they run up. My son is ten and will be coming up to my school next year. His sister is eight and she'll join him a couple of years after that. We called our daughter Tova after a friend of mine. I wanted to call her Megan after my sister but Trevor flatly refused. Our son, Rodney, is named after my father.

Tova's not happy. 'Are you coming to play now?'

I can't play today. 'Not this evening, darling.' I perform a yawn. 'Very tired, but my holidays start now and we can play in the garden all summer long.'

Tova wants to make a fight of it but her brother takes her by the arm. 'Are you deaf? Mum says she's tired.'

He pulls her back down the garden. Tova gives me an accusing look which suggests I'm faking tiredness while my boy gives me a warm smile which suggests it doesn't matter whether I'm faking it or not. It's a blessed relief watching my children play until the light finally fades and Trevor appears to put them to bed. Tova prefers her father to read her a bedtime story because he gets the characters' voices right, apparently, and I don't. Rodney is past the story-reading age.

It's nearly dark when Trevor returns. He puts a stiff drink on the table in front of me, sits down on the bench and takes my hand. His face is in shadow but his grip is firm and his resolve is clear. 'It's Megan, isn't it?' When I don't reply, he goes on. 'Seriously, Josie, you can't let this eat away at you. You've got to move on. Go and see someone and talk about it if you have to, but whatever you do, don't weaken. It'll start all over again, you know that.'

'I'm fine.'

He's not to be fobbed off. 'Fine? I've just had Tova on my case, demanding to know what's the matter with her mother, why she looks so miserable and why she doesn't want to play. And you say you're fine?'

It's now seven days since I broke off all contact with my sister. I did it by text. It occurred to me afterwards that it was cowardly, but Trevor was right when he said that if I did it in person, Megan would use her box of tricks to make me change my mind. And she's got a big box of tricks. The text explained that while it was right for me to cut all my links with her, if she genuinely decided she wanted to turn her life around, genuinely wanted to change, naturally I'd be there to support her. But it had to be a genuine decision this time, not like the 'genuine' decisions she'd taken in the past. I also made it perfectly clear that I was ready and eager to carry on supporting her son and perhaps she'd contact me so we could organise that.

That was seven days ago. I've heard nothing from Megan since, no attempt to change my mind, no accusations of betrayal or any of the other forms of emotional blackmail she uses and no obviously fake attempts to persuade me things will be different this time. Worst of all, nothing about my continuing support for her boy, Sunny.

I pull my phone out of my pocket and wave it at my husband but my voice is hesitant. 'She could have got back to me, even just to say OK, but I've heard nothing.'

He's in despair. 'Of course she hasn't got back to you. She knows exactly how to push your buttons. She's waiting for you to break and try again. She's probably getting drunk at her flat with her druggy friends and they're all laughing at you.'

I know this is true but I resent hearing it.

I don't know why my sister stealing money from me was the final straw. It wasn't a large sum and she's done much worse than that to me over the years. Perhaps it was because she couldn't even be bothered to tell decent lies about it. Megan was once a talented liar. I don't mind being lied to, you're lied to all the time in life. But I do expect people telling me lies to put some effort in. Instead, she claimed that it wasn't her who took the money from my purse, it was Tova. Megan claimed she saw my daughter doing it but didn't want to say anything to avoid embarrassment.

It's been a long time coming but that was the end for me.

Trevor squeezes my hand. 'Please don't get in touch with her. I hate watching Megan exploiting and abusing you. Maybe now she hasn't got you to bail her out, she'll be forced to sort her life out.'

I nod in agreement but think my eyes say no. Perhaps in the darkness he won't notice.

Trevor goes back into the house, leaving me alone with my thoughts, but it seems only a few minutes later, he comes out into the garden again with his jacket on and jangling his car keys. 'I'm really sorry about this, Josie, but I've just had a call from work. Some systems have gone down and the helpline's already running hot. The kids on our help desk are being sworn at and I have to go and sort it out. I'll be back as soon as possible.'

I'm not actually that sorry he's being forced to go to the office. Some time on my own will help, and having my husband around reminding me of the truth about Megan on a regular basis doesn't. After watching him drive off at speed, I try and settle. The TV isn't working for me and neither is music. I can't go into the kitchen to make myself a drink because it means I'll see all those gifts in the dining room telling me what a great person I am and I don't feel like a great person tonight. Eventually, I slump into an armchair staring at the walls for an hour, occasionally checking my phone to see if Megan has texted. Of course she hasn't. Trevor is right, she's playing me again, waiting for me to crack.

Her plan is working. My fingers hover over her number. Perhaps if she agreed to apologise for pilfering money from me? Perhaps that would be something to work with?

Outside, I hear a car pulling up, flashing red lights flickering, strobing into the room. When I look through the window, I see a police car and two cops getting out of their car. Even before they come to our gate and walk up our path, I know who they're looking for and why they're here.

It's Megan. Something terrible has happened to her. And it's all my fault.

# Chapter 2

It is about Megan. Something terrible *has* happened to her. And it is all my fault.

I'm all she has left in the world. Our parents are dead and the only other support she has is drug dealers, drunks, lowlifes and a long line of deadbeat, vile and abusive 'boyfriends'. What was I thinking of, cutting her off like that, leaving my little sister alone in the world?

The policemen's story is a jumble until I realise that it's actually me who's a jumble. They ask if I'm the sister of Megan Campbell. Her next of kin. I think at once that she's dead, found on the street, probably murdered. They tell me she's not dead but she is dangerously ill in hospital and I need to go at once. In a daze, I wake the children and tell them I have to go out but that Alice from next door is coming over to look after them. They're upset but Alice is brilliant, all our neighbours are. I rush out into the night, only just remembering to call Trevor and tell him to leave work at once and come to the hospital.

The police fly me through the night on streets that are oddly empty until I look at my watch and realise it's after midnight. At the hospital, I'm ushered in by the police but they don't hang around. I'm directed to a side room where my sister lies unconscious, hooked up to drips and monitors. She looks oddly peaceful and her face has recovered some of its former beauty. She was always the pretty girl. A nurse is overseeing things and I explain who I am.

'What's happened?'

The nurse makes some adjustments to the apparatus. 'It looks like a drug overdose. We're doing everything we can to make your sister comfortable.' To me it looks like the heart monitor Megan is attached to is huffing and puffing and struggling to register a beat.

'Is she going to be all right?'

The nurse knows but doesn't want to say. 'You'll need to speak to the doctor. He'll be along in a minute or two.'

My sister's hands are cold as if she's already dead. In my handbag are some gloves and I try to fit them on her hands to warm them up. The nurse is baffled but says nothing and lets me do it. She's obviously given up on my sister. When the doctor arrives, it appears he has too. He takes me outside the room and down to an office where he explains in a flat voice, 'It looks like your sister has suffered an overdose, heroin probably. We're doing everything we can.'

'She'll be OK though, won't she?'

He clears his throat. 'We're doing our best but you should probably prepare yourself for the worst. Megan's body is badly weakened by years of substance abuse. She's been a patient here before on a number of occasions. We also understand from the police that there are some highly toxic narcotics on the streets at the moment. We've had a number of cases in the past few months sadly.'

Back in Megan's room, a shifty man has appeared. He's standing well back from her bedside, by the door as if ready to make a quick escape. When the police brought me in, he was loitering around the corridors looking furtive but quickly disappeared. Now the police are gone, he's reappeared. He whispers, 'You must be Josie? Megan's sister?'

'That's right. Who are you?'

He smiles slightly. 'I'm Dixie, Megan's boyfriend.' He hastily corrects himself. 'Well, not really her boyfriend, just more of a friend, in a way.' He corrects himself again. 'Although even that is probably over-egging it a bit.' He gestures at my sister's bed. 'Is she going to be all right?'

'She's had an overdose and the doctor thinks probably not.'

Dixie tries to look sad and to think of something to say. Finally, he manages something. 'It was bound to happen, I suppose.'

I don't want to make a scene by my sister's bedside so my voice is an angry whisper. 'Is that all you've got to say? That it was bound to happen? And you're supposed to be her boyfriend?'

He's upset. 'What do you want me to say? That I'm very sorry? Of course I'm very sorry. But, I mean, come on, the amount of gear she did. It'd kill an elephant.'

Time after time in my life, the same question has come up. How did my beautiful and smart sister ever end up with men like this?

'Were you there when it happened?'

He's alarmed. 'No, why would I be there?'

'How did you know she was in hospital then?'

He cobbles together a story in a hurry. Guys like Dixie know how to do that. 'We had a row this morning. I walked out and left her to simmer down. I came back this evening to kiss and make up and found an ambulance outside the block and the law nosing around. A neighbour told me she was in hospital.' He seems to take the look on my face as an accusation and snaps, 'I'm here now, aren't I?' When he doesn't get an answer, he leans in. 'Listen, are the cops still around?'

'I don't know. Does it matter?'

He rolls his eyes. 'You know what they're like, always looking for someone to blame. They might think I sold her the stuff.'

'Did you?'

When he hears footsteps in the corridor outside, he panics. 'Listen, I'm going to get a coffee. Do you want anything?'

'No.'

Dixie slips quickly out of the room and it's clear he won't be coming back.

But the footsteps belong to Trevor, not the police. He hurries into the room, breathless and in shock. He's divided between trying to understand what I'm saying to him, trying to support me and then inspecting the drips and monitors as if the staff might have missed something that he can put right. Eventually he calms down and the two of us stand holding hands together and watch my sister slowly slipping away.

It occurs to me suddenly that someone is missing. It's my nephew. 'Where's Sunny?'

Trevor knows the answer. 'He's at his grandmother's. The police have gone to fetch him.'

'What's he doing there?'

'The neighbours told the police that when things get too heavy at Megan's place, Sunny takes himself off to his granny's. That happened on a regular basis apparently and you can imagine why.'

If my sister wasn't dying, I'd be upset to hear that Sunny went to his grandmother's for refuge rather than coming to me. I've never met the grandmother. Megan had Sunny with the grandmother's son Kit, yet another of my sister's bad boy lovers and a particularly nasty example of the genre. He's still around and the only things we've got in common are mutual hatred and an understanding that I'm determined to keep Kit as far away from my nephew as possible.

In the distance, from down the corridor, there's the sound of a hacking cough and shuffling feet. When I look out of the door, it's to see an old woman with a walking stick in one hand and Sunny's hand in the other, the pair of them escorted by a nurse. Sunny is thirteen, old enough to know what death means but not old enough to have experienced it at close quarters. He gets a big hug from me and I begin to try and explain what's happened to his mother and what he will see in the room. The grandmother cuts me short with her hacking cough. 'He knows what's going on, he's not a kid. His mum's drugged herself up again and she's taken it too far this time. And let's face it, everyone's surprised the silly bitch has lasted this long.'

I'm beyond disgusted. 'I don't think that's an appropriate way to talk in front of her child.'

The grandmother sneers. 'You're the teacher, aren't you? Yeah, you sound like one. Now where is she?'

Sunny is unmoved by what's being said. He looks from me to this bitter old woman and back again without any expression. He says nothing before they shuffle past me into the room. In the distance, another visitor is walking casually down the corridor as if he were going to buy a newspaper. Kit is over six foot tall and likes to use his height and physique to frighten people. It doesn't work on me though. I might be a teacher now but I'm from the block like he is and I know how to deal with men like him. If only my sister had known how to do the same.

'Hello, Josie, condolences on your loss.'

He looms over me, hoping I'll draw back slightly but he's disappointed. 'She's not gone yet.'

'Yeah, whatever. Is my son here?'

He turns to go through the door but then hesitates. 'Oh yeah, and there is one thing I'd like to get straight from the gate. Whatever happens, I'm taking my son home with me tonight. Those little games you played with your sister to stop me getting custody of my son? That's all over now that she's all over. So don't play any of your little tricks, trying to persuade your friends in social services to keep me away from Sunny. You don't think I know who wrote all those tear-jerking statements she used to peddle to social workers and who carefully trashed my reputation with the authorities? Who made out I wasn't a fit father for my own son? You should be ashamed of yourself, you homewrecker.'

He walks into the room, leaving the door wide open so I can see everyone gathered around the death bed. Kit throws a brief look of contempt my sister's way before ruffling Sunny's hair as if he were a pet dog and whispering, 'Hello, son.'

I don't blame Kit for his outburst. He's right, it was me who helped Megan retain custody of Sunny and keep Kit out of his life.

And if we lose Megan, it's me who's going to do it again.

When I walk back into the room, it's to find that Megan is dead.

# Chapter 3

For the last half an hour, Trevor, Kit, Sunny, the grandmother – Rose – and myself have been waiting in the corridor while a crash team tries to bring my sister back from the dead. No one says a word. Kit holds on to Sunny as if his son were a prize he's won at a funfair. Rose is on Sunny's other side keeping a tight grip on her grandson's arm. Trevor holds my hand.

The door to Megan's room opens and a nurse emerges and walks away. Through the open door, I can hear a doctor. 'Are we all agreed then?'

It's over. The doctor comes out and we gather round. 'I'm terribly sorry but we were unable to save Megan. My deepest condolences.'

No one speaks and no one cries. Even me. All I can think about is the text I sent to Megan a week ago, casting her adrift. All the words I wrote are blasted into my heart. Now she's dead and it's too late to take them back. No one seems quite sure what to do next. I loosen my hand from my husband's and whisper, 'I'm going to say goodbye to my sister.'

'Do you need me?'

'No, but thank you.'

Her room is silent. Everything's been disconnected and the monitors are quiet. Megan is more at peace now than at any time since we were children. I pull up a chair and sit down by the bed and take her lifeless hand in mine. The gloves I pulled over her fingers have been removed. I'm surprised now that the initial shock is over that I don't feel more upset. But it's because the 'boyfriend' was right. It was bound to happen. She knew it and I knew it. You can't play the games she did forever and not expect to make a mistake. She had her faults but she wasn't stupid. She knew where her lifestyle would take her in the end. Perhaps she even wanted it. Instead of being upset I'm angry with her, angry about a lot of things but right now it's because she didn't get back to me when I blew her off. It's difficult keeping my temper. 'Why didn't you get in touch with me? Why? You know I didn't mean what I wrote. You've always got back when this has happened before, why not this time? We could have avoided all this if only you'd reached out. You know I would have folded. Now you're gone. Why? Why?'

Her face is impassively beautiful. The tears begin welling up now. 'You can't blame me for this, Megan. I know you want to blame me for a lot of things but you can't blame me for this.'

She does blame me. We both know it.

In my handbag is a comb. I take it out and use it to pull her hair straight and arrange it and then I use a tissue to fix her makeup. Outside is her son with his violent and criminal father and his batty grandmother. Once, for no particular reason, my sister made me promise that if anything happened to her I would look after Sunny. I snatch at this. 'Don't worry about Sunny, I'll take care of that. We might not have been able to save you but we can save him. He's young enough to be pulled from the wreckage and I know all about children. Is that a deal?'

Megan doesn't answer.

I'm angry. 'Well, is it?'

In the corridor, voices are being raised. I'm glad of it, I'm in the mood for a fight.

Outside, an argument is going on between Kit and Rose about who's taking Sunny home which Trevor is half-heartedly trying to stop. Rose is laying into her son on the one hand and appealing for support from Sunny on the other. The poor kid just looks embarrassed.

'Call yourself a father? You were in prison when he was born and in prison again when he started school. I'm not having my grandson going home to stay with a jailbird.' She turns to Sunny. 'Isn't that right, boy? You don't want to fetch up with a jailbird?'

Sunny doesn't know.

Kit shoves his mother. 'Why don't you mind your own business you mad old woman. I'm his father and a son should be with his father. Why don't you go home, smoke your cigarettes and watch your TV? You can't even look after yourself, never mind my kid.'

Although Rose is a little unsteady with her walking stick, she shoves Kit back. 'Raising your hand to your own mother? That's just about your level, slapping old women. What a dog you are. Are you going to kick your kid around as well?'

This custody battle is cut short by me. 'Neither of you are taking Sunny home. We are.'

I look to Trevor for support but he doesn't seem too sure about my decision. I look to Sunny but he doesn't seem too sure either. But it doesn't matter, we are taking Sunny home. I've just promised my sister.

Kit bursts out laughing. 'I thought as much, you want to kidnap my kid. I've got news for you, sweetheart. Your sister is dead and your day is done. Just keep your nose out of my family's business.'

'It is my family's business. We're taking Sunny home tonight and a decision will be taken on Sunny's future in the long run by social services. Although let me give you a steer on that. With your track record and the injunctions taken out against you already, your chances of getting custody are roughly the same as your chances of staying out of prison.'

At the mention of the words 'injunctions' and 'prison' he bridles slightly but he's still full of bluster. 'We'll see about that.'

'Yes, we will.'

He says no more but backs off slightly from Sunny. It only remains to get Sunny out of the tight grip of his grandmother. She's not giving way. 'Leave my grandson alone. If you want to fight about it, fight about it. I can match you punch for punch, my love.'

An angry nurse comes on to the corridor to remind us that this is a hospital and if we want to argue, can we take it off the premises.

Trevor takes this opportunity to usher me to one side and whisper, 'Listen, Josie, perhaps it would be better if Sunny stayed with his grandmother tonight. He's used to going over there and he'll be in shock at the moment. It might be better for him to be in familiar surroundings.'

This is true, although my husband's lack of support is disappointing. He should be backing me up. But it's still true. 'OK. As long as it's clearly understood that Sunny is coming to live with us now my sister has passed.'

Trevor doesn't look convinced. 'That's a decision that will have to be made by others. Let's see how things play out.'

I'm still angry with everyone, including myself, but this needs to be nipped in the bud. 'I'll tell you exactly how it's going to play out. My nephew is coming to live with us and we're going to give him the best possible start in life.'

'If that's what you want.'

The meeting breaks up. Kit leaves on his own. Rose and Sunny refuse our offer of a lift and get a cab from outside the hospital. Trevor is in a hurry to get home and see the children but I can't do that at the moment. I have to go to Megan's flat first, although I'm not sure why. Perhaps I'm too wired by losing my sister and the guilt and I need something to do. Reluctantly, Trevor agrees to drop me off and says he'll take care of the children. As we emerge into the night, there's a tall figure lurking in the shadows off to one side. As we pass, he calls my name. It's Kit. He asks to speak to me alone and after I tell Trevor it's OK, we talk.

'What do you want?'

He looks even more menacing in the shadows but his voice is soft. 'Listen, Josie, I don't want to fall out with you. I know you're a good person and you just want what's best for Sunny. If I'm being honest, you and your sister were probably right to keep me away from my kid. I wasn't in a good place back in the day. But I've sorted myself out now. I've got a job, a place to live, and a new partner. She's pregnant and I'm ready to take Sunny on. So please, don't get in my way.'

He sounds like Megan. She had the 'I'm really going to change this time' shtick down to a fine art.

'It's not up to us.'

Kit is almost pleading. 'Social services will see things my way if you support me.'

'You must be joking.'

He sighs heavily. 'What's the problem? You worried I won't let you see Sunny? Of course I want you to see Sunny. You're a teacher, you're educated, you can help him with his schoolwork. I want you to take him to places that I don't know about. I want you to help him with the things I can't.' His voice hardens. 'But I'm his father and you're not.'

He's almost as good at this as Megan was. 'You can make your case to the authorities.'

His voice softens again. 'Oh, I will, don't worry about that, but you need to understand something. I want my child at home with me. You're from the street and you know what men like me are like.' He raises his hand and points his finger at my face in the darkness. 'We'll stop at nothing when it comes to our children, absolutely nothing.' His voice turns violent. 'Do you understand? Absolutely nothing!'

# Chapter 4

After trying to persuade me one more time to come home with him, Trevor drops me off at Megan's block. He offers to come and pick me up but I say I'd prefer to get a taxi while he stays with the children.

These flats are in a 1960s building that's slated for demolition as part of a redevelopment. Not everyone locally is happy about that. On a wall by the block someone has spray-painted 'Homes for the poor! War on the rich!' in gold. Others are happy about it. It's widely rumoured locally that these homes are a dumping ground for 'problem families' and they want them out. There's no sign of any police who might be investigating Megan's death. I know the code for the entry system from all my previous visits but it doesn't matter. The door is propped open anyway by a brick. The lift doesn't work because of course it doesn't. I walk the flight of stairs to the third floor to find Megan's front door open and realise there's someone in there.

With great care, I creep inside while keeping an eye on the door in case I need a quick escape. Inside a man is sitting on a sofa with various items of drug paraphernalia on a table in front of him. He picks up his phone and begins to speak into it before realising he's being watched. He gets to his feet and hurries over and bars the front door to prevent my getaway.

'Get out of my way or I'll call the police.'

He starts laughing. 'I am the police, madam. Perhaps you can tell me what your connection with this flat is?'

'My sister lives here. Or rather she did.' I have to get used to referring to my sister in the past tense. 'My name is Josie Thomas.'

He relaxes. 'OK, that's good, I thought you might be a friend of the tenant come here to see what they could pilfer in the way of drugs after what happened. I'm Detective Constable Summers. I'm just here collecting evidence and to seal the flat up. My condolences for your loss. You must be very upset. Can I make you a cup of tea or something?'

'That's very kind.'

Summers goes off to the kitchen. I sit on a chair and look at the table. On it is a hubble-bubble with water and charred matter that's been smoked. Various plastic evidence bags contain pills. There are phones, a number of them, in other bags. Syringes and needles waiting to be labelled and bagged up. Cigarette papers and silver foil littered around. It's a veritable Aladdin's cave of narcotics.

And why did Megan need those phones?

Summers is clattering around in the kitchen but returns empty handed. 'Tea's off unfortunately. There isn't any tea and there isn't any coffee. There's milk but it looks like it's been in the fridge for a few weeks. Do you want a proper drink? There's plenty of that.'

I'm too busy staring at the table to answer. Whenever I gave Megan money, Trevor would always ask the same question. 'What do you think your sister does with the money you give her? Buy Sunny new shoes? Or buy new ways to see the fifth dimension?' It was obviously the fifth dimension. Of course I knew she was a heavy user, but whenever I came here there were never any drugs lying around. Megan had a rule about that. The flat was always tidy too and there was always tea and coffee. Perhaps she needed to keep up the pretence when she was taking money from me. Perhaps after

I pulled the plug on her the previous week she didn't feel the need to do that any more.

Summers sits down next to me and purses his lips. 'Sorry you have to see all this. We'll clear it all up when we're done. We just need it as evidence.'

'I understand.'

'Not against your sister obviously. We just need to try and find out where she bought the stuff and build a case. Megan was an old friend of ours so to speak, for various reasons, but only as a user and we're not really interested in users. It's dealers and the importation end of the market we're after. Although she probably sold any surplus to her friends, that's what usually happens.'

It feels like asking an unnecessary question faced with what's on the table but my anger towards Megan is ebbing away, leaving me wrung out and confused. 'The hospital said she took an overdose.'

Summers sighs and picks up one of the bags with powder in. 'That's right, it was probably this. The paramedics and my colleagues found the syringe and needle. We'll have to run tests of course but it's par for the course at the moment. Was she a regular user of heroin?'

'Not to my knowledge.'

He shrugs. 'It's amazing what you don't know about people close to you though, isn't it? Listen, I'm nearly finished here, where do you live? Do you want me to run you home? You look like you're at the end of your tether if I'm being honest.' When he gets no answer, he takes an address book out of one of his plastic bags and thumbs through it and finds my address in there under 'Sis'. 'I'll run you home, give me five minutes.'

He carries on with his work, scribbling, voice messaging and bagging up. In what feels like a drug-induced trance of my own, I get up and begin to wander around the flat as if I'm looking for something but don't know what. Sunny's room looks like the cell of a desert hermit. It has none of the things you'd expect to find in a teenager's bedroom. He has a bed pushed up against a wall, some empty shelves, a table with nothing on it, a chair and bare walls. His clothes are kept in black bags in one corner of the room. In an alcove is an empty fish tank. All that will change when he comes to stay with us.

Detective Constable Summers comes to fetch me and take me home. He tries various things to cheer me up on the journey. He's doing it all wrong because I don't need cheering up but he means well. He's using an unmarked police car but enjoys showing off the lights and sirens hidden on it. He shares some amusing stories about his adventures in the drugs squad. At least, presumably they're amusing, I'm not really listening. He's incredibly impressed when he discovers that I'm a deputy head and which school I'm at.

'Wow, that's the school everyone wants to get their kids into. My cousin's youngster goes there'.

He drops me off at my house and gives me his card and tells me that if I have any questions don't hesitate to ring him. For safety's sake, he waits for me to get to my front door before driving off but as I'm walking on the pathway, something occurs to me through my emotional fog. I retrace my steps to the car and tap on his window.

'I'm sorry, I'm confused. In the flat, did you say that my sister injected herself with heroin?'

He's baffled. 'We can't say for certain it's heroin yet but she was certainly injecting. The paramedics found the needle mark where she put it into her thigh.'

'That's impossible.'

He's slightly embarrassed for me. 'No, we're pretty sure about that.'

My poor sister. 'No, you're not, you're wrong. She didn't.'

Summers draws breath and drawls 'Okaayyy, look it's very late and you're obviously very upset and everyone can understand that.

I'll be back on duty this afternoon, why don't you come into my office and we can try and address any concerns you might have?'

I've come back to life now that I'm becoming angry again. 'There's no way she injected herself. That didn't happen. And my only concern now is that you find out who killed her.'

# Chapter 5

'Is this really the right time to be doing this?'

Trevor isn't happy with me being on the phone arranging things this morning while I'm totally focused. 'Doing what?'

'Ringing up social services, trying to organise meetings, speaking to your old friends in child protection and all the rest of it? Your sister passed away in the small hours and you spent half the night at Megan's flat chatting to a cop for reasons that still aren't clear. You're in shock and suffering from grief. Shouldn't you be taking some time with that? And letting me help you with it?'

I'm distracted with my phone call. 'No problem, I'll hold for her . . . This is quite urgent. Please, please ask her to call me back asap. Tell her it's Josie Thomas, she knows me, thank you.'

That's the end of my phone calls for now. I reach for my bag. 'Taking time with what?' I ask Trevor.

He sighs meaningfully. 'Processing your sister's death?'

'I've got things to do. We need to get the relevant people to agree to Sunny coming to live with us with a view to making it permanent. And we need to do it quickly before Grandma Rose and Kit can get their oar in.'

Trevor doesn't look convinced and sounds pained. 'OK, but shouldn't *we* be talking about this first?' He sees me shouldering my bag and pulling on some trainers. 'Where are you going now?'

'I'm going to Rose's to check on Sunny and then to the police to have another word with them.'

He doesn't understand. 'The police? You spoke to them last night. What are you going back for?'

My reply is in an undertone. There are good reasons why I don't want to share things with him at the moment. 'Just to make sure they do their job properly. That there's nothing suspicious about my sister's death.'

He's dumbfounded. 'Suspicious? What on earth are you talking about? It must be the least suspicious death ever in the history of unsuspicious deaths. No one would want to be trapped in a lift with Rose, Kit or that Dixie guy but they're right about one thing. The only suspicious thing about Megan's death is that it didn't happen sooner.'

'I just want the investigation done properly.'

He says nothing more before I leave.

I don't get much of a greeting at the grandmother's flat. Rose opens the front door a fraction at my knock and anyone would think from her manner that I'm a cop with a search warrant or some sort of bailiff.

'What do you want?'

As a deputy head, I'm used to occasionally dealing with difficult parents and guardians. 'I want to speak to Sunny and see how he's managing.'

The door closes an inch or so. 'He's fine.'

'I'm sure, but I'd like to see for myself.'

Rose calls out. 'Sunny! It's your auntie Josie. Are you all right?' She doesn't wait for an answer before telling me. 'There you are, he's fine. Now, go away and mind your own business.'

She tries to close the door but I'm too quick for her, shoving my trainer into the crack. She admits defeat and opens up but snarls at me, 'I know what your game is, missy. Now your smack-head sister is dead, you want to grab the boy up and take him home with you. In the same way you and her kept him away from his father. Well, you're not getting away with it. He's perfectly happy here. He likes it in my flat and he's company for me.'

'Sunny's future will be for the relevant authorities to decide and if you want company, why don't you get a cat?'

She sneers. 'Relevant authorities . . . Hark at you, Lady Muck.'

Rose's home is small and poky and the room Sunny uses when he flees here isn't hard to find. Although room is probably over-egging it a little, it's more of a broom cupboard. Rammed up against one wall is a makeshift camp bed with a sleeping bag. Rammed up against another wall is a makeshift desk with a chair under it. My nephew himself is sat on the chair, writing on the top sheet of a sheaf of papers. He turns and looks up briefly when I come in but doesn't acknowledge me. Instead, he carries on writing. I'm not quite sure what to say. I've dealt with traumatised children before as part of my work, but not one from my own family, not my own sister's child. There's no chair for me to sit on so I crouch down beside him and put my arm around his shoulder.

'I'm terribly sorry about what happened to your mum.'

He carries on writing, only shrugging slightly. His hand is gripped tightly around his pen. His voice is flat. 'It's OK.'

'Are you coping all right?'

He carries on writing. 'Yeah.'

'I just want you to know that in the days to come, whatever happens, me, your uncle Trevor, Tova and Rodney are here to help and support you in any way you want or need.'

He's still writing and seems mildly irritated at my interrupting him. 'That's good.'

I ask him what he's writing, partly to keep this stilted convo going but also out of genuine curiosity. He stops writing and puts his pen down as if he's finally given up hope that if he answers my questions I'll go away. 'It's just a story.'

I lift myself up slightly to see the title, which is underlined. The story is called 'The Cub'.

'Do you like writing stories?'

'Yeah.'

'Do you not write your stories on your computer?'

He picks up his pen again. 'I had a computer but Mum sold it to buy drugs. I had a phone as well but she sold that too.'

There's a stab of regret in my guts. I always defended my sister. I always insisted on supporting her through thick and thin, whatever happened. I always forgave her when she did me wrong, right up to the previous week when I cut my links with her. I fought for her right to keep custody of her son, which she might not have been able to do otherwise. Trevor, who despised Megan, always maintained that too much forgiveness, support and love can boomerang on you. She was my sister though and it was my duty to be emotionally generous with her. But on hearing that she sold her son's belongings to fund her drug habit, I can see why Sunny might feel slightly differently. Why her death might not be having the impact on him that I would have expected. I thought it might be shock and it probably is. It could be other things as well though. And it was me who bought Sunny the computer and phone as Christmas and birthday presents.

'It doesn't matter. We'll buy you another computer.'

He starts writing again. 'That's OK, I like pen and paper anyway.'

Looking around the room, I notice something I hadn't seen before. Along the wall by the door is a pile of books stacked up, dozens of them. 'Are these yours, Sunny?'

He turns around. 'Yeah, I used to keep them at home but Mum sold them as well.'

Another stab of regret deep in my belly.

I get up and sift through Sunny's pile of books. There is the standard fare you might expect a boy in his early teens to read if you could get one to read any books in the first place. There are horror and ghost stories and tales of derring-do on the battlefield. But some of these books are of a reading age well beyond Sunny's. They're the kind of stories you might expect a student of literature to study. There is William Golding's *Lord of the Flies* and Graham Greene's *The Destructors*. When I pick up some of the books, I quickly discover where Sunny's been getting them from. They've clearly been stolen from libraries. It's probably not the way a deputy head would encourage a pupil to get reading matter but in view of how hard it is to get boys reading in the first place, perhaps it should be overlooked.

It's obvious that my nephew has read these books. In the margins, there are notes he's scribbled in his scratchy handwriting, in other places he's drawn in smiley faces or exclamation marks. On turning from his books, I can see him writing away at his makeshift desk. I know a clever boy when I see one, it's my job. He's a clever boy. I've done my best to encourage him with his schoolwork but the local school he attends is struggling and it was an unforgiving task. But that's all going to change now he's coming to live with us.

'We'll get you a bookcase for you to keep your books in a room of your own in our house.'

He stops writing for a moment as if brought up short. It occurs to me for the first time that perhaps he doesn't want to live in our house. I put my hand back on his shoulder. 'Would you like that? To come and live with us?'

He starts writing again. 'It's OK here, my gran can look after me.'

I'm disappointed. 'She can't look after you, Sunny, she's of an age, she can't even look after herself, and surely you don't want to live with your father?'

He doesn't answer, which leaves me wondering if he does, but that's not happening. 'I have to go now. We'll talk some more. In the meantime, if you need anything phone me.'

He carries on writing but he finally shows some emotion by laughing. 'I can't phone you, my mother sold my phone.'

# Chapter 6

For the first time since my sister passed I'm alone with my thoughts. No family, no Rose, no Sunny giving me blank answers, no calls to and from social services and no DC Summers totting up the evidence in my sister's flat. My only company is the passing by of cops, witnesses and suspects at the police station where Summers serves in the drugs squad. Summers passed me a message that he has to finish interviewing someone but will be happy to see me when it's over. I'm in a hurry for him to see me so that I can get home to my family. I don't like having nothing to distract me. I'm haunted by the break with Megan a week ago and her sudden death and what role I may have played in it. At times, I'm still looking at my phone expecting a text from Megan saying we need to meet up and sort out our split. The text that never came and now it never will.

I'm still looking at my phone when a grim-faced teenager walks by. He's followed a few seconds later by DC Summers. 'Sorry to have kept you.'

He escorts me into his office while I ask him whether the youngster that he just interviewed was guilty. Summers takes a seat. 'Not in so many words. He's the schoolfriend of a youngster who died in a drugs incident in a park last Saturday night. We're interviewing all his friends to see if they can throw any light on the incident. But none of them can. They either didn't really know him or weren't really there. It's the usual story.'

'How old was the victim?'

'Seventeen. It's an epidemic. Young kids destroying themselves or taking their own lives. It's always a difficult time for young people but it's particularly grim at the moment.'

I think of Tova, Rodney and Sunny. He catches my thoughts. 'Have you got children, Josie?'

'Yes, two or maybe three now.'

He sighs. 'My advice would be to keep them close and keep an eye on them. Now, you said last night that you weren't happy with how things appear to have played out in your sister's flat?'

He has to repeat the question because I'm not concentrating. I choke up. 'Yes, you or your colleagues have decided that my sister took a heroin overdose and used a syringe to inject herself with it.'

He nods. 'Yes, I'm afraid it looks like your sister injected a lethal dose of heroin into her bloodstream and even if she'd been fit and, well, her body wouldn't have coped. It looks like she misjudged the dose and we know there's some high-strength stuff on the streets at the moment so that won't have helped either. Obviously, we'll do our best to track down the guys who sold it to her and put them in prison.'

'I'm afraid that's impossible.'

This amiable cop is on my side and probably thinks I'm in shock or unable to accept that my sister used drugs. He pulls a sympathetic face. 'Listen, I know this is hard, but trust me, we've got considerable experience in this field and while we have to wait for the tests and a post mortem, we can be pretty confident that's what happened. We've got the drugs she used and we've got the syringe and needle. It was clasped in her left hand. We can identify the place on her leg where it went in. Have you got any reason to think that isn't what happened?'

'My sister was terrified of needles. It's been a thing in our family since she was about ten. It's impossible. If the drugs were injected, someone did it to her.'

In the past, I had a preprepared story as to why my sister had a phobia about needles. I didn't need one of course, a fear of needles is as natural as a fear of spiders or heights. I used to keep my story ready in case anyone suspected that Megan's phobia was my fault in some way. My story was that as a little girl she had a vaccination that went wrong which made her arm swell and caused her terrible pain. I'd told that story to myself so often, I almost ended up believing it. It was certainly preferable to the truth. In the end, the story was changed to one sentence that was easier to remember.

'My sister had an accident when she was young and that had something to do with her fear of needles.'

Summers doesn't want to hear an explanation or my story about needles. He's sympathetic but firm. 'Listen, Josie, you're obviously a respectable woman and so you probably don't understand how people get when they need a hit of something. Nothing will stop them, not even the prospect of death or serious injury, never mind a phobia about needles or blood. No doubt your sister was an intelligent and sensitive woman but you can be sure that she'd have put her hand in acid if that's what it took to stop that burning hunger that comes with drug addiction. Trust me, we see it often enough.'

The fact that this guy is so clearly trying to help isn't helping. I knew my sister and he didn't. She would rather have put her hand in acid than use a needle on herself. 'Have you tracked down the boyfriend yet?'

He shrugs. 'We didn't need to. He came in this morning with a solicitor and offered a statement. He was obviously worried we might think it was him who sold your sister the stuff. The boyfriend is an old friend of ours of course but he claims he hadn't seen your sister for a couple of months.'

'He would say that, wouldn't he? He told me he saw her yesterday and they argued. He said he returned to the flat around the time the ambulance was called.'

The cop gives me a wan smile. 'Of course, I didn't say we believed him. But there's some evidence to suggest he hasn't been around much. He's been in a rehab facility on the south coast. He's making good progress apparently, although guys like him are always making good progress shortly before they fall off the wagon again. Perhaps he was back in town and up to his old habits. What's the saying about a dog returning to his own vomit? Anyway, that's a line of inquiry we're pursuing. Perhaps he sold her the drugs, perhaps he didn't.'

'I'm not bothered if he sold her anything. I want to know if he was in the flat when my sister was injected and whether it was him who did it.'

Summers raises his hands. 'Woah, woah, Josie, we're jumping the gun here when there isn't even a gun. We've got no reason to suppose he was in the flat. We'll check his phone records and do all the relevant checks but we're confident he wasn't. The neighbours didn't hear any visitors or a disturbance in the flat that might have suggested an argument or dispute was taking place. Have you got any reason to think that someone might have wanted to harm your sister?'

I jump on this opportunity. 'Yes, I do. Her ex-partner and the father of her son for a start. He's been trying to gain custody of the boy for years. Have you considered he might have wanted to simplify the process by killing his mother? Has he got an alibi? What about his phone records?'

Summers, who had been on my side, now seems to be veering off. He's probably starting to think I'm impugning his professionalism. It doesn't matter to me whether his professionalism is impugned or not. He's not treating my sister's death with the seriousness it deserves. 'And this boyfriend character, Dixie? He comes in with a solicitor to deny any involvement. That's as good as a confession, isn't it?'

Summers sighs. 'It might be in a TV thriller but we're not in one of those. As for the ex-partner, we'll be speaking to him of course but murder with needles or indeed anything else isn't really his style. He's another old friend of ours. He's a violent thug but he's not the kind of person who'd dream up murdering his ex-partner to get custody of his child. He's too stupid for one thing.'

Summers looks at me with weary eyes. He's probably used to shocked relatives turned amateur detective. 'I understand how difficult this is, Josie, I really do. All we can do to help is collect all the available evidence and present it to a coroner who will come to a judgement. If you have any concerns about the process or evidence you want to raise with the court, they will always be willing to consider it. If what you're really concerned about is the possibility that the court might deliver a verdict of suicide, rest assured a coroner will never do that unless . . .'

He doesn't get the chance to finish his sentence. He's cut short by my howling in anguish. When my breath comes back, I get to my feet and choke up on the words. 'Who's talking about suicide?'

He realises he's said the wrong thing. 'No one is talking about it at the moment but it's always a possibility we have to consider.'

I'm suddenly convinced that he has some evidence that it was suicide but that he wants to avoid distressing me with it. I know it. 'Has she left a note?'

Summers gets up out of his chair and takes me by the arm. 'No, we haven't found a suicide note. Look, Josie, you've got my phone number and I've got yours. You've got my promise that we're going to do a thorough investigation. I'm going to keep you posted with any developments.'

He's lying. I know he is. He just wants me to stop making a scene. To his great credit, he doesn't leave me on the street in tears, he takes me to the canteen, fetches me a cup of tea and sits with me for fifteen minutes before escorting me out of the building. When we part, he says, 'Don't get into "if onlys" Josie, and don't accuse yourself of things. This isn't your fault.'

But it's too late for this advice. I'm already convinced my sister took her own life and I'm to blame. And all because of a silly argument we had when we were children.

# Chapter 7

Thirty years had passed since the accident, but for Josie it felt like yesterday. In that time, whether it was days, weeks, months or even years afterwards, the incident sometimes faded to the back of her mind. But it always returned, burning her heart. Anything could spark that memory off: a girl running in the road, a child crying, a news item about a tragedy or simply a bad dream. Then she was back there on that day, living it all over again. Nothing to do with that moment was ever in the past, it was always in the present.

What she remembered most about the accident that put Megan in hospital and led to a long series of medical procedures was how little Josie could recall of it in the years after it happened. Although that probably showed how little she wanted to remember rather than anything else. She couldn't even remember how old they were when it happened, what the weather was like at the time or what the two girls were arguing about. Megan remembered every detail of course but she preferred not to actually mention the accident, just to emotionally blackmail her sister whenever she felt the need. Josie thought she was eleven and Megan was nine or perhaps they were a year or two older or younger. They were walking home from school together when a slow-burning argument broke out that ended in disaster.

Josie tried to remind herself that it was an accident but that never worked in the long run. Sooner or later, how their argument ended that day, the words and actions from those moments would echo around her head and poison her life once again. And it was all over one stupid mistake.

'You're stupid.'

'No, you're stupid.'

'No, you are.'

They were walking home together from school, swapping biting remarks about whatever had sparked the argument.

'You're an idiot.'

'No, you're an idiot.'

As Josie remembered it, the two sisters rarely argued about anything because they had nothing in common. The only point of contact that could have provoked an argument was which of them their parents preferred. Megan maintained that it was her. In particular, their father was prouder of Megan than Josie because Megan was prettier. Neither of their parents ever gave any hint that was true, but deep down Josie feared that Megan was right. They did prefer her. Perhaps that was what the argument was about that day.

On and on they bickered. They were only five minutes from home when things spun out of control.

'You know something, Josie. I hate you. I don't want to walk home with you anymore. I'm going to walk home with my friends. You can walk home on your own.'

'You haven't got any friends, no one likes you.'

This was too much for Megan. She pushed Josie into a prickly hedge that lined the pavement. 'I've got loads of friends. It's you who hasn't got any friends. No one likes you because you're stupid. And you're ugly. That's why our mum and dad don't like you either. Because you're ugly.'

The jabs from the prickly hedge hurt. Her sister's words hurt even more, perhaps because Josie feared they were true. Megan was in front of her with her back to the road. Josie spread her palms and gave her sister the strongest shove in the chest she could. 'No, you're ugly.'

So much seemed to happen in so little time. It was all over in less than a few seconds. The violence of Josie's blow threw Megan backwards. She stumbled on the kerb before falling into the road and rolling halfway over, after which she tried to get up again. From nowhere a car appeared, its horn blasting. Tyres squealed and the car came to halt at an angle but before doing so, it hit Megan with enough force to knock her off her feet again and sent her flying through the air. In the split second between the car hitting Megan and her coming to rest in the road, Josie hoped she was dead. When that split second was over, Josie was sure her sister was indeed dead. She ran up and tried to pull her to her feet. 'Get up! Get up!'

A crowd quickly gathered and that too appeared to have come from nowhere. Josie couldn't hear a word anyone said to her. All she knew was that her sister was dead.

That she'd wanted her sister dead and that she was to blame.

# Chapter 8

'If I find out that you've done this deliberately, I'll never forgive you!' The anger is making my body shake, it's choking me. 'All the things you've done to me over the years, all the pilfering, lying, cheating and gaslighting, I'll live with that. But this? Is that what happened? Your final revenge? Killing yourself to make me drown in guilt for the rest of my life?'

It's a little irregular for grieving relatives to visit the body in a hospital mortuary. It was always my plan to come here and take care of business after seeing Summers, but now that cop has given me another reason to do so. He implied that my sister might have taken her own life while reassuring me there was no hard evidence she had. That possibility had never occurred to me and it's nearly driven me mad. Or am I so angry because, deep down, I suspected from the moment I arrived at this hospital last night that that's what Megan had really done? That it was no accident at all.

The mortuary attendant was reluctant to let me see the body but perhaps he was intimidated by my insistence and he allowed me in. He pulled her body out from a drawer from what looked like a filing cabinet and agreed to leave me alone with her for a few minutes. Now he clearly thinks he's made a mistake. When he hears me breaking the chilly silence by shouting at Megan, he reappears. 'Are you all right there?'

'Yes, I'm fine, thank you.'

The attendant wants to tell me that it's wildly inappropriate to shout at corpses in a mortuary and there's no arguing with that. My fear now is that he might call security and throw me out before I've concluded my business in this office of the dead. I apologise. 'I'm terribly sorry. I'm so upset.'

'Of course.'

'It won't happen again.'

He relaxes a little. 'It's totally understandable, take your time.'

When he's gone again, I get down to work. It's a struggle pulling the sleeves of Megan's top up and along her stiff arms to expose the dead flesh underneath. I run my hands up the cold, smooth skin and inspect it closely. Her arms are unmarked by needles or anything else. They're like the clean limbs of a tailor's dummy with none of the tell-tale signs of someone who injects regularly or self-harms. Her skirt comes up more easily and there's no evidence on her legs of any jabs or abuse either, except one. On her thigh is a fresh welt with slight bruising around it. That must be where the needle that killed her went in. From where this small sore is placed on her body it's hard to tell whether it was self-inflicted or not. It could have been.

All the same, I don't believe it. She might have taken her own life as a sick revenge on me, but not on her own son, who she loved despite everything. And if she had, not with a needle, her phobia so ingrained that she couldn't have overcome it. In one of those silly discussions that teenagers have, she once told me throwing yourself from a cliff or tall building was the way to end it all.

'Just imagine, for a few seconds you're flying and tumbling through space before you go. That must feel great!'

I calm down a little. DC Summers only put suicide in the mix to advise me of the possibility, or perhaps to punish me for suggesting he wasn't doing his job properly, or because he refused to admit that Megan's needle phobia was a thing. I pull my sister's clothes straight and leave with a few parting words in a softer tone than previously.

'Alright, that was unfair of me to accuse you of doing this to yourself. You know what it's like when you're upset, you say things. I can't believe you'd stoop that low anyway. But someone did this to you and we're going to find out who it was. If the police won't help, I'll make it my business and do it myself. I'll speak to you later, Megan.'

My amateur post-mortem is over. On taking leave of my sister, it occurs to me something else needs saying so I retrace my steps. 'And don't worry about Sunny, we'll take good care of him.'

I mean this. I might not have been able to save my sister. All the more reason to save her son.

Megan is lying here dead despite all the times I tried to help her off the road that led to this human abattoir. But her son is alive and well and he's going to stay that way, whatever it takes. It will be a strain on my family and me but we're strong enough to take it. Under no circumstances is he ending up with his father or his grandmother and under absolutely no circumstances is he going into the care system. Outside in the fresh air and sunshine there's a text waiting for me. It's from a friend in social services advising me an interim meeting has been arranged to decide Sunny's future.

When I get home and see my husband, I save the good news about the meeting until I've shared my experience with Summers. Trevor isn't convinced about my theory that Megan can't have injected herself. He reminds me that cops, doctors and coroners are the experts and they don't care for bereaved relatives' unlikely theories about tragic deaths. We should leave it to them. Nor is Trevor buying the idea that Megan's problem with needles could run so deep. He's on the same page as my cop's belief that when it comes to getting a hit of something, phobias aren't really an issue for addicts. They're too desperate. Trevor can't be blamed for that of course. I've never felt able to share the full story of my relationship with my sister, preferring to allude to it as 'troubled' and 'complicated'. He encouraged me to share but respected my decision not to do so. He didn't pry about it with anyone outside of our marriage either, though that wouldn't have helped anyway. No one knows the real story except Megan and me, not even our parents. Now she's gone, that means only me.

Trevor has settled on his own simple explanation for our relationship. Megan was a total grifter who exploited my generosity and good nature and caused me no end of unnecessary heartache which could have ended years ago with a simple text from me ending all communication. Naturally, I prefer him to believe that.

'Anyway, there is good news today. We've got a meeting this week with social services to decide Sunny's future. No doubt Rose, Kit and Kit's fly solicitor will be there but we'll soon see them off.'

Trevor doesn't have time to fix his face after this unexpected news. He looks alarmed. 'This week? This is a bit soon, isn't it? Your sister hasn't even been laid to rest yet and they're arranging meetings about Sunny already. I don't see why he can't stay with mad granny Rose for now, he's happy enough there. Let's bury your sister, take some time with it and then discuss what's happening with your nephew later. You know, take some time with things.'

My husband is the most warm, generous and family focused man you could ever wish to meet. He's more or less the ideal father and husband. Perhaps that's why it takes me a few moments to realise what he's actually saying. 'There's nothing to discuss. Sunny is coming to live with us and that's all there is to it.'

He pulls a sceptical face. 'That's one option we can consider. There are others though that might be better for everyone, including Sunny.'

'One option? What other options are there? That my nephew lives with his crazy grandmother who can't even look after herself? Or he ends up being raised by his violent criminal father? Perhaps you'd like him to go into the care system where he'll probably be bullied and abused. Is that another option you'd like to consider?'

He shrugs. 'I'm not saying any of those things but it's early days. Why don't we just let things settle down first and then afterwards take some time with it.'

'Is that so? How much time do you have in mind?'

Perhaps I'm not meant to hear him mutter under his breath 'about ten years' but I do. I'm exhausted after the past twenty-four hours but I can't let this go. 'I'm sorry, is there a problem with Sunny living with us? If there is, you should say so instead of whispering under your breath.'

He nods firmly. 'Oh yes, there is a problem alright, but perhaps now is not the right time to discuss it. Let's wait until the children have gone to bed.'

Tova and Rodney are playing in the back garden. 'You're worried they might hear us arguing? We don't need to worry about that, it won't do them any harm to realise that parents disagree sometimes and things get said. That's the real world and they're going to have to live in the real world one day. So come on, let's have this out. Are you saying you don't want my nephew coming to live with us?'

Trevor goes over to the window and looks out at Tova and Rodney as if involving them might help his case. He looks like a fugitive caught by the police who hasn't had time to think up a cover story or arrange an alibi. Confronted by my question and seeing there's no way out, he turns on me, but there's no anger in his voice. It's both firm and final. 'Yes, that's exactly what I'm saying. I don't want that child in this house under any circumstances.'

# Chapter 9

'He's not coming here. He can't. It's not right for us and, just as importantly, it's not right for him. You want to do what's best for Sunny? Let him find somewhere where there are people who can actually help him, professional people. And that isn't here.'

Megan and I are of mixed heritage. Our father was black and came from the Caribbean while our mother was English and white. My sister and I grew up in poverty and knew hard times. We were brought up to always be conscious of who we are and where we're from. Trevor is white and so is Kit. And as far as the world is concerned, with only one black grandparent, Tova, Rodney and Sunny might look like white children but in fact they're 'blended' like our families. It's a standing joke with Trevor that I'm more a member of the English professional middle classes than any blonde girl from the countryside who grew up with ponies and jolly hockey sticks. That's partly true but it's also partly untrue. I'm from here but I'm also from there. I'm not from here and I'm not from there either. I'm from everywhere and nowhere. That's how it is.

The fact that we're different ethnically makes less impact on our marriage than people might think. But in one way I am from 'there', where my father grew up. If a child from the extended family needs taking in by relatives, that child is taken in, there's no argument about it. We don't do children's homes and orphanages and the like. I thought Trevor understood this but it appears he doesn't. I've made it repeatedly clear over the years that if Megan was unable to look after Sunny any more, and that was always possible, we'd have to take him in. I solemnly promised my sister that would happen. Even when I broke my links with her, that was still understood. It was an unbreakable promise whatever the circumstances. I thought my husband and I were agreed about that. It's fortunate for me in some ways that this is 'how it is' on my side of the family. It means I don't have to share with my husband the other reasons why I need Sunny to live with us.

The violence of Trevor's refusal to accept Sunny into our family is underlined by his determination to keep his voice down to avoid disturbing our children. It's only now that it becomes obvious that this is how he's felt since the moment my sister passed away. He's quiet but vehement. 'Have you any idea what that kid will have seen in your sister's flat? Any idea what he will have heard while your sister and her druggie friends were having their crazy parties every other night? Who will have come to the door? Who he will have seen trooping in and out, as well as bailiffs, the police, and the debt collectors? Do you know how disturbed he will be? We'll be lucky if he doesn't turn into a serial killer. You want to bring a child of that sort into our house, under the same roof as our children? You're out of your mind. I absolutely want to support Sunny but he needs specialist help and support and we're not equipped to do that. We'll only end up making things worse. Wherever he goes we can help and support, but we can't be helpers and supporters in this house. Of course, he might be able to pay us a visit now and again.' Trevor can't resist adding, 'Occasionally.'

Who is this man? The kind, compassionate and generous soul that can't do enough to help strangers, never mind his own family. Who wants to turn my sister's son over to the tender mercies of his father, grandmother or the care system? What's happened to him?

'All the more reason for us to take him under our wing,' I insist. 'All the more reason for us to give him a stable, loving and supportive home where he can work things through, supported by his aunt and his cousins. I thought his uncle Trevor might have felt the same but perhaps I was wrong about that. I would have thought too that his uncle Trevor might have shown Sunny how to be a better sort of man than his own father. Perhaps I was wrong about that as well.'

My husband comes and stands behind me. He places his hands on my shoulders and steers me over to the window so we can both watch Tova and Rodney playing in the garden. His voice is hurried, urgent as if there's no time to lose. 'You see those children, Josie, they're yours. I'd love to claim the credit for the fact that they're happy, well-adjusted and flourishing. Perhaps I can claim some of the credit but it pales into nothing compared to yours. This is mainly on you and the work you've done with them. They don't suffer from the complexes and syndromes other children in their school playgrounds are already plagued by. They're smart and they understand things. That's on you. Now you want to bring someone like Sunny in to our house to mess them up. What are you thinking? Why are you doing this? Why do you want to turn them into props in your nephew's redemption story? What's the real reason? Is this your sister playing you in death just like she did when she was alive? Tell me, I want to know.'

I turn away from the garden until I'm facing my husband. 'I'll make a deal with you. I'll tell you the real reason why I'm determined to have Sunny here, if you tell me the real reason, you're not.'

'I don't know what you're talking about. Those are my real reasons. You think there might be others? You're deluding yourself as you always have with anything to do with your sister.'

'Are you sure?'

For a moment I think he's going to agree to tell me the real reasons for his flat refusal but he thinks better of it. 'You do what you need to do, Josie. But I'm telling you now, if you force me to come to this meeting with social services, you'll find me sitting on the other side of the table with mad Granny Rose and her son Kit, supporting their case, not yours. Don't think I won't.'

He walks out of the back door into the garden, calling to the children, 'Hey, kids! What's your poor old father got to do to get a game around here?'

He's right in certain respects. It was totally wrong of me to decide Sunny's future without discussing it with him first. We should have waited until Megan was buried and then talked about it calmly and rationally, deciding together what was best for my nephew and what was best for our family. It isn't wrong of him to worry about Sunny's presence in our house. I'm worrying about it too. Sunny is a traumatised young boy and that will have an impact on all of us. But, unlike Trevor, I'm confident that any problems can be worked through. I'm a professional teacher after all. I have experience with traumatised kids. If I didn't think we could accommodate Sunny and his 'issues', I wouldn't consider it. Perhaps admitting anything else would be going down a dark road that would mean admitting I'm being played by my sister again. But Trevor's no more willing to discuss it than I am. What's his reason? His reaction is so unlike him, it's difficult to believe he's the same person. What's his secret?

We told the children that their aunt had gone away to heaven so they wouldn't be seeing her any more. Tova seemed to accept it but Rodney rolled his eyes as if we were talking about Santa and his reindeer. They both liked Megan and she always behaved herself in front of them. She was good with children. It was only me and other adults she had a problem with. The children only saw her when she came over to our house on the cadge. I was too worried about what they might find if we visited her home. She rarely brought Sunny with her so they barely know him. Trevor has always kept his views on Megan quiet in front of the children but they must know he didn't like her. Tova noticed once that her father always seemed to be 'out' when her aunt called round. Rodney explained to her that their dad didn't like me lending their aunt money. I'm sure they'll be good for Sunny.

I pick up the keys from the table and go into the garden and beckon to Trevor telling him I'm going out. It also feels like the right time to lay my cards on the table.

'I'm not compromising on Sunny. It's my duty to take him and I can't allow you or anyone to drive me off that path.'

He fixes on my eyes. 'That's how it is?'

'That's how it is.'

He looks away. 'What happens if I decide I don't accept that?'

'That's for you to decide.'

This conversation sounds alien, like someone else's. We don't talk to each other like this, with veiled threats of walk outs and splits. It's as if we're reading lines in a script on a film set. I hesitate before walking off, as if someone off-stage might shout 'cut' and stop this from happening. When no one shouts 'cut, that's a wrap people', I begin to walk away, but Trevor calls me back.

'Do you see what's happening here? Sunny and your sister's ghost aren't even in the house yet and they're already destroying our family. And you're not just letting it happen. You're making it happen.'

# Chapter 10

Megan's block is even grimmer in the twilight than in the dead of night. Nothing except a determination to find out what really happened to my sister that night would bring me here again now that she's gone. The escalating words of the row with my husband are still echoing around my head. I really want to go back home and start our argument again and turn it into a discussion that's resolved peacefully. But it's too late.

The entry phone is working again but the lift isn't, so it's another slow walk up the stairs to the third floor. Megan's flat is already boarded up to stop squatters and a simple note on the boards tells any visitors to contact the police if they need entry. Given the sort of visitors she had, it's unlikely any of them will be taking that advice. Bailiffs and debt collectors will probably be writing off any money she owed already.

There are six flats on this landing, three on one side of the landing and three on the other. Megan's flat was the middle one on the left as you come up the stairs. My intention is to knock on the other five to see if they heard or saw anything the night she died. In my bag is a notebook to note down anything of interest. DC Summers might have written her death off as another drug overdose but I won't, not without a fight anyway. I knock on the door of Megan's immediate neighbour to the left.

From behind the door, a gruff woman's voice calls out, 'Who is it?'

'My name is Josie Thomas. I'm the sister of Megan Campbell, your next-door neighbour. I was hoping you might help me by answering some questions about last night.'

Very slowly a bolt is unlatched and a chain is taken off the door. When it opens, a middle-aged woman appears. She folds her arms across her chest in a distinctly unfriendly way. She casts a glance over me and appears to be slightly disappointed that I'm smartly and respectably dressed.

'You're her sister, are you?'

'That's right. I don't want to trouble you but . . .'

That's as far as we get before she interrupts me. 'Have you any idea what it was like living next door to your sister?'

I should have expected this and should probably expect it at the other doors too. 'She probably wasn't the ideal neighbour, I understand that.'

The woman is outraged by my choice of words. 'Ideal!? A constant procession of criminals, drug addicts and all-round lowlife coming up and down our stairs at all times of the day and night. Arguments, foul language, things being thrown around in her flat, fights, parties and the police turning up, on and on it went.'

She sounds as if she thinks my visit is an effort to justify my sister's behaviour or garner sympathy. 'I understand, but—'

She shakes her head with venom. 'No, no, you don't. She made my life a complete misery and did anyone ever do anything about it? Fat chance!'

'Yes . . .'

'I felt sorry for the boy of course, what's his name? Sunny? Poor kid never stood a chance in a home like that. We never had a problem with him anyway.'

I know I'm going to sound like a teacher trying to bring an unruly pupil into line but she's leaving me no choice. My voice is pointed, loud and won't take any interruptions this time. 'Listen, I'm not here to justify my sister's behaviour. I just want to know if you heard or saw anything next door last night that might throw some light on what happened.'

Years of work in schools have given my voice a genuine ring of authority. But it doesn't work this time.

She sneers. 'Oh, that's what you're here for, is it?' She smiles sarcastically as she says, 'I've already spoken to the police, my love. If you've got any questions, why don't you go and ask them?' The smile ends. 'Now get off my doorstep!'

With an almighty slam, the door is closed.

I'm not unsympathetic. I know how it was being Megan's sister so it's not difficult to imagine what living next door to her must have been like. Looking at the other four doors, it's not difficult to imagine the response I'm going to get at those either.

'Who is it?'

The neighbour to the right doesn't open the door, preferring to hide behind it.

'My name is Josie Thomas. I'm the sister of Megan Campbell, your next-door neighbour. I was hoping you might help me answer some questions about what happened to her last night.'

The door doesn't open. 'Not tonight, thank you.'

'Would another time be convenient?'

The voice retreats from the door and calls out the same words again, 'Not tonight, thank you.'

Presumably this means another time wouldn't be convenient. At the next door, my knock is answered by a middle-aged man.

This guy is more sympathetic but refuses to answer my questions. Given the nature of the visitors to Megan's flat, he doesn't want to get 'involved'. He does add though that he too felt sorry for the boy who lived there. 'He was a nice kid.'

At the fourth door, it's another grim-faced woman. She listens patiently to my questions but she can't help either. 'I didn't hear anything and didn't see anything. Look dear, we've already had the police round asking about this, so I'm not quite sure why you're doing the same thing. Don't you like the police?' Once again though, Sunny gets a thumbs up. 'Good kid, he used to bring my shopping up the stairs when the lift was out. It must be terrible for him losing his mother like that. Poor boy, what will become of him? You can't blame him for his mother, can you?' She becomes quite chatty. 'I'm going to be honest with you, there won't be many people in this block who are sorry to see the back of your sister. I know that sounds harsh but she was just one wagon load of trouble.'

I don't hold out much hope for the final door either. It's directly opposite Megan's flat.

'Who is it?'

I repeat my opening lines. The door has a chain on it and opens a fraction. An elderly woman peers out. She opens the door and scans the landing to check if there's anyone with me. Satisfied there isn't, she listens to my questions intently but she can't help either. Or can she? She's an honest soul and remarkably reluctant to say flat out that she didn't hear or see anything, apparently hoping I'll think that's what she's saying.

'Of course, people came and went at your sister's flat all the time, so I wouldn't like to say for certain that there was no one in there last night or there weren't any arguments.'

She looks at me as if that might be enough to make me go away. There's a little part of me that wishes it was. 'Is it possible that you might remember if anyone came to Megan's flat last night and if there were any arguments or fights?'

She has a think. 'It's possible, dear, anything's possible.'

Her name is Frieda and it feels like she and I are negotiating about whether she saw anything or not. 'Did you see or hear anything?'

She looks ashamed when she says no. She obviously doesn't like telling lies and I'm pretty sure this is a lie. 'Are you sure?'

She is sure and I've no way of proving otherwise. I've drawn a complete blank. I wish her well and thank her for her time but she's obviously unhappy with herself. 'Wait one minute, dear, I might have something that might help you.' She disappears back into her flat and scans all the rooms before coming back out again to tell me she hasn't got anything after all. Who knows what that was about.

In my car, I pull out my notebook and look inside. There is a heading on one page that reads 'Neighbours'. Of course the page is empty apart from that single word and it's not going to be filled by anything in the future by the look of it. On another page is the title 'Megan's Phones'. I saw that my sister had several phones that DC Summers had put in evidence bags on the night she died. No doubt the police will want to check them for evidence first but as they're my sister's property, I'm assuming they will come back to me at some stage. When they do, I'll be able to check them myself. Summers assured me that I could ring him at any time, and although things are now a little frosty between us, I take him up on it. He's not surprised at all to hear from me but it's a firm 'no' on the phones, not only now but in the future too. They're evidence and they may be evidence again in future enquiries so they won't be returned.

'To tell you the truth, Josie, one of the phones is locked anyway and we can't get into it. We're assuming that's the one she used to phone her friends in the drugs trade.'

'If you can't get into it, why don't you just give it to me?'

Summers laughs. 'Believe me, Josie, if we can't get into it, you won't be able to. No, it's procedure, we're holding on to them for now.'

When the call is over, I look at my notebook again. The final title on an empty page reads 'Next Steps'.

But I've got no next steps. My promise to find out who killed my sister is over before it's even begun.

# Chapter 11

'I take it your husband will be joining us shortly Ms Thomas?'

Next to me at the interim meeting with social services to decide Sunny's future is an empty chair. Trevor should be sitting there. But he isn't and he won't be.

The past few days have seen a marriage that a week ago might have served as the model of a happy couple in a TV advert go into deep freeze. We've barely spoken apart from a few terse remarks about this meeting. Trevor initially refused to come and support our application to take charge of my nephew. When I warned him that he was putting our marriage at risk by refusing to attend, he finally gave in. Last night though, he announced he couldn't come due to 'pressure of work'. After a bitter row, I decided to let it go as it probably wouldn't help to have him here scowling next to me. His reaction to my request that he provide a statement supporting our application was to scoff.

'You're joking!'

'It will harm our case if you don't.'

'If we're lucky, it will.'

We've both tried to hide what's going on from the children but it isn't working. I've had Tova tugging at my leg asking what the matter is with her daddy. At other times she tugs at Trevor's leg and asks what's the matter with her mummy.

I didn't ask for this and I don't want it. But I have to take charge of my nephew. I owe him and my sister. I've made promises. I understand Trevor's position and I'm well aware of the challenges taking my nephew in will pose. But it's happening and no one is going to stop it.

Around the table at this meeting are a number of social workers, Kit, Kit's solicitor and Sunny himself. It's decided Sunny is old enough to contribute to the discussion although it's hard to believe he is. He's small, lean and looks younger than his age. He looks bored and he's already fidgeting. There's no sign of Rose. Presumably she's already out of the running to be my nephew's new guardian. Sunny was already here when his father arrived and he looked deeply embarrassed when Kit performed a big hug on him for the benefit of the professionals sat around the table. Kit's ripped torso and legs are squeezed into a suit that's a little too small for him and his tie is arranged around his neck as if someone tried to strangle him with it. He leaves his solicitor to make his case to take over the guardianship of Sunny. This pinch-faced woman is probably more used to talking the cops out of charging her client with various offences than persuading social workers in a meeting like this. She does a good job but if you heard Kit's case for ownership of Sunny before, as I have, it's all wearily familiar.

His solicitor performs her act. Kit apparently has turned over a new leaf. He's made a fresh start. He's no longer out under licence from prison and has cut his links with the criminal fraternity. Yes, it's true that he's had challenges, issues and problems in the past but after prolonged counselling and anger management, he's moved on. He has a job as a roofer and a flat that he shares with his pregnant girlfriend, who fully supports bringing Sunny into the family. Kit has testimonials from various professionals that will attest to his changed character and his fitness for the role of parent. When the solicitor finishes, it's difficult to tell what the team make of her statement. Fortunately, Kit is unable to resist wagging his finger in Sunny's direction and adding, 'One other thing needs to be said. My boy needs a firm hand on the tiller or he'll go off the rails. No disrespect to Josie or Trev but he needs his father to keep him in line.'

I assume the social workers realise that 'a firm hand on the tiller' means violence. Kit's solicitor certainly does as she gives him a kick under the table to shut him up.

I keep it short and brief when my turn comes. I offer a stable loving home with financial security to back it up. I remind them of my background in education and my experience working with children who have challenges. My own two children are happy and flourishing and are a testament to the environment they've been brought up in. I press all the buttons I know from experience that other professionals like to hear. I regret having to use the fact that I know how to play this game and Kit doesn't. But he poses a mortal threat to Sunny's future and he has to be stopped at all costs. I remind the team that Sunny is of mixed heritage and that I am too and so will be in a position to provide help, support and guidance on this issue. Kit loses his temper at this line and interrupts in fury.

'Mixed heritage? As far as anyone is concerned, my kid is white. Look at him! He's got curly blonde hair and grey eyes. What's mixed heritage got to do with the price of fish?'

The social workers are appalled. The solicitor, who at first closed her eyes in horror, jumps in to repair the damage. 'What my client is trying to say is that while obviously issues of identity and heritage are of vital importance in Sunny's future wellbeing, they have to be balanced with all the other concerns to get a rounded picture. Naturally, my client is looking forward to working closely with Sunny's aunt Josie on this matter.'

As my pitch finishes, I feel uneasy. Even while trotting out these forms of words that I know so well, it suddenly occurs to me why it is. I keep saying 'I offer' and 'my family' rather than 'we offer' and 'our family'. I'm talking about myself and not my husband or children and this makes me even more uncomfortable. I'm even more unhappy when I notice that Kit has a smug look on his face. That means he might have something up his sleeve for his final comments. Before that, Sunny is offered the chance to say who he wants to live with. He merely shrugs and says he's happy enough where he is although he's been told he can't stay with Grandma Rose. If he can't do that, he doesn't care where he ends up. Despite gentle prompting from the social workers, he has nothing else to add.

We're all asked if there's anything else we wish to be taken into consideration. The solicitor has a couple of points. She understands that there might be concerns over whether Josie's family is a safe environment for a child. Ears prick up. What concerns are these? She tells the story of the time that Tova was taken to hospital with arm injuries and the hospital suspected that they might have been inflicted by someone in the family. I'm shocked for a few seconds. Where did Kit get this from? The only person outside the family who knew about that incident was Megan and she was told in confidence. She must have told him about it. For a moment I sympathise with her neighbours. What a total bitch my sister could be. My explanation is that hospitals making such enquiries is standard procedure these days for safeguarding reasons. The staff spoke to Tova in private and were completely satisfied that her injuries were the result of an accident. My daughter fell off a swing, injured her arm and that's what happened.

The solicitor pulls a face. 'No doubt, although of course small children can be very loyal to their parents in these situations.'

It doesn't bother me that she's trying to wind me up. It bothers me that she's succeeding. 'What's that supposed to mean?'

'Nothing, Mrs Thomas, there's no need to get upset. If the hospital were satisfied, there's nothing else to add.'

But she isn't done. She notices that Trevor hasn't joined us. She raises the possibility that perhaps my husband isn't as supportive of our becoming Sunny's guardians as I am. Perhaps he's against it? Even strongly against it? I'm even more shocked by this than by Kit's hospital stunt. Where did he get this from? Not from Megan, she's dead. Everyone looks at the empty chair. I don't want to lie but Kit has to be stopped and Sunny has to be saved. 'My husband is completely supportive of our decision and only work commitments prevent him from joining us today.'

The solicitor asks with mock sincerity. 'His work commitments are more important than your nephew's future?'

'It won't help Sunny's future if my husband is made redundant. He's completely behind my decision.' I stumble while correcting myself. 'Our decision.'

'And your children are equally happy to have Sunny living with them?'

To my horror, I realise I haven't even asked them about it.

'Yes.'

The meeting is closed. The team feel a decision on Sunny's future needs to be made as soon as possible. Kit knows he's lost but he at least enjoyed trying to screw me over there at the last. When our paths cross in the corridor outside, I let fly at him. 'That was a dirty trick you pulled in there with my daughter's injury.'

He plays the innocent. 'I don't know what you're talking about. That was nothing to do with me.' He takes me to one side. 'Enjoy your win, Josie, but you're going to bitterly regret what you've just done to me in there. I'm going to make you pay for it and I'll bring my son home. It might take me a while but one way or another it's going to happen, I'll see to that. We'll see where your fancy words get you then.'

'Is that a threat? That would be a shame after everything we've just heard in that meeting about what a wonderful father and reformed old con you are these days.'

'Sneer all you like, babe. But your words will turn to ash on your tongue sooner than you think.' He turns and walks down the corridor with his solicitor, but remembers something as he goes.

He turns and calls out to me, 'Give my regards to Trevor.'

# Chapter 12

'Child snatcher.'

It's not much of a welcome from Granny Rose but perhaps it was too much to hope for anything else. At least she leaves it at that and doesn't make a fight of it.

'Where is he?'

'In his room.'

It's only an hour since a formal notice came through that our family is to be given temporary custody of Sunny until a final decision is made. There was agreement though that in the light of the evidence, Kit would be allowed contact. That means we'll have him turning up at our home on a regular basis. And who knows, maybe he really is a reformed character, anything's possible. I already knew about the decision as a friend in social services tipped me off early, so at home everything is prepared. Despite my phoning ahead to warn Rose I was coming for Sunny, she clearly hasn't bothered to tell him. Sunny is in his room, sat at his makeshift desk scribbling away on his sheets of paper. He doesn't stop working when I knock on the door and come in, or turn around or say hello. He's totally absorbed in his writing.

'Hi, Sunny, has anyone told you you're coming to live with us yet?'

It's a stupid question. They obviously haven't. Nor does he seem in a hurry to make it happen. He carries on writing. 'OK.'

'Shall we help you pack?'

He's annoyed at being interrupted and doesn't say anything but he puts his pen down and helps me put his things together. 'Pack' is probably an exaggeration. There are a few clothes to be put in a suitcase and some odd bits and pieces but he's travelling light. He takes great care though with his books, which he puts in the box that I brought with me. You might think he's laying a baby in his cot the way he neatly arranges them.

'I promise you this, Sunny. Whatever happens in our house, no one will ever sell your books like your mother did.'

He looks up at me with a mischievous glint in his grey eyes that I know well. It's the same one Megan had when she was up to something. 'That's OK. She had her reasons.'

'Yes, but they weren't very good ones.'

The glint becomes even more mischievous as if he's sharing a joke somewhere with my late and unlamented sister. 'Yes, that's true.'

I never judged my sister. To do so would have meant a fusillade of abuse, but I didn't feel in a position to anyway. We both knew who she really blamed for the way things turned out. She always insisted that her chaotic lifestyle, what she called her 'extra-curricular activities', didn't affect Sunny. She learned the phrase 'extra-curricular activities' from me and my career and used it as a slight. She always insisted that Sunny never saw her substance abuse or was ever forced to mix with her unsavoury friends and associates. Perhaps she even believed it. Perhaps she had to. She loved her son and always maintained he was a smart kid who was going places. She welcomed my attempts to broaden her son's horizons by taking him to museums, events and shows. He didn't though, he hated it no matter how 'fun' I tried to make my own version of extra-curricular activities.

When he's done, Sunny stands by the small suitcase, black bin liners and his box of books as if he were a refugee. It dawns on me slowly as we stare at each other just what I'm taking on here and it seems odd that it didn't occur to me before. But I suppose fire fighters don't think about what it means to bring a child out of a burning building because they're too busy saving a life. This is what I'm doing – saving my sister's son from the burning house of Rose, Kit or the care system. Of course. But it's also true that guilt and a bad conscience play some part in my 'rescuing' Sunny.

'Shall we go?'

He doesn't reply. It's already obvious that Sunny isn't big on answers.

Across the front of the house is a banner which says 'Welcome Sunny!' I had it made after the meeting with social services. I knew it was a done deal despite Kit's attempt to trip me up at the end. Trevor helped me put it up. After the decision came, the subject of Sunny was dropped between us but we breathed in the atmosphere from our arguments like acrid smoke. Once my friend tipped me off that Sunny was ours, Trevor and I had a brief meeting to discuss things. We compromised. I agreed that if it didn't work out with my nephew living with us we'd make other arrangements. In return he promised to welcome Sunny and not let his 'doubts' affect his relationship with him. It was obvious neither of us meant what we'd agreed but it allowed us to move forward.

When Sunny and I arrive, Trevor is standing on the doorstep holding the hand of Tova on one side and Rodney on the other. They're all smiling with varying degrees of sincerity. The children have both been primed for Sunny's arrival and warned what to expect: that Sunny is to be welcomed into our home and supported in every way as a member of the family because, as their cousin, he is a member of the family. Yes, he may come across as a little odd at times and his manners and behaviour might not be what they're used to but he's just lost his mum so we all have to be on his side.

A little party is prepared in our dining room where all my gifts from school have been cleared away. It's the usual fare dished up for children. In the middle of the dining table is a cake which also says 'Welcome Sunny' in icing. Afterwards, I show him around the house. Our spare room is now Sunny's and I behave like an estate agent asking him to admire the view from the window over the garden, the spaciousness and in particular the new desk, chair and computer on which he can now write his stories. There's a new phone for him too, which he seems surprisingly disinterested in. But perhaps he'll like the new shelves that are now in place for him to put his books on. Considering it important that his mother is namechecked in his new space, I've hung three photos on the wall. One of Megan, one of Megan and Sunny together and a third of the three of us at the seaside when he was a small boy. Rather like a prospective buyer who wants to 'go away and think about it', Sunny doesn't seem overly impressed.

'If you want to add your own touches to your room, Sunny, some decoration, that's fine.'

He doesn't answer.

After leaving him to unpack his things, I tell Tova and Rodney to invite Sunny into the back garden when he comes downstairs. They can play ball or frisbee together before it gets dark. Sunny doesn't come down. When I go up to fetch him, it's to find him sitting at his new desk, bent over, scribbling on his sheets of paper.

The computer lies dormant. After some coaxing, he's persuaded to go and play with his cousins in the back garden. When he leaves, I look around the room. His books are propped against the skirting board as they were at his grandmother's rather than on the new shelves. His clothes are parked in a corner of the room still in their bin liners rather than in the new chest of drawers. The three photos of his mother, myself and him that were hanging on the wall have been taken down and look like they've been dropped facing the wall.

But that's OK, all this is new to him.

In the back garden, the children are doing their best with Sunny but he's rather like an exchange student struggling to speak a different language. I stand back and let them get on with it rather than join in. From time to time Sunny tells Tova and Rodney that he's going up to his room, but when he turns and sees me standing there watching, he reluctantly turns around and tries again.

Trevor joins me by the back door. He stands by my shoulder watching the three children playing for a while, then he raises his hand and gestures at Sunny with his finger.

'Just remember, this is all on you.' He turns his hand towards me and waves his finger at me. 'Whatever happens, it's all on you.'

Then he's gone.

Sunny finally gives up playing at playing and comes up the garden. It might be a stupid question but it gets asked anyway. 'Are you settling in all right?'

Sunny looks up at me with those mischievous grey eyes. 'He doesn't like me, does he?'

'What? Who doesn't like you?'

Sunny appears to be enjoying himself for the first time since his arrival. 'Uncle Trevor. He doesn't like me. He thinks I'm trouble.'

I give a light laugh. 'Don't be silly, whatever makes you say that?'

He merely walks into the house, saying as he goes, 'He thinks I'm trouble. Perhaps he's right, perhaps I am trouble. Big, big trouble.'

He stops at the door and gives me a rueful smile and his eyes twinkle the way Megan's did when she was feeling sorry for herself. I'm angry with Trevor for making him feel this way and am all the more determined to ensure that he doesn't.

# Chapter 13

'If you can't sleep, why don't you pull on a shroud and go and haunt the house or something?'

Trevor's being rude but he's right, I haven't had a wink. 'How do you know I can't sleep?'

'I can feel you on the other side of the bed, trembling.'

The clock says half past two. I decide not to pull on a shroud but I will go and haunt the house. After climbing out of bed, I shuffle across the room to the door. As I go past his side of the bed, I can't stop myself whispering angrily, 'What did you say that for?'

'Say what?'

If you can whisper in a loud voice, that's what I do. 'Saying it was all on me, whatever happens. That was a wicked thing to say.'

'Well, it's not on me, Tova or Rodney, you can't blame us. Who else is there to blame?'

As if this night isn't bad enough.

'Blame for what?'

'You'll see.'

'I don't understand you and the Sunny thing. He's a good kid. How do you know there will be anything for anyone to take blame for? You've barely spoken two words to Sunny since he was born. Why don't you take him out and do some boy things with him? Get to know him a little.'

This is true. Trevor despised Megan and would have nothing to do with her. Early on and for a while, he tried to persuade me to break all links with her and when that didn't work, he gave up speaking about her altogether. It was because he refused to have anything to do with Megan that he refused to have anything to do with Sunny either. He wouldn't join us when we went out to broaden Sunny's horizons. Trevor insisted that Megan used Sunny as a bargaining chip whenever we fell out. 'You won't help me, OK, but will you at least help my son?' By helping Sunny of course that was helping Megan too and she was back in the game.

He's becoming sleepy now there's no trembling woman lying next to him. 'You'll see.'

The house is dark and quiet. On the landing are two steps that join one half of it to the other so that's where I sit for a while. I'm feeling ill, which isn't helping. Trevor and Sunny didn't eat any of the party food and the children weren't really hungry either so it was left to me to hoover it up. It was considered a sin when we were children to leave food uneaten. We were poor kids and poor kids are told not to waste food. Now I've got a belly trying to digest crisps, nuts, nibbles, rolls and cake and it's not dealing with it very well. This is going to end with me heaving over the loo. But that's not the only reason I'm feeling ill. It's everything else too.

Three men have now told me it was a bad idea to take my nephew in. Kit with his warning I was going to regret it, Trevor with his 'it's all on you' and Sunny himself with his 'big, big trouble' line. It's true that Kit wasn't threatening Sunny would be 'big, big trouble', instead he was threatening to retaliate against me. Or was he? What did he mean when he said Sunny needs 'a firm hand on the tiller'? What do these three boys know that I don't? What's the big secret that they don't want to share?

It's not any of them that I blame for this though, not ultimately. I know exactly who's to blame. It's Megan again. My sister doing to me in death what she regularly did to me in life. It's got her fingerprints all over it. She must have known that getting herself killed by a needle would prompt me to realise that she couldn't have done it herself. Someone else must have and she would have known that if the law didn't want to find out who it was, I would. She must have known that getting herself killed by a needle would mean that I would have to take Sunny in in the face of opposition from my husband. She knew full well how much he despised her. She knew even from the other side of the grave that she could exploit my good nature and guilt over what happened when we were children. It feels like she probably planned this.

This would all sound crazy to someone who isn't crazy. Those who aren't crazy don't understand what my life has been like. Decades of living with, and by, my sister means crazy is all I have left to offer in the midst of the peace and harmony of the rest of my life.

My ears prick up. There are noises somewhere upstairs where everyone but me is asleep. I can hear shuffling. The landing is dark like the rest of the house with only a little street light coming in through the windows. I get up and listen at various bedroom doors but can hear nothing. Perhaps it was nothing. When I'm back on the landing, I wonder what my next steps should be. If I can find out how Megan got herself killed then perhaps I can exorcise her ghost for good. This is her final hold over me. And she did get herself killed. The life she led, the things she did and the people she mixed with meant her death was inevitable.

We both knew it, which is why as her life ebbed away in that bed, it was no surprise to either of us.

But there it is again, the noises above. I don't know why I bother to check at Tova and Rodney's doors, I know full well whose room it's coming from before even pressing my ear against his door. I've been warned by three men what might happen. It's Sunny's room. There's no light under the door but inside his room there are whispers and footsteps that sound more like the padding of an animal than something human.

I notice something else in the gloom. On the door is a series of marks that look like a logo, only of a rather sinister kind, like a pentagram or an occult symbol. It's done in black and is about a foot tall and a foot across. We didn't put it there, so it must have been Sunny. I try rubbing it off with the back of my hand but it's indelible marker ink, the sort we use at school. I tap on Sunny's door. There's a brief silence before the sound of hurrying, as if something is being hidden inside. Finally, my nephew answers the knock. He doesn't seem in the least surprised to see me, although perhaps he wouldn't be. He's used to adults keeping irregular hours. He's fully dressed.

'Yes?'

I point at the 'logo'. 'What's this, Sunny? Did you put it there?'

He comes out and surveys the marks. 'Yes, it's my name. It shows it's my room.'

When I look again by the light on my phone, it becomes clearer. It's the five letters of his name superimposed on each other in swirling strokes. I'm stumped. 'OK, the thing is we don't need you to mark the door to know which room you're in. We already know.'

He's not happy. 'Tova's got her name on her door.'

He's right, but hers is a little plate that says 'Princess Tova lives here' and it's hanging discreetly from some coloured thread. I want to keep my voice down as I'm worried that we're going to wake the house but it's hard. 'Yes, but the thing is as a family we agreed on that, we didn't agree on this, whatever it is.'

He shrugs. 'You said I could do my room how I liked.' He's right I did. When I don't answer, he has a suggestion. 'Don't you like it in black? I can do it in a different colour.'

He can see I'm unhappy so reluctantly he makes a half-hearted attempt to rub his name off the door with the palm of his hand but is no more successful than I was. He shrugs again and looks at me. His face bursts into a smile and his charming eyes widen as if we're sharing a joke together and he reminds me of Megan and all the things she got away with with her smile and eyes.

'OK, Sunny, let's talk more in the morning.'

Without another word, he goes back into his room. I listen, and shortly after the shuffling, moving and whispering inside begins again.

My stomach begins to contract, my lungs gulp for air and I realise that I'm going to be violently sick. In the bathroom, after, retching and almost choking, I wash my face and sink to the floor, resting my back against the bathroom wall. I wonder what's really made me sick. Is it the party food or is it having watched my sister die, already in the knowledge that her death is going to wreck my life. Or is it Sunny who's going to play by his own and his mother's rules and not ours. Or perhaps it's really my sister again continuing her campaign against me from the grave, directing her son and trying to organise me and my family's destruction through him. That would be classic Megan.

Struggling out of the bathroom, I spend a full ten minutes slumped against Sunny's door with my ear pressed against it but all there is to hear is total silence in near total darkness.

# Chapter 14

'Hello, miss. Do you remember me? I'm Frieda.'

The autumn term at our school doesn't begin until next week but we run all sorts of activities during the holidays for our students. There are sports, libraries and breakfast clubs which allow them to come on to the premises. This morning I'm on duty. I've already arranged for Sunny to join the school next term and I've brought him in to show him around and introduce him to my colleagues, his new teachers. I'm on the phone to the police when Frieda interrupts me, and at first I don't remember her. I'm still shattered after last night. I decided not to mention Sunny's artwork to him again this morning. I'm merely going to get some cleaning materials and wipe it off. If he wants a sign on his door, he can have a plate like Tova with 'Prince Sunny lives here' on it. Anyway, Frieda looks different in the daylight than she did the half-light lurking behind the front door of the flat opposite my sister's.

'Of course, could you excuse me one moment?'

On the other end of the line, there's no help from my new friend DC Summers. He's bored as he runs through the latest developments because there are no real new developments. He runs through his list. Door to door enquiries have revealed nothing that would help his inquiry. The toxicology tests have confirmed Megan died of a heroin overdose which she injected into her thigh. As far as the police can tell, she was alone all evening. He promises to keep me posted but it's a pro-forma promise. Once again, he refuses to let me have my sister's phones.

I turn back to Frieda. 'Sorry, I didn't mean to be rude but I had to finish that call.'

Frieda is holding the hand of one of our young pupils who doesn't look very happy about it. 'This is Laura. She's my granddaughter. Her mum would bring her to school usually but she's busy today so I've done it.'

'Of course, I know Laura.'

Sunny's standing next to me. 'This is my nephew Sunny, your neighbour Megan's son.'

Frieda looks at Sunny with regret while he looks back at her with what some might think was malice. There's no need for introductions. Frieda already knows him. 'Yes, of course, hello again, Sunny. I was terribly sorry to hear about your mum.'

She gets no answer. After waiting a few seconds for a reply, Frieda turns back to me. 'I didn't realise you were an important teacher at Laura's school. When she saw you, she was telling me how good you are and everything.'

She's probably surprised that Megan has a sister who does a job like mine. 'That's very kind of Laura.' I smile at her. 'You can tell your grandmother what a good student you are.'

Laura looks embarrassed but Frieda isn't interested in her granddaughter's studies. She pulls in closer to me. 'I'm terribly sorry I couldn't help you the other night when you called. If I'd known who you were, you could have come in for a cup of tea and a chat. Perhaps I could have thought of something to help.'

Sunny has also drawn closer. He's watching and listening intently which I'm not very happy about. 'Either you can remember something or you can't, Frieda.'

She looks wistfully at Sunny. 'Deepest condolence to you, miss. It's a terrible tragedy for your poor nephew here. He's a good boy.'

Sunny doesn't appear to be taking on board these words of sympathy. I try and work out if there's something Frieda actually wants to say about Megan's death. 'Thank you.'

'Are you working at the school today?'

'Until lunchtime.'

Frieda looks as if this is some vital piece of information that she needs, and gripping Laura's hands she walks away without saying goodbye. Sunny watches her go with a look of complete contempt.

They're out of earshot now. 'You didn't get on with Frieda?'

Sunny's still watching her go. 'Nah, she was always knocking on my mother's door, complaining about the noise, threatening her with the police and trying to get us evicted. Don't be fooled by her old lady act. I hope she drops dead, the moany old bag.' He adds through his teeth with as much venom as he can muster, 'She's a dumb bitch.'

Despite these being the most words that I've heard from my nephew since he arrived, I take him by the arm and warn him, 'We don't use words like "old bag" and "dumb bitch" at this school and we don't use them in my family either. Please remember that, Sunny.'

He looks up at me, completely baffled. 'Why not?'

Perhaps this is a conversation for another day. 'We just don't.'

Despite me being eager to get any sort of conversation going with him, he falls silent again as he's shown around the school and meets some of my colleagues. I've decided not to ask him how he's feeling about losing his mother the way he did. If he wants to talk about it, I've explained already that we're available at all times, but only if he feels he wants to. If he wants to talk about his experience living at Megan's, we can do that too. Or about his father, or school, or his books or indeed anything at all. I'm here for him.

Of course, it would help me work out what might have happened to Megan if he could talk about the days, weeks or months before she was lost, but I'm not going to press that matter and I hope in the course of conversations I might glean a few things. He was interviewed by Summers but couldn't help him. He went straight to his grandmother's flat from school that day, as he had all week. He told Summers that things were a little 'lairy' at home but he didn't want to say what 'lairy' meant. That's one of the things I'm hoping to discover.

Sunny is unimpressed by the impressive sports, music and other facilities our school offers, much of it paid for by our wealthier parents, of whom there are quite a number. But he's completely wowed by our library. We have computer suites, of course, but it was me who insisted that we also have proper books on proper shelves. Sunny is in Aladdin's cave as he eagerly sees what titles are on offer. He almost has to be dragged out of it. I make a mental note to remind him that he's not to steal books from our library for his collection. But perhaps that's also another conversation for another day.

At lunchtime my duty is over and the pair of us go to the car park to drive home. When we get there it's to discover Frieda is waiting for us. There's no sign of Laura. Frieda is carrying a plastic bag and asks if she can have a word in private. I tell Sunny to pop to the gents' toilet so he's not caught short on the way home.

He obviously doesn't like being bossed around by adults and it shows. 'I've already been.'

'Well, go again.'

He looks from me to Frieda and back to me again with that Megan-esque look in his eyes. 'OK.'

When he's gone, Frieda looks mournful. 'Your nephew doesn't like me.'

That's putting it mildly. 'He's a troubled young man. It's not your fault.'

'I know I complained a lot and neither of them liked it, but you've no idea what it was like living opposite them. It was a nightmare.' She adds hurriedly, 'I don't mean any disrespect to you or your sister.'

'None taken.'

She holds out the plastic bag for me. 'I was going to give you this the evening you came round to see me but then I thought better of it.'

'What is it?'

She's shamefaced. 'I often used to complain to the local authority about your sister's behaviour so they could do something about it. Not to get her thrown out or anything, not that, but just to get her to keep the noise down and keep some of the undesirables she attracted away. That's all. Anyway, they told me to keep an anti-social behaviour log that they could use as evidence. You know, a record of every instance when it was kicking off in your sister's flat. Names, dates, details all that.'

'And?'

She shakes the bag at me. 'This is it, the log. You might find it useful. It's no use to me any more. Or her come to that.'

In the bag is a thick blue notebook. Frieda snatches the bag back. 'Only you need to do one thing for me. Don't give it to the police. I like to keep myself to myself. I don't want any trouble with anyone. When the law came round, I told them I never heard anything.' I smile when she says, 'I don't want them arresting me for perjury or anything, I'm a respectable woman.' She gestures with her thumb in the direction that Sunny went. 'And don't show it to him either, he might come after me because he thinks I'm a snitch or something.'

I take the bag she offers. 'The police won't arrest you for perjury for telling a few fibs on the doorstep but I won't show it to them or Sunny.'

'Thank you, dear.' She turns to go but then turns back. 'It's strange to think that you're her sister. You're completely different people, what with you being an important teacher and so respectable and polite.'

My voice is wistful. 'We weren't always so different.'

When she's gone and while waiting for Sunny, I thumb through the log.

It's obvious at once that it's a goldmine.

# Chapter 15

***11.15 p.m.***

*Lots of noise opposite. Men and women's voices. Look out of the peep-hole on my door and see people going into the flat. Looks like they're the police and paramedics, some shouting going on.*

***11.25 p.m.***

*Through my bedroom window I can see an ambulance and police cars down below with their lights flashing. Open my door and ask a policeman what's going on. He says he can't tell me. Hear someone in the flat saying, 'Can you hear me, Megan?' That must be a nurse. She's obviously ill.*

***11.35 p.m.***

*A knock at my door. It's the police. They ask if I know the woman opposite and I say not really to be honest. They ask if anyone else lives in the flat and I say her son, Sunny, he's about thirteen, I think. They want to know where he is. I don't know but the neighbour next door to their flat says he might be at his grandmother's flat because he stays there sometimes. Don't know how she knows that. The police talk to her.*

***11.55 p.m.***

*See them carrying a stretcher out of the flat. Out of my bedroom window, see them put the stretcher in the ambulance. The police are still in the flat though. The woman opposite's a nightmare but hope she's all right.*

Those are the final entries in Frieda's anti-social behaviour log that cover my sister's final hour. There's plenty more though, what seem like hundreds of notes going back over twelve months, all carefully written in blue fountain pen. Some of the entries are a line or two. *More noise in her flat.* Others go on for pages. Long and painful descriptions of the chaos in Megan's home. These are a difficult read for me and will have to wait for another time. At the moment, it's the day she died that actually matters. The police were wrong to think there was no one in the flat that evening. In fact, the log shows that Megan had a number of visitors.

***7.10 p.m.***

*Argument in the flat opposite. Sounds like the woman and her boyfriend.*

***7.20 p.m.***

*Argument on the landing and down the staircase. Lots of foul language. The woman is telling the man not to come back. They're finished. He says she'll call him up again just like she always does. She's calling him 'Dirty Dixie'. More foul language.*

Definitely Dixie then.

***8.10 p.m.***

*The ex-husband is back again. Hammers on the door. Says he wants to see his son. Woman shouts through door, says her son is not there. Ex-husband doesn't believe her. Demands she opens the door so he can search the flat. Don't know what happens next but think she must have let him in. Goes quiet.*

She must mean Kit although he's not her ex-husband. Another visitor to the flat who told the police he wasn't there.

***8.45 p.m.***

*Argument opposite again. Ex-husband leaving. Says he's got rights. Says woman won't get a penny out if him until she lets him see his son. That poor boy. Says if she wants money, why doesn't she go to her dumb bitch of a sister. Says the sister is the woman's personal ATM. Can't hear what the woman says back but he shouts from stairwell saying if she's going to kill herself again, to make a good job of it this time. Says how many times is it that she's killed herself now?*

The page shakes under my trembling fingers. Megan never mentioned taking her own life to me. Not even once. Yet here's an entry in the log that suggests she was constantly threatening to commit suicide to Kit. My first thought is to wonder what Kit said to the police when they interviewed him. He lied about being at the flat that evening but did he tell DC Summers that Megan repeatedly threatened to take her own life? Is that what prompted Summers to tell me there was no evidence to prove that Megan took an overdose deliberately? Because there was?

***9.10 p.m.***

*Put the chain on the door and open my door a fraction. The ex-husband is sat halfway down the stairs, all hunched up. Decide to go out and speak to him to see if he's all right. He's crying. When he sees me, he gets up and looks embarrassed. Tells me to mind my own business. Goes down the stairs a bit more but stops and is a bit nicer. Tells me not worry, there'll be a new neighbour in the flat opposite soon and I'll get some peace and quiet.*

Is that a death threat? If it is, you can be sure that Kit won't have mentioned that to Summers.

***9.30 p.m.***

*The ex-boyfriend is back. Hammering on the door saying he wants his stuff. She's refusing to answer. Ex-boyfriend says if she doesn't give him his stuff, he'll bring some guys round and kick the door in and take it, plus the gear she owes him, and sort her out. He doesn't get an answer. Ex-boyfriend goes off in a huff shouting to the woman that she's been warned.*

Is that another death threat? I'll bet Dixie didn't mention that to the police either.

***9.35 p.m.***

*I'm looking through my peephole. Woman opposite comes out and walks up to my door. Shouts she knows I'm in here listening. Why don't I mind my own business and watch the TV or something instead of poking my nose in? Sounds like she's been crying too. She sounds a bit mournful. She goes off again. I call the police and say I'm being threatened by my neighbour. They say they'll send someone over.*

Has Summers got a record of that call and didn't bother to tell me about it when I spoke to him? Did the police send someone over in a car? Did it occur to them to press the neighbours about what they saw and heard that night instead of taking their claims they heard and saw nothing at face value? Did it occur to them that two despicable lowlifes like Dixie and Kit might have lied to them about visiting the flat that night? What has Summers' investigation into my sister's death actually amounted to?

There's one final entry before the emergency services arrive.

***10.30 p.m.***

*Sitting by my door on a chair. Have my walking stick in case woman opposite tries to get in and attack me. No sign of the police. Expect they won't come. They don't care about an old lady like me. Hear some noises opposite. Get up and look through my peephole. The door to the woman's flat is open. Someone's gone in there. Hear a man's voice but it's quiet so can't tell which one of them it is or what he says. When I look again the door is now ajar but can't hear any more voices. Can't hear the woman either. Can't see anyone leaving from my bedroom window but hear a car drive off.*

That will have been three quarters of an hour before the emergency services arrived.

I'm not sure who to be angriest with. The neighbours, Kit, Dixie, the police, Frieda for not gathering more information or my sister herself. I had no idea that things were getting this bad at her flat and she never said a word to me. On my visits, the flat was always in a reasonable state and she and Sunny seemed happy enough. There were no boyfriends, associates or Kit loitering around. Or did I know? What did I think was going on over there?

Cheese and wine parties, followed by bridge and scrabble? Maybe I'm angry with myself as well.

I'm not sure what to do now. Someone killed my sister, I'm sure of it, and there are already two prime suspects. I will never believe that she took her own life no matter what Kit heard from her. Yes, Summers is the professional, he knows his job and he's used to dealing with distraught relatives who can't accept any evidence that goes against what they 'know'. His conclusions all make sense. Yes, none of us who gathered at Megan's deathbed were shocked or even particularly surprised that my sister's life had ended the way it did. Yes, she was an addict and no number of phobias or complexes are going to stop an addict when it comes to their next hit. Perhaps someone else 'helped' her with the jab in good faith. I know all that. I'm a rational person who follows evidence and is willing to be proved wrong.

But I also know about my sister and needles. At the same time, perhaps it suits me to believe Megan was murdered so I don't have to face the possibility that my breaking links with her the previous week prompted her decision to end it all? I grit my teeth and think about that. Is this what's driving me? Do I need a murderer here so I don't have to feel like a murderer?

Perhaps, but I'm not going to stop, whatever my motivation may be.

My first instinct is to call Summers, provide him with the new information that Frieda has given me and demand to know why he didn't find it out himself. The trouble is that I promised Frieda that I wouldn't do that. Is it unethical to betray a promise like that? Is it ethical to leave the police without this vital information that might lead them to the person who murdered my sister?

It's seven o'clock in the evening now. The three children are downstairs playing Monopoly. Trevor isn't home from work yet and it's probably best to wait until he comes home and see what he thinks. It will give us something else to talk about apart from Sunny being in the house. Perhaps if we're quarrelling about Megan, we won't be quarrelling about Sunny. And to be totally honest, it'll make me happy to prove that Trevor calling my suspicions about Megan's unnatural death 'conspiracy theories' was wrong.

I begin to flip through Frieda's notebook to see the entries from the days before Megan's death when I hear what sounds like angry words from downstairs. Out on the landing, it soon becomes clear that a terrible argument has broken out among the children about Monopoly.

# Chapter 16

I hurry downstairs and into the dining room where the children are at the table.

'What is all this shouting? What is going on?'

A furious Tova points at Sunny. 'It's him, he's cheating!'

I've always encouraged my children to play board and card games. We play them together regularly as a family. I know Tova and Rodney will be 'digitalised' eventually but before they are, why not try and convince them that playing games with other humans in real life is a good idea? Tova usually wins. She's quite the card sharp. Her father, who used to play for money in clubs in his irresponsible youth, once told me that he wouldn't dare play poker against Tova, she'd have the shirt off his back. She's that quick and that clever. On occasion, Trevor and I have worked together to ensure that Rodney wins the occasional game so he doesn't feel too left out. But Tova's not winning today, one look at the board proves that.

Sunny has plenty of the toy money on his side of the table. Ruefully, I notice he's tied the pretend banknotes up in elastic bands as if they were drugs money. He has most of the cards, including the most valuable properties, which he has houses and hotels on. Tova and Rodney meanwhile seem to have very little money, very little property and very few houses. Either Sunny is a potential property magnate or he has indeed been cheating. Tova notices that I've said nothing and repeats even more loudly, 'He's cheating.'

I exchange glances with Rodney, who rolls his eyes and shrugs as if to say that Sunny has indeed been cheating but it's not worth making a fuss about.

'Perhaps there's been a misunderstanding?'

Tova is disgusted. 'No, he's cheating. Look at him! He steals money from the bank, takes cards out of community chest and chance and puts houses and hotels on the board when he thinks we're not looking.'

I'm totally lost. My own children know their limits and boundaries because we as a couple enforce them. Some of my pupils might not know theirs but they're other people's children and that's a different situation. I'm not sure how to enforce limits and boundaries with Sunny. I've just been reading about what limits and boundaries meant at my sister's flat. 'Right, well, let's see if we can think of a way to resolve this.'

Tova is beside herself with fury. 'Tell him off! If I cheated, you'd tell me off! Tell him off!'

Sunny is watching this dispute as if it's about someone else, not him. I ask my children to join me in the next room and explain to them that we need to understand that Sunny comes from a different place to us and we need to give him time to learn how to share our space as we do. Tova is unimpressed and walks out. 'What a joke! He's a cheat!'

Back in the dining room, Sunny is still sitting at the table when I return. He's staring at the Monopoly board as if it might give him a clue as to what the argument was about. I sit down in Tova's place and ask Sunny if he understands why his cousin was so upset.

'Sure.'

At least we've made a start. 'Why?'

'Because she was losing.'

Not a start then. 'No, it's because you weren't playing by the rules. Games don't work if everyone's not playing by the same rules. It's not fair.'

'Why doesn't she cheat as well and then it would be fair?'

I try again. 'Do you understand why lying and cheating are wrong?' When he doesn't answer I add, 'They're wrong, Sunny, because they destroy our trust in one another. Families, friends, schools and the world in general doesn't work without trust.'

'Who cares?'

When I was at university, one of our professors invited us students to consider a question in a tutorial. Why is murder wrong? One of the students, a Catholic girl, had a simple answer to that. It was against the ten commandments, number six I think it was, and forbidden by her religion. That was enough for her and she said nothing further. The rest of us were left tangling with various moral angles, the main one being a world where murder wasn't forbidden would soon become a dystopian nightmare of all against all, cruelty, suffering and killing. Our professor was unimpressed. 'In nature, animals kill each other all the time. No one says that's dystopian.'

'But human beings aren't animals.'

'Yes, we are, we're part of nature just like other animals. So why is murder wrong?'

Afterwards some of my fellow students expressed envy of the Catholic girl.

I feel like I'm in that tutorial again now and don't want to be. 'Who cares? Look, Sunny, let me explain things to you.' Looking into his eyes, it suddenly makes sense to leave this as another conversation for the mounting list of other conversations that can wait for other days. 'It's simple really, we don't cheat in this house, please try and remember that when you're playing with your cousins.'

'OK.'

Tucked in between his legs is a book which he pulls out. It crosses my mind that he may well have been reading it while he was cheating at Monopoly. He shows it to me. 'Can I go and read my book now?'

'Yes, of course.'

There's a key in the front door and Trevor appears. When I ask him if we can have a word, he looks alarmed. 'It's about Sunny, isn't it? What's he done?'

'It's not about Sunny, at least not directly.'

He's relieved. 'OK, let me sort myself out, go and see the children and then we can talk.'

It's half an hour before he reappears. 'What's up?'

I show him Frieda's log, tell him how I got it and explain the situation to him. How it proves that Kit and Dixie were both lying about not being at Megan's flat that day and that they both made threats within a few hours of her death. The police were wrong to say she was there alone that evening. I admit there might be grounds for thinking she was suicidal but insist again it would never have been with an overdose with a needle. I also tell him about keeping Frieda's confidence. What should I do?

He reads the entries intently before handing me the log back. 'It's obvious what you should do. You need to take it to the police.'

'I can't take it to the police, I promised Frieda I wouldn't.'

He's aghast. 'I don't understand you. You've been maintaining from the start that your sister was the victim of foul play. Now you've got your hands on some evidence that might suggest something funny was going on and you don't want to take it to the police? I don't get it. If you want my opinion there's nothing funny going on here, it was a long-expected overdose, but if you do take that to the police, I'm sure they'll want another word with Kit and Dixie. They can sort it out.'

'I was thinking of telling the police what was in the log but not telling them how I found out to safeguard Frieda.'

He looks at me in disbelief. 'I'm not a lawyer but that's just hearsay, isn't it? What are the police supposed to do with that?'

'A promise is a promise.'

'It's up to you. Is there anything else? Are we all right with Sunny and everything?'

The question sounds pointed. 'Yes.'

He gives me a knowing look. 'You weren't going to tell me, were you?'

'About what?'

'About Sunny cheating at a board game and really upsetting your daughter when you didn't stick up for her? Tova's just been telling me about it. She hid behind the door while it appears you were doing moral philosophy with her cousin. She wanted to make sure you were putting him straight but of course you weren't.'

I'm caught and I don't even know why I didn't tell the truth. But Trevor does. 'You don't want to admit it, do you? What a terrible mistake it was to bring that boy into our house? Let me tell you something, the day is going to come when that kid reducing our daughter to tears is going to be remembered as the good old days.' He makes to leave. 'And another thing. You weren't going to tell me about Sunny's artwork on his door either. You did a good job wiping it off but the outline is still there. You're a fine one to talk to Sunny about trust and good faith and the rest of it. Although I suppose I can't blame you. The real culprit is upstairs in his room with the ghost of your sister. They're probably laughing at you, the same way Megan always did.'

There's just enough truth in there to make it hurt. But he doesn't know the real truth about my sister and me. It was my decision early on in our relationship not to tell him. Perhaps the real culprit has been me all the time. Perhaps it wasn't Sunny or the ghost of my sister upstairs.

'And another thing, Josie. What was this problem she had with needles anyway?'

I choose my words carefully this time. 'It was just a phobia, that's all.'

'I get it with kids but not with adults. Why not just close your eyes tight while you're getting the jab?'

I don't answer. He's right, I've told enough lies for one day.

# Chapter 17

## Thirty Years Earlier

'What happened?'

This question was asked all the time from the panicked moment Megan and Josie's parents arrived at the hospital where Megan was taken after the accident, with a broken leg. They kept asking because Josie didn't seem to know even though she'd been there. Their father became angry at his older daughter. 'It's not a difficult question, Josie. What happened to your sister?'

Josie turned her head for a moment to where her sister was howling in pain behind a curtain while a doctor and nurse offered soothing reassurances. The medical staff were promising Megan that her leg would soon mend. Josie fumbled, desperately trying to find an answer that wouldn't mean she was to blame. 'She was hit by a car in the road.'

This wasn't enough for their father. 'She was crossing the road then, not looking where she was going? Is that right?'

Another howl and sob from Megan behind the curtains, more soothing words from the medical team. There was no point in lying, Megan was going to tell them anyway. She was probably looking forward to doing so. But there was also no point in telling them the truth and seeing their faces when they discovered Josie had pushed her sister under a car. There was no answer. Her father bowed down so they were face to face. 'Have you lost your voice, girl?'

Their mother pulled him back. 'Don't, she's upset. There's a policeman over there, ask him what happened.'

The cop was under the impression it was all a terrible accident. 'We've breathalysed the driver and from what we can tell from an eyewitness, he wasn't speeding or anything. He says one minute the two girls were on the pavement and the next, one of them was under his wheels. He doesn't know how that happened, but he's pretty shaken up, he thought he might have killed her. I'm afraid that unless your daughters have got anything to add, it's just one of those things unfortunately. We'll take statements to be on the safe side.'

Josie overheard the words 'take statements' and thought she would be in trouble with the police now as well as her parents. Mercifully a doctor appeared from behind the curtain and their parents descended on him. He was reassuring. 'Your daughter will soon be on the mend. Her leg is broken and it is an awkward fracture and there's some tissue damage, so when it's healed, we'll need to bring her back in again from time to time for some procedures. They won't be comfortable ones, I'm afraid, but we'll make sure she's properly sedated before we get to work. So, it's six weeks in plaster and then she can come home and we'll see her regularly after that. Don't worry, she'll make a full recovery, it's just slightly more tricky than a typical broken leg.'

The curtains around Megan's bed were drawn back to reveal her propped up in bed, her plastered leg dangling in the air. She wasn't crying or howling any more, she was quiet but she had a sullen, resentful and unquiet expression. Her parents took up positions on either side of their youngest and each took one of her hands. Josie stood at the head of the bed staring down at her sister.

It was, Josie felt in the years after, like a death bed scene where a confession was about to be announced. Once they'd done their share of reassurances, sympathy and promises that she would soon be home, the dreaded question was asked. Their father put on his most sympathetic voice. 'What happened?'

Megan looked up at her father with a curled lip and then at her mother before finally looking down the bed to where Josie was standing. She fixed her eyes on her for a long time before turning back to their father but without saying a word. He tried again. 'Don't you remember?'

Their mother wondered aloud if Megan was in shock. Once again, her sister's eyes drifted to where Josie was standing and finally, she spoke. 'No, it's all right I remember. I tripped up on the pavement and fell in the road and the car hit me.'

Their father wasn't convinced. 'How do you trip on the pavement and then fall into the road?'

Megan snapped bitterly, 'I tripped up on the pavement and fell into the road. What do you want me to say? That Josie and I were having a fight and she tried to kill me by shoving me under a car?'

Their father was convinced now and was apologetic. 'No, no, of course not, if you tripped, you tripped.'

Megan turned her eyes and looked again at her sister with a stare. It had a simple message.

You owe me.

# Chapter 18

I'm still working out how to pass the information from Frieda's log on to Summers without compromising her. But he saves me the trouble by ringing me himself. I take a seat at the table where the Monopoly board that sparked the argument the previous day is still set up. Summers uses the sensitive tone that he presumably keeps for distressed relatives, for relatives who can't face facts, but his message is plain. As far as he's concerned, his inquiry is over. He goes on to explain.

'We know you're not happy with the idea that Megan would have used a needle on herself but the evidence is overwhelming. There's no reason to suspect foul play. What we're going to do now is pass all this information on to the coroner so we can get a death certificate issued and then you can lay your sister to rest. As far as we're concerned that's our role over. You can rest assured though that we're close on the tail of the people who sold her the drugs. As I've said, you can rely on the courts to be very sensitive on these matters.'

I haven't made a decision on the means so I go straight to the ends. 'You might have to wait a little while before closing your file. I spoke to a neighbour of my sister's and she said both Megan's boyfriend Dixie and her former partner Kit were with her the evening she died and there were a series of arguments. There was also a final visitor shortly before she died. My understanding was that my sister was alone in the flat on the evening she died and Dixie and Kit both denied having seen her that day.'

Summers is curious at once. 'Oh really, that's very interesting. Those two charmers did indeed both say they weren't there while the neighbours all said they heard and saw nothing.' He sounds as if he's reaching for a notebook. 'Which neighbour was this?'

'Unfortunately, I can't say, she told me in confidence. She doesn't want to get involved in any inquiry.'

Summers sighs heavily. 'There's not much we can do with that, Josie. If she's not willing to put her name to anything, we don't have much to go on. We can bring Kit and Dixie in for another chat, but they're old hands at the interview game and they'll soon be able to tell if we've got any evidence against them. If they know we have nothing, they'll just drink tea and smoke cigarettes until we let them go. To be honest, I wouldn't be surprised if they were in the flat that evening, that they were arguing, and it might have been one of them who sold Megan the drugs. That sounds plausible but I'm not quite sure what you're suggesting. That Dixie or Kit killed your sister with a jab? Neither of them are that sort of offender.'

I don't know enough about Dixie to say but I'm pretty sure that Kit is. When I say nothing, Summers goes on, 'Look, if you can go round and speak to the neighbour and persuade her to sign something, I'll bring the pair of them in and lean on them a little.'

I'm certainly not going to try and persuade Frieda to speak to the police. It's obvious how paranoid and suspicious she is already. If I speak to her about the cops, she'll probably demand her log back and I can't do that, at least not until I've read it thoroughly and copied it. I'm not looking forward to her calling me a liar and a cheat either. My husband doing it last night was enough. Speaking to Dixie and Kit myself is a more promising approach, and although Kit hates me, there's no reason for Dixie to. I know where to find him. Megan told me a few weeks before her death that her current boyfriend was the classic mug punter. All the money he made through honest stealing, dealing and sponging, he wasted in betting shops. There's a list online of the local places within a five-mile radius and with that in my bag, I set out in my car to find him.

It's early afternoon before my searching finally pays off. Perched on a stool in a high street betting shop he's watching horse racing on a TV, clutching some betting slips.

He's surprised but not alarmed when he sees me come in.

'Hello, Dixie, can we have a word about my sister's death?'

He shakes his head. 'I've got nothing to say to you. I've said everything that needs saying about Megan to the police and they're happy enough. That's the end of the matter as far as I'm concerned.'

'What about if I buy you a drink or two?'

He looks at the racing and then at his betting slips. 'What do you want to talk about?'

'About my sister. For a start I'd like to know why you lied to the police about being in her flat the night she died.'

He bursts out laughing. 'My word, you're naive. The police don't expect you to tell them the truth. All they want to know is whether you're guilty of anything or not and they know you're not going to tell them. That's our world, it's just a game really.'

On the TV, a horse race is finishing. Dixie looks down at the grubby floor in despair and lets the betting slips fall through his fingers. 'Alright, you can buy me a drink, I've got nothing to hide.'

We go into a pub next door and he has a double, swills it back in one go before we've even sat down and then looks at me expectantly. It's no problem buying him another one. It's more likely he'll tell me the truth if he's had a few drinks.

'What do you want to know, Josie?'

'You told the police you weren't in my sister's flat that evening but you were. You told me that you were at her flat earlier in the day and then only went back there again much later in the evening and that's when you saw the ambulance outside.'

He shrugs. 'Sure, I went round there in the early evening. So what? We smoked some stuff, had a bust-up and she kicked me out. She said for good this time. I had a few things left in the flat so I went round to collect them a little while later when I thought she might have been in a better mood. One of the neighbours told me Megan was in a bad way so I followed on to A&E.'

'That was good of you after you threatened earlier in the evening to bring some people round and kick her door in.'

He's puzzled. 'Where did you find all this out?' Dixie has a lightbulb moment. 'I suppose it was the old dear in the flat opposite. Megan had some history with her, she thought the old woman was spying on her. I don't know what she told you but she makes things up.' He shows me his empty palms as a way of assuring me he's being honest. 'So, yeah, sure, Megan and me had a row. Big deal. You know what a row's like, don't you? Things get said that probably shouldn't be said, it doesn't mean anything.' He looks me up and down. 'Or maybe not in your case. Maybe you and your husband don't row, no doubt you're the type of couple who sits down and works through their issues in a sensible, adult way. Good for you. After the row, I cleared off when she warned me Sunny's father was coming round. He's a piece of work that guy, if you think there was foul play with Megan's death, he's the one you need to speak to. Anyway, that was the last I saw of Megan. When I came back later, the ambulance was outside.'

He shakes his jacket with one hand. 'Look at me. Do I look like a foul play kind of guy? I'm just a high plains drifter that's all and don't pretend to be anything else. That Kit, on the other hand,

I wouldn't like to say. What makes you think there was something not quite right about your sister's death anyway?'

'The police say she injected herself with heroin. She might have been injected but she didn't do it herself. She had a phobia of needles.'

Dixie has another lightbulb moment. 'Yeah, you're right, she did! She snorted and smoked a lot of stuff but she had a big problem with needles. She didn't use heroin either. Find out where she got the needles and smack from and you might get some answers.' He catches my eye. 'She certainly didn't get them from me if that's what you're thinking. That's a bit out of my league. Where'd her needle problem come from anyway? That's a kid's kind of thing not an adult's.'

If I can't tell my nearest and dearest, I certainly can't tell a guy like Dixie. When he doesn't get an answer, he supplies his own. 'You can't really explain a phobia though. Bit like fear of flying.'

Dixie wants to get back to his betting shop. He asks me if I can lend him fifty quid, promising me that he'll give it back when he's got it. It shows what kind of mug punter I am that I very nearly do.

'Come on, Josie, you're good for it. You gave Megan loads of money.'

I don't know where he got that idea from. 'I helped her when she was in trouble but only when she really needed it.'

He's surprised at this. 'Really? According to Megan, you were her ATM. Some gratitude, eh? Mind you, people like us can always raise money one way or another, legal or not so legal. You can always sell on if you've got some extra.' Then Dixie remembers he's supposed to care about people. 'What's happening to the kid?'

'You mean Sunny? He's come to live with us.'

Dixie is horrified. 'You've got him in your house? Well, good luck with that.'

Yet another person warning me about Sunny. 'What the hell is that supposed to mean?'

'Don't get upset, I'm not saying anything bad about him. It's just he's a bit of a weirdo, that boy, cooped up in his room with all those books. He's a very strange kid who holds grudges over the strangest things. He once asked Megan if he could have boxing lessons. She naturally assumed he was being bullied by bigger boys. But he told her it was because a teacher at his school had told him one break time to walk on the path and not on the grass. He wanted to learn how to box so when he was big enough, he could go back to the school and punch the teacher out. The thing is he admitted that this incident happened the previous term, which meant he'd been brooding about it all that time. That's not normal, Josie. Sunny's what my grandfather always liked to call 'a lad made for the gallows'.

# Chapter 19

It's half past midnight and the lights have just gone out in our house. Truth to tell, they've well and truly gone out in our house now.

I'm in the marital bed that Trevor has now moved out of. He's sleeping on a sofa downstairs. He claims this is because he has to get up early for work and doesn't want to disturb me. I'm not sure whether I'm meant to believe that or not. Of course I don't. It's up there with 'working late at the office' to cover an affair. He assured me the children wouldn't notice but of course they did. I understand my husband's reasons for not wanting Sunny in our house, not least because I share them to some extent. But his dislike of the situation we're in appears to have turned into a real dislike of poor Sunny himself. He refuses to explain what Sunny has done to deserve this. Yes, he puts symbols on his door and cheats at games but that hardly justifies this reaction. Whoever's to blame, it isn't Sunny. So why do I feel the same? It's almost as if we can feel Sunny's presence in the house even when he's quiet in his room. I feel Megan's presence too, as if Sunny has brought his mother's shade with him. Sunny has only been in our house a week but when Trevor comes home, his first question is always the same. 'Has Sunny been up to anything?'

He's almost disappointed to hear he hasn't. My husband appears to be clinging to the possibility that at a later, more formal stage social services will decide to move Sunny on, perhaps to a reformed and cleaned-up Kit. He also clearly resents what he regards as my veto on his opposition to Sunny coming to our home. He doesn't say it out loud but there are sniping remarks about decisions which should be joint being 'up to you, Josie, after all, you have the final say . . .' Perhaps he was worried that in the event of my being forced to choose between Sunny and him, I'd have chosen Sunny. Perhaps I worry about that too.

Tova decided to stop talking to Sunny after the board game incident. For a day or two she only spoke to him through Rodney. She was told to stop doing that as it was unkind to her cousin to freeze him out. As a result, she stopped talking to him at all and had to be told to pack that in as well. She thinks he's a cheat. Some students of family life might think it shows what a good job her parents have done that she's so outraged by cheating. Now Tova also thinks I'm a bad mother because I didn't bawl Sunny out for being a cheat and didn't take her side. She also thinks I've upset her father, presumably over the cheating business, which is why he's sleeping on the sofa. Perhaps she thinks I threw her father out of the bedroom over the board game incident. Poor Rodney is gamely left trying to help Sunny adapt to family life and reconcile his sister with her cousin. He's also concerned about his father's showy move on to the sofa downstairs.

All this over one unfortunate board game.

Because the lodger hasn't done anything to anyone. It would actually be quite difficult for him to do so. He's either in his room 'reading' or occasionally in the back garden 'reading'. He only shows up for meals when he's instructed to do so. He doesn't understand why he can't have his meals in his room so he can read at the same time. When he was asked how he was managing with his new computer and whether he needed any help with it, he seemed to have forgotten that it was there. A sneak peek around the door when he leaves it slightly open shows he's keeping his room surprisingly tidy, with only a pile of loose papers and his pen on the desk.

Meanwhile, I've been reading Frieda's log from the beginning in an effort to see if there are clues in it that might explain what happened to Megan. There aren't any. Dixie was a useless part-time partner cum sponger and Kit is a dangerous thug. But I already knew that. There are other bit-part characters whose names and nicknames only get recorded in passing as Frieda logs the shouting matches and abuse at my sister's flat. There are two other characters. One is Sunny, who appears from time to time when Frieda writes 'that poor boy' or 'that poor boy – what must it be like for him in that chaotic flat?'

There's another person also mentioned in passing. That's me.

***8.10 p.m.***

*The ex-husband is arguing with the woman opposite. He's asking if she's going to get her dumb bitch of a sister to write one of her fancy letters to the authorities to get him thrown in prison.*

I don't read anything about Sunny holding grudges but Kit certainly seems to. He was right to this extent. It certainly was me who wrote all the letters to the authorities and represented Megan in all her meetings when she was in trouble or trying to keep Kit away from her son. I did a good job too. It was essential to keep mother and son together. At the end of the day, Sunny was all she had.

It's not hard to see where Sunny learned the term 'dumb bitch' either.

I can't read all of Frieda's log at one go. It's too hard for me, so it has to be read in bite-sized pieces. The carefully curated image Megan created for me of the lone single mother bravely defying a brutal and oppressive state system and cruel and abusive men might have been half of the truth. The other part though she kept secret from me. The brutal and oppressive state system was also trying to help her and save her and her son from themselves. The cruel and abusive men she tolerated and encouraged into her home when it suited her. A long procession of nameless lowlifes who came to her parties and all-night drug fests. She was a terrible neighbour. Dixie thinks Frieda made things up but it all has the ring of truth. An innocent old woman like Frieda couldn't make those things up.

And where did all the money come from?

Frieda again:

***2.30 p.m.***

*The woman opposite is carrying a new designer handbag. She doesn't work so where's the money coming from? Cheating the social security while honest people like me go without. I'm going to report her to the social.*

That's one possibility but there are others. Petty crime, a sugar daddy, drug dealing. Sex work.

I still can't face going to Frieda's and asking her to make a statement to the police. I don't know how I'm going to persuade Kit to tell me his story of what happened while he was in the flat that night either. But, according to Dixie, the police know that people like him and Kit lie so they've probably factored that in already. And what if they were in her flat? That doesn't prove they had anything to do with Megan's death. Maybe threats were bandied around but, as Dixie told me, things get said in rows.

The weight of all this finally pulls my eyelids shut and I'm in a twilight world of half dreams that might be real and might not be. In one, Megan is lying in her drawer at the morgue when her eyes slowly open. She raises her arm and points an accusing finger at me. In another, Kit is trying to stab me to death with a syringe and needle, chasing me through our house until his clammy hands close around my neck and he plunges his deadly weapon into my arms and thighs. How can he do that with both hands round my neck? I wake, unsure whether the screaming I can hear is me or not. It's a few seconds before it becomes clear that there is screaming in our house and it isn't coming from me. It's Tova, howling like an animal.

I rush into her bedroom and flick the light on. Tova is scrunched up in a corner of her bed with the duvet clasped in her hands, pulled up tight around her neck. She looks terrified. Standing next to the bed is Sunny. Trevor bursts into the room. 'What the hell is going on?' He takes one look at our daughter and another at Sunny and decides for himself what's going on. He flashes a look of hatred at me before rushing over to Tova. 'What happened?'

Tova is trying to draw air into her empty lungs. She points at Sunny. 'It's him! He was leaning over my bed staring at me in the dark!'

Trevor is lost for words. I hurriedly usher Sunny out on to the landing and close the door behind me. 'Sunny! What on earth were you doing?'

He's bemused. 'I got up and went to the bathroom. On the way back, I couldn't remember which room was mine and I didn't want to wake anyone up by putting the light on. I went to Tova's room by mistake and only knew when I leaned over the bed and saw Tova in it. Then she wakes up and starts screaming the place down. Stupid.'

I can hear Tova sobbing, Trevor comforting her.

'Go to your room, Sunny,' I instruct. 'I'll talk to you in the morning.'

He shrugs before returning to his room and closing the door behind him.

The bathroom is on the landing. When I look inside, there's no evidence that Sunny has used it. It has an ancient cistern dating back to when the house was built. It takes around fifteen minutes for it to refill after the chain is pulled. We've had many plumbers in over the years trying to fix it and end the slow monotonous trickle of water into the ornate ceramic bowl. They all failed and told us there was nothing we could do and to treat it as a feature. The cistern is silent now, none of that tell-tale sound of slowly running water that shows it was used in the last quarter of an hour. Sunny hasn't used it at all and he hasn't been in here.

He's lying.

# Chapter 20

'He's gotta go!'

Trevor doesn't wait for a response.

'No, I'm not arguing about it, he's got to go. Ring Social Services today and tell them to come and collect him. Tell them to bring one of those vans with a cage in the back like they use for wild animals.'

I'm upset too but Trevor's response is still wildly out of proportion. 'He said it was an honest mistake. His mistook Tova's room for his own. That's how it happened.'

Who is this person arguing with my husband? I know full well that isn't how it happened. Who is this person excusing Sunny's behaviour? This is my daughter we're talking about.

Trevor looks up at the ceiling in despair. 'Oh man . . .' His eyes are turned back on me. 'I don't care whether it was a mistake or not, whether it was honest or otherwise. He's leaving.'

The stranger arguing with my husband is still working my controls. 'The new school term starts in a few days and he'll be socialised into a totally different environment to the one he's used to. He'll settle down and move on from his time at Megan's.'

Trevor is savage. 'Listen to yourself! Socialised in a different environment? You know, Megan was right about you all along.

You use your fancy campus words to paint over reality because you can't face the truth.'

'How do you know what Megan would say? You hardly spoke a word to her the entire time we've been married.'

He's uncomfortable. 'Don't be cute, Josie. You don't think I don't know what she was like?' He looks around. 'Where is he anyway? What's he up to now?'

Rodney and Tova appeared for breakfast. They didn't stay long though. Tova feels ill and Rodney is taking on the atmosphere in the house. They both leave the table without a word. They're probably looking forward to going back to school and it's hard to blame them. 'I'll go and fetch him. We'll talk and sort things out.'

'Oh no, I'm not talking to him, there's nothing to talk about. I'm going to work. You need to sort things out with yourself not him. Don't think I'm joking about this, Josie. I mean it, he's got to go. If he doesn't go, you'll have to go as well and take him with you. If you refuse, I'll find somewhere else to live and take the children with me. We can fight it out in the courts if need be. I'm not having my children living here with that little psychopath upstairs.'

There are three of us in this savage battle. Trevor, me and the woman making excuses for Sunny who also appears to be me. Why am I doing this? I don't have time to figure it out. 'Don't be ridiculous, he's not a psychopath. I'll speak to him, he'll understand that he made a mistake and why Tova is so upset. He'll promise not to do it again.'

Trevor has a toolbox in one hand and a screwdriver in the other. 'Why are you doing this? Is it something to do with your relationship with Megan? Do you feel like you owe her or something? You don't owe her anything. Are you really going to let her exploit and manipulate you in death as she did in life? Tell me, I really want to know.'

'Why are *you* doing this? You haven't given Sunny a chance since before he came here and you don't want to help him or support me at all. Why is that?'

He doesn't answer. All the questions in our house are going unanswered. 'This is my final word on the matter. He's leaving. If you want to destroy your family and our marriage as a favour to your dead sister that's up to you but I won't go along with it. In the meantime, I've got to go put a lock on the door to our daughter's room to keep her safe. You have a think about what that means.'

He walks upstairs and slams Tova's door behind him. Soon there is the sound of hammering and drilling. With leaden feet I go upstairs and knock on Sunny's door. He doesn't answer but I go in anyway. Sunny is lying on his bed reading a book. I think it's Mary Shelley's *Frankenstein*. He looks up at me when I come in but then goes back to reading his book. I sit on the edge of his bed.

'That was very upsetting what happened last night, Sunny.'

He carries on reading. 'Yeah. You need to have a word with Tova, screaming the house down like that. I was upset.'

'She was screaming because she was terrified Sunny, because of you.'

He's still reading. 'Whatever. It was a mistake. She must have heard of mistakes before.'

I take the book out of his hands and put it down. 'What were you doing in her room?'

He repeats his story from the night before. He's not fazed at all when he hears that it can't be true. Instead, he quickly supplies me with another version. 'I had a piss in the sink. I didn't want to use the cistern because I know it makes a noise. I was trying not to wake anyone up.'

It's the sort of answer my sister would have given. 'I don't believe you and this is causing a lot of discord in our home.'

He looks hurt. 'I don't like discord either. Can I have my book back now?'

Trevor was right. This is a waste of time. I think of all the times Megan should have apologised to me but she never did. All the times I apologised to her for things that weren't my fault. 'Things are going to get very difficult in this house if we don't all learn how to get along. One way we get along when we've upset each other, we say sorry. It would help if you said sorry to Tova.'

The words are sticking in my throat. Deep down, I'm as angry with him as Trevor. The truth is I want him out as well. It's that third person in our argument and marriage who can't let him go and she doesn't make any sense.

'OK.'

He gets off the bed and follows me downstairs where he waits while Tova is summoned from where she's watching her father fit a lock to her door. She doesn't want to come so she has to be shepherded to where her cousin is waiting for her. She stands with her arms folded looking deeply unhappy. 'Have you got something to say, Sunny?' I press my nephew.

He looks at me with eyes both innocent and full of Megan-esque mischief. 'Yes.'

He has to be prompted. 'What is it?'

There's nothing sarcastic in his words, it's a flat monotone. 'I'm sorry you were upset that I came in your room Tova. It was a mistake.'

Tova just glares at him. She has to be prompted too. 'What do you say, Tova?'

'OK.'

I push things too far by saying, 'What about we hug it out?'

It's my turn to be glared at by Tova and she stomps off, leaving Sunny to ask, 'Can I go and read my book now?'

I need a friendly face and someone to tell me that this will all work out in the end. Rodney's playing computer games in his room. He avoids my eyes when I go to see him. He freely admits he heard what happened the night before because he must have done. When he hears about Sunny's explanation, he's not convinced either, while at the same time being disgusted by the idea that Sunny relieved himself in our bathroom sink. Rodney decides that was too vile to make up. 'Perhaps it's true.'

Now I'm prompting my son. 'Yes, there are bound to be a few bumps in the road when someone joins a family. Sunny doesn't know about playing games so it's not surprising that he couldn't cope the first time he played with us. Perhaps his story about going into Tova's room by mistake is true.'

Rodney doesn't answer. The only noise is the clicking of his mouse as he plays his game. I try again. 'Don't you think?'

He stops and turns to face me. 'I don't know. All I know is Dad and Tova want him out and you don't.'

'And what about you?'

He turns away again. 'I don't know.' There is more clicking before he turns to me again. 'The thing is that it's not about the Monopoly or Tova. It's that you kind of know he's in the house even when you can't see him, even when he's in his room. It's like he's everywhere. Like he's up to something all the time but you don't know what. He's like the troll under the bridge in "Billy Goats Gruff". You know he's there even when he's not.'

I'm almost pleading with my son for help. 'You're nearly the same age as Sunny. Can't you try and engage with him? Get him interested in things, do some boy stuff with him? Anything at all?'

He's too good a son to say no outright. 'I'll try.'

This hasn't helped. I decide to go and face the next instalment of Frieda's log although that's not going to help either. Two emails arrive in my inbox. One is from Social Services confirming in writing that the team have decided that Kit can have contact with Sunny. They'll be supervised though. That's all I need. Kit coming to my front door. But maybe I could use these visits to my advantage. I begin thinking of ways to trap Kit into admitting that he was at Megan's flat the night she died and telling me what happened while he was there. The other email is from DC Summers. It's an official notification that the investigation into Megan's death is now closed and the evidence is being sent to the coroner for a provisional verdict and a temporary death certificate so we can bury Megan. He includes a personal note telling me that he's still confident that their initial assessment is correct and that Megan's death was an accident. He notes that as there's no sign of the neighbour's statement he obviously can't investigate any further. If I do get one, though, he will certainly look into it.

I can't read the helpful summary of the evidence that Summers had provided. I only catch the phrase 'no reason to suspect foul play'. If I do read the whole thing then it might just convince me that my sister's death was indeed a tragic accident and my suspicions are just a useful diversion from worrying about what's happening to my family. Summers' evidence might be solid but it excludes one vital fact that I won't let go of. The searing memory of my sister screaming whenever she was faced with a needle.

Time is slipping away but that memory is just as much a part of any evidence as anything Summers has uncovered and I'm leading with it.

# Chapter 21

## Thirty Years Earlier

Josie came to dread the procedures on her sister's leg almost as much as Megan did herself. The pattern was always the same. An appointment would be made at the hospital and in the days leading up to it Megan would become increasingly sullen. On the day itself she would have to be dragged out of the house like an arrested fugitive, insisting her leg was fine and didn't need any more 'work'. On one occasion, while Megan was being manhandled out of the front door to a waiting hospital vehicle, a neighbour called the police because she thought Megan was being kidnapped. At the hospital itself, Megan had to be sedated before procedures so the doctors could begin the treatments. Megan would spit the tablets out. When they tried to inject pain killers into her, Megan would struggle, scream and kick. One nurse thought that Megan regarded injections in the same way that a man about to be executed reacts to the sight of the noose. Afterwards, an exhausted and wrung out Megan would be taken home and it would be over. Until the next time.

Josie was a witness to these hospital trips. Their parents insisted she come to support her sister. 'It might help Megan cope if you're there.'

Josie was hardly in a position to say, 'It won't help her and it certainly won't help me, either.' That might mean admitting who was to blame for the broken leg in the first place. Megan still wasn't telling the truth about it. That meant Josie was there for the kicking and the screaming, the howling and the struggling. Each and every time these sounds cut another scar into her soul and reminded her of what happened. 'This is my fault.' One stupid shove in the heat of the moment that on any other occasion might have led to a grazed knee had ended in disaster. Her traumatised sister, who couldn't get over the last visit to the hospital because there would be another one in a few weeks. A sister who was left with a lifelong phobia of needles and syringes.

The visits to the hospital only lasted a few months but they seemed to Josie to go on for years. Afterwards, Megan's leg was back to normal, although sometimes Megan would perform a limp to get sympathy. She soon stopped that though when her parents wondered if a return visit to the hospital might be necessary. The horror of needles continued into adulthood. Megan flatly refused to be vaccinated for anything.

'But Megan, do you want to get tetanus?'

'I'll take the tetanus, thanks. I'm not having any jabs and that's final.'

At first, the same drama that had unfolded at the hospital repeated itself for Megan with every childhood injection. As she got older, though, the family and the medical profession gave up. Foreign trips that involved inoculations were ruled out. She took drugs before visits to the dentist rather than be jabbed there. Although later she drifted through the world of narcotics, she took a dim view of those who hunted for a vein to inject into.

'Disgusting.'

In time, the accident and the broken leg slowly stopped being a subject of conversation within the family. It was nearly forgotten about and only mentioned when Megan needed an excuse for something. Megan's horror of needles came up from time to time but then almost only as a family joke. She made a full recovery and soon caught up with her lost schoolwork in as far as she was ever going to and certainly not as well as her sister, who excelled. When Megan put in another disappointing performance in an exam, she tried at first to blame the accident.

'It's hardly surprising. I lost a year of schoolwork thanks to my broken leg.'

'It was two months, Megan, not a year. Stop exaggerating.'

If Megan ever used the accident as an excuse to get out of an activity, Josie would freeze in fear that her sister would next point a finger at her in front of their parents. 'And you know who was to blame for that? She was. Josie pushed me in front of that car. Deliberately.' There were times when Josie couldn't stop herself feeling that it would have been better if Megan had been killed in the accident, which only added to her guilt.

But Megan never told anyone about the accident. It was their sordid secret. Their parents might have forgotten but the sisters never did. When Megan was given the chance to blame her sister for what happened she never took it. But she always gave Josie a meaningful and unmistakeable look as a reminder.

It always said the same thing – you really owe me.

# Chapter 22

The start of a new term is always a demanding time for a deputy head but I've never had one like this before. I brought Sunny in with me this morning for his first day at my school. He was introduced to his new class and it felt like a racing certainty that his classmates would agree with Trevor that Sunny was a little psychopath, or with Rodney that he was the billy goats Gruff's troll. Of course he was warmly welcomed. All morning I sat in my office worrying that one of my colleagues would come in and say Sunny was going to be suspended on his first day for cheating in PE or harassing girls in his class. At lunchtime when I anxiously enquired how Sunny was managing in lessons, my colleagues assured me he was settling in, maybe a little shy and awkward but that's only to be expected. It's the first moment of relief I've felt since he arrived in our house.

I'm still worried in the afternoon, however. I know what Rodney means, even when Sunny isn't 'there', he's still 'there' at the back of our minds. At four o'clock the school day ends and Sunny still hasn't been sent to the head teacher, suspended, expelled or arrested. In a corridor I bump into Sunny's English teacher who looks concerned. It turns out she was thinking of some other issue and, if anything, she's a little over the top in her praise for Sunny.

'He's very bright and incredibly well read for a child of his age, especially for a boy. You know he's read *Moby Dick*? It looks like he's going to be a real asset to the class. He's a talented mimic too. When he reads aloud in class, he does all the voices!'

I'm so relieved I have to head back to my office for a few minutes to compose myself. I arranged to meet Sunny in front of the school at close of lessons to take him home. He doesn't show. Worrying again, I stalk the school corridors looking for him. Our school provides plenty of after-school activities. There are sports, music and additional lessons for those who want or need them. He's not in any of them. Panicking, I eventually find him in a corner of the library where his head is buried in a book. It's about crime and punishment in England in the Middle Ages. Over his shoulder, I spy an illustration of a hanging, drawing and quartering at Tyburn. The library is open until six o'clock and some of our students do their homework there. Talking is strictly forbidden in the library so I have to whisper angrily.

'Sunny? We were supposed to meet out front at four o'clock.'

You would think it was the first he'd heard of it. 'Yeah?'

Something occurs to me. 'Are you happy to stay here until six?'

'Sure.'

'Outside the school at six then.'

I drive to our local police station and demand to see Summers. I should have rung ahead but thought he might fob me off. The cop on the desk tells me he's not available. Unfortunately for him, I can clearly see Summers gesturing to someone about what appears to be football in the back office. When his name is called, Summers comes out, looking sheepish.

'Josie, this is a nice surprise. Look, I'm a little tied up at the moment, could we talk on the phone, tomorrow perhaps?'

'This won't take five minutes.'

'Alright, five minutes,' he says reluctantly.

Summers thinks I'm here to try and persuade him again that Megan was murdered because I can't accept that she would have died from something as trivial as a misjudged heroin jab. In his office, he tries to give me what amounts to a brief speech on coming to terms with grief and learning to value the time you had with the deceased and so on and so forth. He also clearly thinks I was bluffing about the neighbour with new information. He's nonplussed when he's told that's not the reason for my visit. 'Oh? What's up then?'

'I want my sister's property back.'

He looks like I've just accused him of stealing. 'We haven't got any of her property.'

'You've got her phones.'

The penny drops. 'The phones? As I explained to you, Josie, we can't let you have those, they could be a vital element in our investigation.'

'You've sent me an email saying your investigation is over and you've forwarded the details to the coroner.'

He's not feeling sorry for me any more. 'Yes, but what you have to remember is that the phones could be key evidence in our understanding of the drugs network in our area. You can't have them I'm afraid.'

'I don't appreciate being made fun of. You said the most important of the two phones was locked and you couldn't get into it so it's no good to you anyway.'

He's not happy. 'There's no need to take that tone, Josie. You're right, it is locked and if we can't get into it, you certainly can't. Even the spooks couldn't get past these sorts of locks, so I don't know what use the phone would be to you.'

'It doesn't matter. I want it.'

He shakes his head. 'Sorry, Josie.'

My sister wasn't a very imaginative person. I'm sure I'll be able to guess whatever codes she used and who knows what might turn up on that locked phone that could help me. 'You're going to force me to take legal action?'

A note of admiration creeps into his voice. 'You're hardcore, Josie, I'll give you that. Get a lawyer if you want to. It'll cost you a lot of money but it won't help, a court won't let you have the phones back either.'

I get up. 'We'll see.'

'We will.'

Is it even possible to get a court judgement to return evidence the police hold? I sit in my car and try and google my way to an answer. Things take a disappointing turn when it turns out a lawyer, which I don't have, would need to tangle with the Police Property Act 1897.

There's a tap on the window of the car. It's Summers again. 'Would it make things easier for you if you tried and failed to get into Megan's phone?'

'Yes.'

He sighs and reaches into his pocket. 'It's a bit irregular but if it helps, you can have them.'

He hands me two phones. 'We might need them back though, so don't sell them on the high street when you give up on the locked one.' He walks off and says as he goes, 'You're trying to prove Megan was murdered? Years of experience in the service tells me you're wrong about that but if I can help you with your enquiries, you let me know.'

I'm like a kid with a present she doesn't want to open because the anticipation is almost as exciting as the present itself. It's annoying that I have to waste time picking up Sunny before I can open it, but it has to be done. When we get home, Rodney is loitering and waiting to say hello to his cousin. It's not going to do any good, but

I'm sure he's trying to help me by 'engaging' with my nephew. This gives me the chance to head into the back garden and start examining the phones. The open one is a dreary list of phone numbers for the utilities, social services, helplines and other public services. There are nearly no texts on it and very little in the way of numbers for individuals. Megan knew how to keep business separate from the personal. It was used hardly at all in the week before her death. There's nothing there to help me.

The locked phone is what I'm really after as this is where Megan kept things she wanted to hide away from prying eyes. To get in it needs a passcode or thumbprint. The thumbprint is in the mortuary now but the passcode should be easy enough. Her birthday doesn't work, nor do the birthdays of our parents. Mine doesn't either, or perhaps mine is a longshot. This isn't like Megan at all, she always chose the easy option so why hasn't she done that with her codes? There must really be things on this phone she didn't want anyone to see. With mounting frustration, I keep pumping in numbers that could be the answer. But it seems that Summers was right, there's no obvious way in. While it was true that she always chose the easy option, it was also true she was crafty with it.

Someone will be able to get in though. The head of maths at my school knows about these things and has helped hapless teachers recover data they've wiped or to access phones they've locked themselves out of. He could have a thriving sideline business going if he wanted to. On our high street are other businesses that might help. Every other shop sells phones, tablets, computers and other gadgets while providing the services that go with them. No doubt most of them are fronts for stolen property or money laundering, but if they can get into Megan's phone without losing the data, that's no concern of mine.

I put it down on the garden table in front of me. It's a great present but I can't open it. My mind roams randomly over all sorts of things. What secrets might be unlocked by a pin or password that I don't have? And about what Trevor has said to me as the days pass by. I'm sure the answers I'm looking for about my sister's death will be on this phone.

The answer to the other question of why Trevor and I are behaving as we are might be more difficult to resolve.

# Chapter 23

'Can't help you with this, madam. What I can do is sell you an updated model with a two-year guarantee and a charger thrown in for a price that can only be described as self-robbery.'

The head of maths couldn't help me. In fact, he seemed to think asking him if he could access Megan's phone for me was something of a silly question. 'I'm afraid not, Josie, only the police could get into a phone that's locked up like this.'

'They couldn't help either, it's my late sister's phone.'

He'd pulled a sympathetic face. 'Right, in that case you're not getting into it unfortunately.'

It's unprofessional, but the obvious next step was to enquire with some of my geeky tech-minded students if they knew how to access a locked phone. After all, if teenagers don't know about these things, who does? They seemed to think it was a silly question too. Of course they could. One after another though, they gave up, usually by explaining that it was an old model that only a tramp would use or that they had to hurry off to lessons.

On the high street, one shop after another, from the guys who sell off stalls to the chain stores, couldn't help either, although I've learned more about selling digital items than is really healthy for someone in my position. I've also read more blogs, technical pages and forums on the Net in an effort to solve my problem and I'm up to speed on a lot of things I didn't know, but at a grinding halt with Megan's phone. Summers was right. This phone is no use to the police but it's no use to me either. Sitting in my car after my fruitless tour of the high street, I hold it in my hand and am taunted by its screen prompting me for the secret formula to open it up. What secrets are hidden in my hands that might help me discover who killed my sister?

There'll be phone calls, texts and emails, maybe some from the night she died. They could help me unravel the mystery. Names of people who I've never heard of but who might hold the key to the puzzle. Appeals for help? Expressions of fear? A relationship with someone who might have resorted to deadly force when backed into a corner? Who did she owe money to or betrayed one time too many? This phone could have the answers but it's not sharing and I've no other way of knowing. I let it slip through my fingers into the well of the car. Some good fortune is needed here and there doesn't appear to be any coming.

In my bag is Frieda's log. That's not helping me either. I have to confine myself to reading five pages a day and I'm now only a month away from Megan's death. If I were a cop I'd sit and read the whole thing in one go, link names and incidents, cross reference and pursue any leads it gives me. But I'm not a cop and I can't face it. It seems on every page there are examples of the games Megan played with me. Incidents that prove I was made a fool of. Snatches of arguments that show Megan's contempt for me, all told in Frieda's spiky handwriting. On her visits, my sister pleaded poverty and gaslit me into giving her money when the log shows she was actually never short of cash, rather the reverse if anything. When my name is mentioned in this log, it's like a punch in the belly.

***9.30 p.m.***

*Shouting match between the woman opposite and the boyfriend. She says he owes her money. He shouts that if she needs money why doesn't she just 'borrow' it from her dumb bitch of a sister as usual. Woman shouts that her sister might be dumb and a complete bitch but at least she's not a sponger like he is.*

I'm starting to think if I'd been in Megan's social circle of druggie deadbeats my street handle would have been 'dumb bitch'. Where did she get her money from? From me, obviously, and from social services, but that couldn't have covered all her expenses. Her drug, alcohol and party habits alone must have run bills of hundreds of pounds a week. Keeping Sunny must have cost, although you wouldn't think it to look at him. Her expensive tastes would only have added to the bills. It crosses my mind to think about going back to her flat, which is still locked up, to look through the paperwork inside. If I were a cop taking my sister's death seriously that's probably the first thing I would have done. But I'm not a cop and this is all new to me.

I carry on reading the log.

***9.30 a.m.***

*After the woman opposite's party last night, there's broken glass on the landing and stairwell. I knock on her door and point it out to her. She becomes aggressive and says if I don't like it, I should get a broom and dustpan. She says that I might be an old crone at death's door but surely that's not beyond me. Then she slams the door in my face.*

How often Megan plucked at my heartstrings by telling me how she was persecuted by the neighbours. I close the log, unable to read any more. There may be secrets in here too but I'll probably be too upset to read them or work them out.

I dropped Sunny off at home after school before continuing my hunt for miles around in an effort to break into Megan's phone. He was in the library again and had to be virtually dragged out. Trevor was at home when we arrived and gave Sunny the same familiar look as if my nephew were a debt collector or undertaker. The only promising thing to happen today was when I checked in with Rodney on his efforts to 'engage' with his cousin. It appears to have worked. Clever Rodney has picked up on Sunny's reading obsession and offered to show him his own shelf of books. Sunny took him up on the offer but was unimpressed. He thought Rodney's books were 'stupid' and 'for kids'. Instead, he took his cousin and proudly showed his own collection and agreed to lend one or two to Rodney. It's not much but it's a start.

When I get home, I can feel the argument going on inside before I hear or see it. Coming up the garden path into the house, I can see Trevor and Sunny in our living room shouting at each other. Or rather Trevor appears to be shouting, while Sunny is alternately shrugging and smirking. They don't hear me open the front door so I catch Trevor's final words on the matter before they register my presence. 'This is all a game to you, isn't it, Sunny? Well, you're not playing games in my house with my wife!'

Trevor falls silent when he sees me, clearly embarrassed.

'What on earth is going on?'

Sunny mumbles, 'Nothing.'

He looks forlorn, as if he's in a world he doesn't understand and where nothing makes sense. As if he's being blamed for things that aren't his fault and he doesn't know what the things are or where the fault lies. His expression is one of apology to me but as if he's not sure what he's apologising for. The look on his face seems almost a plea for my help. He walks off slowly and goes upstairs to his room.

Trevor invents ingenious questions to test how much I heard of the argument, as if what he's going to tell me about it depends on my answer. When it becomes clear that I only caught the end of it, he looks relieved. 'You want to know what's going on? I'll show you what he's done this time and we'll see if that's enough to persuade you to throw him and his book collection out of the front door.'

# Chapter 24

He too walks off, leaving me alone. I run upstairs and find a frightened Rodney. He heard the argument but claims he doesn't know what it was about. Tova is at her friend's and missed everything. When I come back down, it's to find Trevor standing by the back door with a book in one hand and a drawing in the other. He beckons me into the back garden where he pushes the book at me. 'Do you know what this is?'

The book Trevor gives me is an American novel with a cover showing a silhouette of a youth in a ski mask carrying a gun and a holdall. There's a bookmark in chapter three, which means someone is reading it.

'This is a book Sunny lent our son. I've been skimming it, quite a good read actually. It's about an American high school kid. He's bullied at school by the sporty boys and laughed at by the cool girls. You can probably guess how the hero reacts to that. He steals guns from his grandfather, learns how to make bombs on the internet and then plans to stage a massacre at his high school, which he does very successfully. His moment of triumph comes when he lures a SWAT team into the place where he's hiding and blows them, the school and himself up in a massive grand explosion by way of a finale. You know what's interesting about this book? It's written from the boy's point of view and it's actually very sympathetic to him. Its line is that shooting and bombing your school is a valid response to bullying and social isolation. Is this the kind of material we want our ten-year-old son reading?'

Since I asked Rodney to try and engage with Sunny, my son has done me proud. As the weeks have passed, Rodney has been making an effort with Sunny and my nephew has responded. Rodney has been sharing books with Sunny and vice versa. I've noticed the two of them playing cards together and thus far there have been no reports of cheating. On the contrary, Rodney's rather enjoyed learning card tricks from his cousin, although no doubt that includes some that he picked up from his father or Megan's friends. On one occasion I've even noticed the two boys returning from the park with their arms draped around each other's shoulders. Rodney's efforts appear to be working.

Now this.

When I say nothing, he hands me the drawing. 'Do you know what this is?'

The drawing is of a gravestone adorned with flowers. The picture is in black and white but the flowers are coloured in. I hand it back to him. 'No.'

'Sunny did it in art class today and brought it home. Did you read the writing on the gravestone?'

I didn't. Trevor hands the drawing back and tells me to study it. The writing is very small, ornate and curly. It reads 'Tova Thomas RIP'.

'Sunny pinned it on the fridge when he got home. Mercifully I found it before Rodney and Tova did. Sunny's claiming it was a joke and he doesn't know what the fuss is about.'

I'm inert, both because of what's happened and because of what's going to happen next. I know what Trevor is going to say and I don't know how to refuse him. The anger drains out of him. 'I don't want to keep saying the same thing over and again but he's got to go. He can't stay here. You understand that? We've got our children to think about. Call social services, do it tomorrow morning.'

'I'll talk to him.'

Trevor groans in despair. 'Talk to him? Can't you see what he's doing? Are you determined to drink this cup right down to its last dregs? He's going to destroy us.'

No doubt the argument between Trevor and Sunny was about the book and the drawing to start with, but that's not what they were arguing about when they were interrupted.

'What did you mean when you said to Sunny that this is all a game to him? That he's not playing games in this house with your wife?'

'You work it out. I can't be bothered. Just get rid of him before it's too late.'

He tears up Sunny's drawing, throws the book on the compost heap and mutters under his breath, 'You'll see soon enough if you don't wake up and get over this whole Megan thing you've got going on, whatever that may be.'

'What's that supposed to mean?'

But he says no more and leaves me alone in the garden.

Upstairs, Sunny is lying on his bed reading a book. He's obviously anticipated my visit and has his answers ready.

'Trevor didn't like me lending Rodney that book and he didn't like my jokey drawing with Tova's name on it. Anyway, he told me off, that's all. It's over.'

He thinks this should be the end of the matter but listens patiently while he's told why lending that kind of reading matter to Rodney and making a very cruel 'joke' at Tova's expense isn't acceptable. I already know this is a waste of time and that Sunny will accept what he's told without understanding what it means. Deep down, I also know Trevor is right that Sunny can't stay in our house. But that's not the real reason for my visit. 'What were you arguing about with Trevor when I came through the door?'

Unlike Trevor, Sunny has had time to prepare for this question. 'I told you, the book and the drawing.'

'Probably, but that's not what you were arguing about when I came home. What's all a game to you and why are you playing games with me?'

'I don't know, ask Trevor, he's the expert.' After a pause he adds, 'He was probably talking about the joke on Tova.'

'That was your idea of a joke on Tova, not on me.'

He has his answer at the ready. 'Yeah, but you're Tova's mum so it was sort of a joke on you too.'

He's lying, the way his mother used to lie to me, but I'm on to their lies now. Then I notice something. 'What's that on the side of your face?'

He turns his head away. 'Nothing.'

I use my hand to turn his face towards me. 'It's a bruise.'

'Is it?'

'Where did that come from?'

He looks around the room for an answer. 'I had a fight at school. It's nothing.'

'You didn't have a fight at school. My colleagues would have told me.'

He corrects himself. 'I mean after school.'

'You were in the library after school.'

He tries again. 'That's right. Me and another boy had an argument about borrowing a book and we slapped each other about a bit. It's nothing.'

He has a twinkle in his eye because he knows what I'm thinking. I know that twinkle. It's the same glint Megan had when she was playing me but which was so warm that I couldn't blame her for what she was doing. 'It wasn't Trevor. He wouldn't do something like that. Trevor's a nice guy.'

Sunny's almost laughing now. Is this what Trevor meant about Sunny playing games? There's a knock at the front door. Sunny gets off the bed. 'That'll be the social worker.'

'Social worker?'

Sunny reminds me it was I who told him that she was coming for an informal chat this evening about how he was managing and to make arrangements for Kit's visits.

It's a bad time for Marylin the social worker to pay us a visit. She's disappointed when she hears that Trevor is working and won't be able to join us, that Rodney is doing his homework and won't be able to join us and Tova is with her friend so she can't join us either. But she enjoys her tour around the house, constantly stopping to say how spacious it is and what a lovely garden and how lucky Sunny is to be joining such a lovely family in such a lovely house. Our guest doesn't notice the funereal atmosphere, nor the stony expression on Sunny's face when she's speaking. Only when Marylin explains how important it is for children of mixed heritage to be in a blended household does she see him pull a face, which earns him a dirty look from her.

Marylin sits down with Sunny, who knows from past experience what questions he's going to be asked and how to answer them. He's indifferent to his father's upcoming visits despite our guest trying to drum up some enthusiasm for them. Arrangements are made for Kit to come once a week, although I insist that he's not coming through the door and will have to wait outside for Sunny. I'm not having him in the house. Marylin is disappointed by this. The poor woman is so desperate for the extended family to come together after our sad loss. I don't have the heart to tell her that as far as we're concerned Kit isn't family.

Finally, Marylin asks Sunny whether he's still seeing Carla. It turns out that his old school had arranged, in concert with Megan, for Sunny to see a child psychologist and that's who Carla is. Now Sunny's moved to my school and Megan is dead, the arrangement has lapsed. Marylin is eager for the sessions to resume. It comes as no surprise when she asks Sunny whether he'd like to continue seeing Carla and he just shrugs.

It's starting to look like we can take Sunny's shrugs as read, much to his social worker's disappointment. Nonetheless, I take Carla's phone number.

We're done and I take her to the door. She's still upbeat and positive. 'Families can be so complicated, can't they, Josie?'

They certainly can.

When she leaves, I notice something further down the road. A van is parked up with ladders on the roof. The driver is sitting there behind tinted glass, waiting for something. In normal circumstances I'd think nothing of it, but there is nothing normal about my life these days. From our front gate, I can see the lettering on the side of the van. The name of the company is unclear but the words 'roofer' and 'all work considered' are. There is only one roofer I know of and if it's him, I want to know what he's doing parked up on our road. I open the gate and begin to walk towards the van. When he sees me coming, the driver hastily turns his engine on, does a three-point turn and takes off at speed.

I still couldn't see the driver. But I knew who it was.

# Chapter 25

I've called in sick at work. The school secretary was quite shocked because I've never taken a sick day before, I'm the ultimate healthy professional. And in a way I am sick, sicker than I've ever been in my life. My family is falling apart and it's all my fault. I know Trevor is right and that Sunny is steadily and progressively undermining us, but it's not his fault. Even if it was, my nephew is my responsibility. I can't let him go. Not only that but it's making me worry that this suburban idyll we've created here could have been an illusion all along. Trevor was right that Sunny would mess things up but I don't understand how he was so right so quickly. Perhaps he was warned beforehand but that's impossible. Who could have done that? He's always believed the apple doesn't fall far from the tree and he detested Megan so it might be that. Yes, he was right about Sunny but he was prematurely right. Meanwhile, Sunny has denied that Trevor hit him and I refuse to believe that he did. Though he denied it in such a vehement fashion that it sounded more like an accusation.

I decide to speak to the child psychologist that Sunny was seeing, but it's difficult not to feel it's about me as much as it is about him. I ring Carla with a view to a meeting about her continuing to see Sunny now that he's changed schools and families.

That's what I tell her but what I really want to know is how to prevent the growing discord in our house. I pour out my story and desperately seek some advice, anything to prevent a looming disaster.

'To tell you the truth, Ms Thomas, Sunny came to see me for a number of months and I think that perhaps he needs more specialised help, more expertise than you or I can offer. With the passing of his mother, his new school and new home, he's in a wholly different environment and this might be the right time for him to seek a new service elsewhere.'

It doesn't sound as if it's been going too well. She wants out and I need to know why. 'Of course, but perhaps if you could give me a briefing on how things have been going now that I'm going to be his guardian?'

'My conversations with Sunny are confidential and my notes will be available to any future practitioner.'

My voice is trembling. 'Please.'

Carla gives in and agrees to see me. I leave Sunny at home and drop a silent Rodney and equally silent Tova at their school. I can't look at their faces in the rear-view mirror as they get out of the car. It's too painful.

Carla welcomes me by asking if I'm feeling unwell, I must look so depressed. I reassure her I'm fine. She tells me she was consulted by social services about Sunny's future and informed them that she felt my family might not be the right way forward despite what we could offer. We're only 'civilians'.

Carla gives me a brief summary of her work with my nephew. She found it very difficult to get him to talk and he only came to see her because he was compelled to. But by piecing together what he did and didn't say she was able to build a picture of what his emotional life was like. He was reluctant to criticise his mother and didn't want to hold her to account for anything. Nonetheless, he was a bitter and vengeful young man when he felt the need. It was clear that his experience in Megan's flat was traumatic and left him a deeply troubled young boy. He took refuge by going to his grandmother's or barricading himself in his room reading books. She breaks confidence by giving me an example of what he went through.

'The only time I ever saw him show any real emotion was on one occasion when he broke down in tears while we were talking. I tried to encourage him to tell me why he was so upset and he told me that his fish were, as he put it, murdered, by one of his mother's friends. I asked him what he intended to do about the friend and Sunny said he was too small to do anything now. But one day that guy would pay. Sunny said he could wait as long as it takes. He was obsessed with taking revenge on the man and the subject cropped up in other conversations we had.'

I remember how that story began but not how it ended. It was me who bought the fish tank and me who took him to a shop to buy the fish. He was younger then and promised to feed the fish every day and clean their tank regularly. He was quite excited to have something to look after. On another visit, later, I noticed the fish had gone and the tank was empty. Sunny told me they'd died but said no more.

'There are a number of other stories of a similar nature but the point is, Ms Thomas, there's no reason that with the right support and help Sunny couldn't go on to lead a useful and productive life. But to be frank, I'm not sure that you'd be in the right position to offer that support. You're too close. My own view is that your nephew would probably benefit from a spell in residential care where he can access a tailored programme of therapy. He's a very clever boy and things could still work out. Perhaps not only are you too close to things but perhaps your relationship with your late sister clouds your judgement?'

She's right. My relationship with Sunny is indeed my relationship with my sister at one remove. If there were a way of resolving that, I could really help my nephew and myself by moving him out of my home. But I can't resolve things with a dead person.

'I'm not in the predictions business,' Carla explains. 'I've seen children from dysfunctional homes become model and creative adults and I've seen other children from what might be considered model and creative families where things go very badly wrong indeed. We can't say. What we can do is flag up various markers that might be indications of how things might turn out if they're not addressed. I can see there's an undertow of violence in Sunny's personality. He respects and admires violence. He's shared his feelings with me and it's something we've discussed. We need to try and head that off if possible.'

I'm shocked, disgusted and a little bit frightened, which makes me snap at her, 'Sunny has got his problems but he's not violent, not at all. Why would you say that?'

Carla doesn't answer directly, which is even more alarming. Perhaps she has got some evidence for that and won't share it with me. 'These are just things for you to consider but if I were you, I would consider them very carefully to prevent tragedy happening in the future. A tendency to violence along with a high IQ and street smarts can be a toxic and lethal combination. Perhaps you too could also use some support untangling your relationship with your late sister.'

The vague nature of her warnings and the caveats she's added are more disturbing than if she'd called my nephew a potential killer or psychopath. I'm in a hurry to get away before she says something else that I might believe.

After leaving Carla, I drive a long distance to where it all started between Megan and me. It's a quiet suburban road and it's changed a little since we were schoolgirls. It's roughly halfway between our childhood home and our school. The area has been somewhat gentrified, the older houses spruced up, extensions and lofts added and the parked cars are more expensive, but it's still all vaguely recognisable. The actual place where the accident happened was just beyond a postbox which still stands. I always called it the 'accident' but Megan preferred other words, finally settling on the 'episode'.

I drop down and sit on the kerb. As if on cue a car drives past just as it did that afternoon and my eyes begin to moisten and fill with tears. After the accident, we'd still walk to school together but it became a tug of war between us. I insisted on using a different route whereas Megan insisted we carry on as before, her way of reminding me about what happened. When she won, she liked to slow down by this spot. We'd walk by in silence. Even then she knew how to play her older sister.

I sit here for a long time staring at the road and wondering if I'm strong enough to do the right thing. I devise a strategy. It's to stop thinking about my children as my two children and imagine them as Megan and Josie instead. I would do anything to turn back the clock and stop the pair of us walking down the road that day but it's too late. But it's not too late to stop Tova and Rodney walking down this road. They can still be saved. The only way to stop them is to get Sunny out of my house. I need a strategy. It doesn't involve doing what Trevor wants and ringing social services and asking them to take Sunny off my hands. But I do need to explore other options as to where he might go, still with my full support.

When I stand, my back straightens and my mind is made up. Sunny is leaving my home and taking my sister with him. I'll speak to my husband first, then Sunny and finally my children. And I'm leaving this street and not coming back. It's the end of being manipulated by Megan. I'm going to manipulate myself instead.

# Chapter 26

## Three Years Earlier

'He's a weird little kid, your boy.'

It was another one of Sunny's mum's crazy parties and it was always hard to tell how long they would last. Sometimes they petered out before midnight and other times they lasted until day-break. By now, Sunny had a routine to help him keep his own peace. He wrote a message on a piece of paper and sellotaped it to the door of his bedroom.

'Sunny's room. Private. Keep Out.'

After that, he stuffed cotton wool in his ears to drown out the noise and made sure he had some water so he didn't have to leave his room and see 'them', by which he meant his mother's 'guests'. Sometimes it was only half a dozen of them, on other occasions it was a flat full of people. After making sure his tropical fish in their tank were tended to, he would climb on to his bed with a good book from his collection and read until he fell asleep. When he awoke in the morning, there would be only the wreckage of the night before and the odd stranger asleep on a sofa to show what had happened while he slept.

This night, though, was different. An unkempt-looking guy pushed his door open and looked inside to see Sunny reading his book. He was clearly drunk or high, or both.

'Megan! Babe! I said your boy's a weird little kid. He's got cotton wool sticking out of his ears. He looks a bit simple.'

An angry Megan marched in and grabbed the guy by his arm and pulled him out of the room. 'Don't talk about my son like that or I'll throw you out on the landing and down the stairwell.'

It looked like the man was doing as he was told until he noticed the fish tank. 'Oh look! He's got an aquarium! I love tropical fish me!' He broke away from Megan's grip, crouched slightly and pressed his nose up against the glass panel of the tank and called to Sunny, 'Are these guppies?'

Sunny didn't answer. Megan took the visitor by his arm again and dragged him this time. 'Alright, that's enough, get out.'

This time the guy left without putting up a fight, only muttering, 'He don't say much your kid.'

Megan closed the door behind her and Sunny was alone again. Ten minutes later the man was back. Swaying gently to and fro with a bottle of vodka pressed into a jacket pocket and a glass of something in his hand, he came to sit down on Sunny's bed. 'You're not very friendly, are you? Why don't you come and join the party?'

All the man got in return was a blank stare and no response, but he didn't give up. 'What's your name, son? Do you want a drink? Here, let me give you a drink.'

He pulled the bottle of vodka from his pocket and poured a large measure into Sunny's glass of water. 'Go on, drink it up, I won't tell anyone.'

The man seemed to be largely talking to himself. 'What's the book you're reading?' He snatched the book out of Sunny's hands and examined it despite Sunny's attempt to grab it back. Sunny had recovered it from a skip where some old books had been dumped. He'd thrown most of them back but kept this one. It was called *Wisdom of the Ages* and was made of yellowing pages and a spine that had fallen to bits. Inside were various quotes and stories from round the world that made up a collection of wisdom for Victorians. The drunk flipped through the broken pages and wasn't impressed. 'You should throw that in the bin. You'll catch something off it.'

He gave it back and got up, tired of trying to engage this weird kid in conversation. On the way out of the room, swaying, he stopped by the tropical fish tank and peered inside. 'Your fish look a bit miserable mate. I think they need cheering up.'

To cheer them up, he pulled the vodka bottle from his pocket, unscrewed the cap and began to pour the liquid into the tank and then watched to see what happened next. Horrified, Sunny jumped from his bed and launched into an attack on the drunk, kicking and punching him, shouting and screaming. He didn't do much harm because the guy put a big hand on Sunny's head and held him back while laughing at him. 'Woah, tiger, woah!'

The noise brought Megan into the room. When she realised what had happened, she grabbed the drunk by the scruff of the neck and threw him out of the flat, screaming abuse at him. A panicking Sunny unplugged the tank and, cradling it in both arms, took it to the kitchen, weaving his way through the partygoers and the fug of smoke and fumes. At the sink, he used a jug to try and scoop out the vodka-soaked water and poured in fresh water from the tap. As carefully as he could, he brought his precious fish back to his room and plugged the tank back in and waited to see if he'd saved them. For a while it seemed to have worked but then slowly, one by one, the fish began to lose their balance. They drifted to the surface before finally turning belly up and dying. When it was over, he turned to the bedroom wall behind which the party was still going and looked at it with hatred. But it wasn't hatred for the man who'd killed his fish, it was all of 'them' outside, including his own mother.

He remembered a line from the *Wisdom of the Ages*. It was from China. It read that if you waited by the river long enough, eventually the body of your enemy would float by.

# Chapter 27

'You want to talk to me?'

Sunny has joined me in the back garden as dusk is falling.

I called Trevor earlier and told him I want to speak to him about my nephew when he comes in. When I picked up my children from school, I couldn't resist telling them that things would be changing soon around the house.

Tova, bright as ever, asked hopefully, 'Is Sunny going?'

I didn't answer directly but it was written all over my face. It feels like forever since I last saw her smiling.

My nephew stands in front of me, his slight frame nearly a shadow in the twilight. I gesture at the chair on the other side of the garden table. 'Yes, sit down, we've got something we need to discuss.'

He sits down and looks at my hands. 'Is that my mother's phone?'

Megan's phone has become like an ironic fidget toy or a set of worry beads ever since Summers reluctantly handed it over. It stays in my pocket from where it's fished out every time the stress in my life gets too much, which is now pretty much all the time. I press increasingly unlikely patterns of numbers or characters on the keypad in an effort to get in. I'm rather like someone trying to guess the next set of lottery numbers, safe in the knowledge it's a million to one chance, while at the same time in some sort of hope things might be different.

I wasn't even conscious I had it in my hands. Sunny peers over the table between us. 'Do you want me to open it for you?'

'You won't be able to, Sunny, it's locked.'

His smile is slightly sinister in the gloom. 'I can open it.'

He stretches out his hand to take the phone. Without even thinking, I hand it over to him. He studies the screen for a moment and then gets up from the table and walks into the house. I sit in the garden alone for a while until the back door opens again and a hangdog Trevor appears. The days of kisses and hugs between us have drawn to a close. He takes Sunny's seat on the other side of the table. 'What's up? You said on the phone you wanted to speak about something important. Come on, what is it? I'm hungry, I didn't get anything to eat at work.'

Are we really going back to how things were before? 'I spoke to Sunny's child psychiatrist today.'

He interrupts me. He never used to do that. 'Really? What's the diagnosis? A complete psychopath who should be locked up permanently for everyone's good. Am I getting warm?'

'No, but we did discuss Sunny and she felt it would be better for him if he went somewhere that might be able to offer him more specialised care. Afterwards I spent some time on my own.' I don't tell Trevor where I went because he doesn't need to know that. He's never needed to know. 'On reflection I decided that she was right and that would be the best way forward.'

Trevor is baffled and perhaps slightly shocked, as if he's just discovered he's won the lottery. 'I don't understand. Are you saying you want Sunny out of our house?'

'I wouldn't put it like that, but yes, we need to look at other options.'

He stands up and walks to the back of my chair, where his arms entwine around my waist and a kiss is put on my cheek. We're back to hugs and kisses. 'You're brilliant, you won't regret this.' His voice becomes hurried and slightly excited as if he can't decide what to spend his lottery win on. 'Don't get me wrong, I feel sorry for the kid, I really do, and I get the Caribbean thing, but it's not good for him being here either. Look, I'm not saying you shouldn't have anything to do with him, you can go and see him anytime you like. Give him extra lessons or whatever, I mean there's no need to write him off.' He untangles himself from me. 'I'm going to tell the kids, they'll be ecstatic.'

I grab his arm as he tries to get away. 'Don't do that, I haven't told Sunny yet, although I think he's probably guessed.'

Trevor becomes alarmed and snaps, 'You're not going to back down here?'

'No.'

He nods violently. 'OK, OK, as long as you do it. If you can't face it, I will.'

His path crosses with Sunny who's come back into the garden with Megan's phone. They exchange glances as they pass but say nothing. Sunny sits down opposite me and hands me the phone. The screen is ablaze with colours and the shapes of its apps. The wallpaper on the phone is a photo of Megan and Sunny when he was a baby. I'm dumbfounded. 'You got into it then.'

'Yeah. She always used the same variations on codes for things. This phone was our postcode with one slightly different number in it. It's just a question of going away and sitting down for ten minutes and going through them all.'

He's saying something to me but I'm not listening. I'm already scrolling through the texts, messages and phone calls. Who are these people and what's being said? There's a mountain of information here. 'Sorry Sunny I didn't catch that?'

'The passcode is gone now. You can put your own on.'

I don't know where to start with the phone, so I go to the last calls and messages from the night Megan died, as I did with Frieda's log before rewinding to the days before and back again. Sunny says something else which I don't hear either. 'Listen, Sunny, could you give me a little while alone?'

'You said you wanted to talk to me.'

'Yes, that's right but if you could let me have a few minutes?'

He's nearly in darkness now. 'OK.'

He gets up and leaves the garden, and me alone. In the house, someone is playing music. Music vanished in our house shortly after Sunny arrived, now it's back. Some sort of joyful pop sound, which must be Trevor. He's started his party already. Somewhere else in the house, I can hear Tova and Rodney calling each other but there's a different tone to their voices now, as if they're wondering if Father Christmas will be coming down the chimney tonight. They should be in bed but it's hard to get children to bed when they're excited and no doubt Trevor won't be up for the job anyway. He's probably swilling champagne and crunching nibbles in his hidey-hole. Lights are on in the house full blast, whereas since my nephew arrived it seems to have been in darkness even in the daylight. A spell has been broken.

Only Sunny and I aren't joining in the festive spirit, only we're still under the witch's power, only we can hear the flutter of my sister moving invisibly from one room to another. Only Sunny and I are still in darkness. I scroll through Megan's phone, darting from one message to another. I take deep breaths and start again.

What do I make of the text messages between Kit and Megan the night she died? Is what he wrote to her a death threat? Who is this 'Bill' that Megan called late that evening and what was that call about? Why a few hours before that did Megan write to Dixie telling him that he could have his things back when she was dead.

Why did she call a helpline for those considering self-harm or suicide that evening? What was the 'duke' that Megan accused Kit of trying to steal from under her nose on his visit mid evening? The one that, according to Frieda, ended with Kit crying in the stairwell. The 999 phone call is the last number called that night but how can I even be sure it was Megan who called it?

'Do you want to talk to me or not?'

Without my noticing, Sunny has reappeared in the garden. The light from the house means he throws a shadow over the table, as if he's much taller and looming over me. 'Yes, why did your mum call your grandmother the night she died? Did she want to talk to you?'

Sunny's aghast. 'That's what you wanted to talk about?'

'No, but that's what I want to ask you now.'

He gives me one of his trademark shrugs. 'She never spoke to me that evening. If you want to know what she said to my gran, ask her. What does it matter anyway? My mother's dead.'

'Your grandmother won't talk to me. Can you ask her why my sister called her?'

I can't see his face but I suspect he's laughing at me. 'I can ask her if you like. Is that it?'

There's a long silence. All the things that were decided earlier in the day are melting into thin air. My sister has done it again. 'No, that's not what I want to talk to you about but it can wait for another time, it's not urgent.'

# Chapter 28

Trevor has rejoined me in the marital bed. He probably thinks I've already told Sunny that he has to go. Him coming back is probably my reward. I haven't told my husband yet that that's not the case. I am going to tell Sunny but not now.

Megan's phone is uncomfortable in the pocket of my pyjama bottoms but it's not going anywhere until I've read everything and made detailed notes and then compared them to Frieda's log. You don't leave a winning lottery ticket lying around. I decided to leave a detailed examination of the texts, calls and voice messages until the following morning. My state of mind isn't right tonight. Unfortunately, the phone keeps waking me up by digging into my thigh. When it does, the temptation to pull it out and start reading it again is overwhelming. It's half past two when it really catches the flesh on my leg and my own yelping wakes me up. My hand flails around and drifts over to Trevor's side of the bed. He isn't there. Perhaps he's popped to the bathroom after drinking to celebrate Sunny's departure or maybe he's guessed that I didn't really say anything to Sunny after all and he's gone back to the sofa as my punishment.

Unable to sleep myself, I take the phone to the bathroom to sit and study it some more. But on the way, the strangest thing happens.

The door to Sunny's room is slightly ajar. When I stand and listen, it begins to look as if he's not actually in there. A quick peep around the door proves he's not. Downstairs, it becomes clear that not only is Sunny not there but neither is Trevor. He's not on the sofa. His car is still outside so they haven't gone anywhere. Clutching Megan's phone, I search the house looking for them while trying to avoid worrying about what they're up to. They're not in the attic. Tova's door is securely locked and unless they're operating in silence, they're not in Rodney's room either. When I've finished a thorough search of the house, I begin to panic. Where the hell are they and what are they doing? It's only when I look out of a back window from upstairs that I see them.

They're semi-hidden, sheltered under a tree on a bench at the bottom of the garden. Clouds are scudding across the sky, so the moon appears then disappears, lighting them up and then casting them in shadow. It's as if they were sitting under very slow-moving strobe lights. I'm tempted to go outside at once and demand to know what they're up to but decide I can ask them that later and separately. Instead, I watch them deep in conversation. There's no sign that Trevor is angry or that Sunny is sullen. Rather the reverse, they appear to be talking through a problem together. Finally, the two of them emerge from their hiding place and begin walking up the garden. Almost unbelievably, Trevor puts his arm around Sunny's shoulders and appears to be explaining something to him.

My immediate thought is that this little convo is something to do with Megan's phone. It can't be, however, because it was Sunny who was quite happy to crack it for me and Trevor doesn't know about it unless Sunny told him, and why would he? The two of them disappear through the back door. I hurry back to bed. A few minutes later, there are soft footsteps on the staircase and the door to Sunny's room is carefully closed. I lay still with my eyes closed when Trevor returns and creeps around the room before getting into bed as gently and quietly as he can.

After a few yawns and some stretching, I pretend to wake up. My question sounds as completely innocent as it could be, given my suspicion that he's about to start lying to me.

'Having trouble sleeping?'

He stops his attempt to disentangle the bedding and hesitates for a few moments. 'Yeah, I just popped downstairs to get something for a cold.' He performs a few half-hearted coughs in an unconvincing attempt to back his story up.

'Do you want me to go and find something for it?'

He fronts it out. 'No, no, it's nothing, don't worry, go back to sleep.'

I'm not worried. I spent a lifetime being played by my sister.

I'm used to being lied to.

I'm still off 'sick'.

I took Sunny, Tova and Rodney to school and Trevor left for work as usual. Before he went, he asked me if Sunny had his marching orders yet but was untroubled when he didn't get a straight answer. He's confident he's won his battle. Now, the children are back home and I've wasted a day with Frieda's log in one hand and Megan's phone in the other, trying to decipher what it's all saying to me about the night she died. She was arguing with Dixie and Kit and they both visited the flat. She also phoned 'Bill' around the time she was dying. There's no way for me to know who he was or why she was calling him but he was obviously important to her. Was it a desperate appeal for help in her last minutes of consciousness from someone she trusted?

The vile texts between Kit and my sister are filled with abuse and don't help at all. It's not even clear what they're arguing about as the texts are filled with acronyms and slang which make no sense to me. I get the 'LOLS' and the 'GTF'. But what is the 'duke' that Megan accused Kit of trying to steal from her flat that evening from right under her nose? That's shortly before Frieda's log says that Kit ended up on the stairwell of the flat crying at around 8.10 p.m.

I left the children alone when they came home and got back to work at my desk, developing ever more elaborate and unlikely theories as to what it all means. But there simply isn't enough information here for me to work with.

From my desk I can see a van parked outside our house with 'Kit's Roofing: No Job Too Small' emblazoned down the side in red. Kit is at the wheel, waiting. This evening is the first of his contact visits. He was supposed to arrive at six but he drove up an hour early and has been sitting outside ever since like a malevolent goblin. He, of course, could answer some of my questions and it's tempting to go outside, tap on his window and ask them. I'm resisting it. He was involved in some way with my sister's murder and I'm not going to let him know what I've already discovered. Instead, I Google the urban slang for 'duke'. My guess is that it's drugs of some kind but I can't find any evidence of that.

At six o'clock precisely, Kit climbs out of his van and checks his watch. He adjusts his tie and smooths down the suit he's wearing, which he probably thinks is what a responsible father would wear to visit his son. He pushes open our gate and strides up to the door and hammers on the knocker. He looks me up and down with distaste when I answer but is all smiles when a reluctant Sunny appears. He gives his unresponsive son a big hug.

'Hello, boy! How you doing? Pleased to see your old dad?'

He doesn't get an answer and nor do I when I ask him where the social worker is. He's vague. 'I don't know, she's busy or something. Does it matter?'

He puts his arm around Sunny's shoulder and escorts him down the garden path as if he were a suspect in a murder case. 'Come on, Duke, let's go and catch a bite to eat.'

I watch them drive off. Kit's answered one of my questions after all, although I should have known the answer straightaway. The 'duke' that Kit tried to steal from under Megan's nose on the evening she died was Sunny.

He wasn't at his grandmother's. He was in the flat with Megan all the evening long.

# Chapter 29

It took a while for Megan to choose Sunny's name after he was born. In the end, she settled on 'Sunny' because she felt her baby had brought some sunshine into her life. While she was making her mind up, she called him Marmaduke. That was shortened later to 'Dukey' or 'Duke'. I don't know why she chose that. Even after he was called Sunny, she occasionally reverted to 'Duke', which became a kind of pet name for her child. A pet name that I had somehow forgotten.

*'Dukey couldn't sleep last night, he kept me awake until the small hours.'*

Megan and Kit were still a couple when Dukey was born although they were already in trouble.

Now I'm wondering who 'Bill' might have been a pet name for.

My first response is to call the police. Sunny's an eyewitness now to what happened in the flat that evening and he needs to be thoroughly questioned about what he saw and what he heard. My second reaction is to be furious with Summers. He took Sunny's story that he was at Grandma Rose's that evening at face value and didn't probe any further. Some cop he is. My third is to be beyond angry with Sunny himself. The little bastard, knowing full well that there were questions he had answers to and he said nothing except to make up a story about being at his grandmother's. I add Granny

Rose to the list of lying shysters. She knew he wasn't with her but still backed his story up. He was obviously at Rose's when the police came calling for him later though, that much was true.

The front door opens and a harassed-looking Trevor comes in. I can add him to my ever-lengthening list of dishonest, hypocritical accomplices who I want answers from. He skips the formalities. 'Have you told him yet?'

I don't want to speak to him. It's Sunny I want to speak to. The clock says only ten past six. Who knows when he'll be back. I'm seized with panic. How do I know he'll be back? How do I know Kit isn't going to steal his 'duke' out from under my nose as he tried to do at Megan's that evening? The clock says eleven minutes past six. It's going to be a long and fretful evening.

'Told who, what?'

Trevor is pained. 'Sunny, who do you think?' When he doesn't get an answer right away his face turns red. 'Don't tell me you haven't? Does this mean you haven't called social services either to come and collect him? What the hell have you been doing all day?'

The great thing when you discover someone has been lying to you is that you no longer feel any obligation to be truthful with them. 'He's with his father at the moment. I'll speak to him later.'

I'll be speaking to him all right, although it won't be about his future. Not the least of the questions that needs answering is what Sunny and my husband were having a cosy chat in the garden about last night and what prompted it.

Trevor is only slightly happier. 'Make sure you do. I mean it, Josie. He's got to go. If he doesn't then harsh decisions will have to be taken about the future of our family.'

The clock doesn't even say a quarter past six yet. This is going to be a long evening. I decide not to stay and watch time drag, I've got business to attend to.

Trevor watches me pick up my car keys. 'Now where are you going?'

I use the formula that I've heard Kit use when he's telling someone to mind their own business. 'I'm going to see a man about a dog.'

I drive to Rose's flat. When I knock on her door, I hear a slow shuffle and a voice calling out from behind the closed door. 'Who is it?'

'It's Josie, Sunny's aunt.'

'Well, you can piss off for a start.'

I'm finding lying to liars is even more pleasurable when you think you're doing it for a good cause. 'I understand how you feel, Rose, but I've come to apologise and offer my thanks to you.'

There's a silence on the other side before curiosity gets the better of her. 'Apologise for what?'

'If you open the door, I'll tell you.'

She opens the door a fraction, peers out but says nothing. My expression is suitably hangdog and guilty. 'You're owed an apology for the way I behaved when my sister passed. It was rude and totally unacceptable. I hope you'll understand that I was in shock and distress and it got the better of me and my behaviour towards you was completely inappropriate.'

'It certainly was, totally out of order.'

It looks like my apology is accepted. 'May I come in?'

She thinks about it. She's lonely without Sunny, probably. 'I suppose.'

She opens the door and leads me into her front room which I begin scanning for conversation openers. Meanwhile, Rose takes a seat and makes herself comfortable while waiting for me to expand on my apology. But I'm too fast for her. On the mantelpiece is a black and white photo of a soldier. He's rather handsome and is wearing a number of medals on his chest. 'Is this Kit's father? He's a very striking man.'

'That's Kit's grandfather, my father. Kit's not that old. His grandfather was a soldier. He fought the reds in Malaya. Dirty fighters those reds. We called my boy Kit after one of my father's comrades who was killed in the fighting.'

I nod. 'And I bet your father and his comrades didn't get much thanks for it from the government.'

Rose is outraged. 'Thanks? That's a laugh. Do you know what a war widow's pension is? Wouldn't keep a church mouse in cheese slices! The posh scum who run this country send young men off to war and then spit on them when they come back. You wouldn't catch them dodging bullets themselves though, mark my words.'

She joins me by the mantelpiece and begins explaining who's who in the various photographs. Little by little, she gradually softens. 'Do you want a cup of tea, dear?'

She goes off to make tea and when she returns, Rose is bombarded with my apologies about my behaviour and my sincere regrets. Finally, she buckles. 'Oh, that's alright, dear, I understand, no one likes to lose a family member. One of my aunts died of TB when she was only a girl but, you know, life has to go on.'

'And I wanted to thank you for keeping Sunny out of it.'

She becomes suspicious again and puts her tea down. 'What do you mean keeping Sunny out of it?'

'By telling the police he was here all evening. There's no reason why he should get the third degree from the police about what happened, we all know what they're like, putting words in people's mouths.'

She leans forwards and whispers so that we're not overheard by people who aren't there. 'You're not wrong there, dear. He's a good boy, my Sunny. It wasn't his fault your sister decided to top herself with drugs.' She adds hurriedly, 'No disrespect to your sister obviously.'

'You mean she did it deliberately?'

Finally, this crafty old bird begins to rumble what I'm up to. 'I wouldn't know about that, dear. If you've got any questions on that subject, you ought to ask Sunny.'

She needn't worry about that, I intend to. 'Of course.'

Rose puts her tea down. My interview is over and I'm dismissed. 'Anyway, thank you very much indeed for coming round and offering apologies, that was very honourable of you.'

I give her another barrage of apologies in an effort to prepare the way for my final question but there's no innocent way to ask it. 'I don't suppose you remember what time Sunny arrived the evening my sister died or how he got here when it was so late?'

Unfortunately, I'm done. Rose can't remember anything about that, in fact, when she thinks about it and in retrospect, she's not even sure Sunny was here. 'I'm an old woman, dear, and my memory isn't what it was.'

On the doorstep, I give her a final 'sorry' for my behaviour as a way of saying thanks for talking to me. In the short journey from her armchair to the front door to see me out, her suspicions have grown and finally ripened. 'Just one thing, dear, you understand anything we've discussed is strictly between us whether I remembered properly or not?'

'Of course.'

She grabs my wrist with her bony hand. 'Only in my family, we take a dim view of snitches. Just ask my boy Kit, he'll tell you all about that.'

# Chapter 30

When I return home, on the road near our house the van with 'Kit's Roofing: No Job Too Small' is parked. Kit is dropping off Sunny after his visit. Except he's not. Pulling over under a tree before reaching them, I sit and watch what's happening. Kit is at the wheel with Sunny in the passenger seat. The pair of them are deep in conversation but it doesn't look like a father saying goodbye to his son. It looks exactly like the conversation Trevor was having with Sunny in our back garden the night before. Kit appears to be explaining something to Sunny who sits with his head bowed, occasionally nodding earnestly. When Kit looks up and sees me parked up, he takes fright. He nudges Sunny with his elbow who also looks in my direction. After a few more words, Kit climbs out of the driver's seat and goes round to the passenger side and opens the door. Sunny climbs out himself and becomes the victim of another one of his father's performative hugs before being released to go back into our house.

Kit walks up the road and his looming height appears over my car door. He taps on my window. 'Run out of gas, have you, Josie, parking up on the street like this? Or are you spying on me and my son?'

'It's none of your business what I'm doing.'

'No? I'll tell you what is my business. I've just had my mother on the phone. She tells me you've just been round there asking lots of nosy questions about the night your sister died. Is that right?'

Rose obviously had time to think about things after I left. 'I just went round to apologise to her, nothing more, nothing less.'

'Did you now? That's nice.' He rests his big hands on the car. 'Alright, perhaps you can answer another question for me. What's this you want to talk to my Sunny about? He says he was ordered into your back garden for a conversation but you lost interest when he kindly opened your sister's phone for you. Playing private detective, are you? Or maybe assisting that dopey cop Summers with his enquiries with a view to getting me put in prison?'

'That's none of your business either.'

His leans into my open car window so he's only a few inches away from my ear. He hisses, 'You're in way over your head, babe, you know that?'

He doesn't wait for an answer, walking slowly back down the street, but I call him back. 'By the way, Kit, perhaps you could help me with another one of my questions. Do you use the false name "Bill" at all?'

He's smiling at me now. 'Don't know what you're talking about, sweetheart, I don't know any Bill.'

He gets into his van and drives slowly away, giving me a smiley look as he goes.

He's not the only man who's not happy with me this evening. As soon as I get through the front door, Trevor appears from nowhere. He gestures with his thumb at the staircase. 'He's back. Go upstairs and tell him now.' He doesn't wait for an answer. 'No, no, we're not arguing about it, go and tell him now.'

He disappears as quickly as he came.

My feet are heavy and slow on the stairs. Sunny isn't going anywhere until he tells me what happened to my sister and who did what. I don't knock on his door, I just walk straight in.

The first thing I notice though when I walk into his room is not Sunny himself but the smell of fresh paint. On a shelf sits a tin of black paint with a brush balanced on top. Sunny's been decorating. Covering the white walls are lurid painted shapes and symbols that you have to study for a few seconds to understand. Some are outlines of a youth running with what looks like a weapon in his hands. Others are horrified faces, screaming, images that you might only see in nightmares. Along one of the walls are some generic fish being chased by a larger fish. Others are puzzling outlines, the keys to which might help make sense of what they are but I don't have the keys. Misshapen bodies and limbs, spirals, eyes that follow you around the room, all in various shades of black. Distorted, deranged, illusional images dragged from somewhere deep in Sunny's subconscious. I'm angry, but much, much more than that, I'm scared.

Who is this kid?

Sunny is sitting at his desk writing when I come in and doesn't seem to notice that I'm there. Only what I've just studied on the walls would take priority over asking him about Megan's death.

'Sunny! What the hell is this?'

I gesture at his artwork, which completely surrounds me and feels as if it's already seeping into my soul. He doesn't understand the question. 'What is what?'

I run my fingers across the wall, which leaves still tacky paint on my fingertips. I run them across his cheek, leaving black smudges. 'This is this.'

He still doesn't understand. 'You said I could decorate my room, so I did. Last night. Don't you like it?'

This isn't a normal question, so there isn't a normal answer. 'No, I don't like it.'

He seems genuinely curious. 'Is it the colour?'

'No, it's not the colour.'

He nods. 'OK, maybe I'll redo it in dark green or something. It is a bit out there as it is. I'm sorry you don't like it.'

There's silence for a few moments. This conversation has gone as far as it was going to go. 'Why didn't you tell anyone you were in the flat on the evening your mother died?'

He's still scribbling away. 'I wasn't, I was at my grandma's.'

Before I know what I'm doing I've grabbed him by the scruff of his neck and yanked him off his chair. 'No, you weren't, you were in the flat.'

His body, which was light and relaxed when I grabbed it, becomes heavy and tense. 'Was I? I can't remember.'

'Yes, you were and you know what happened while you were there. What did you see and what do you know?'

He turns his face towards me. There's no mischief in those sly eyes any more. He's worked it all out. Perhaps he knew that I would find out he was there. 'You're getting upset over nothing. I didn't see anything and I don't know anything. Is this why Trevor is upset as well? He's been in my room while I was out with my dad. He was searching for something.'

Trevor will have seen Sunny's decorating. Any lingering doubts he might have had about evicting Sunny will have been well and truly extinguished. For the moment, though, that doesn't matter. I let Sunny drop back into his chair. 'I know you didn't like your mother very much. I didn't either, we had our problems. But she was murdered, someone did it and I want to know who. You can help me.'

He goes back to writing. 'I know you had your problems with her. She told me about them, and that's why you should be glad she's gone. No one liked her.'

His hand is running backwards and forwards over the page, which prompts me to suggest something. 'You like writing, Sunny. Here's an idea, why don't you write down what happened in the flat that night. Who was there and what they did and why you think they did it.'

'That won't help. It's true that I was in the flat and went to my grandma's much later but I can't remember what happened and I don't know anything.'

This is too much for me. He knows and he knows that I know he knows. This time I pounce and grab him by his shirt and pull him to his feet so we're face to face. 'You're an evil little runt and I'm going to make you tell me what you know.' I let go of him, suddenly appalled by my violence, the words coming out of my mouth, but he's laconic.

'I know a lot of things. A lot of things about you, a lot of things about my mother and a lot of fruity things about Trevor. Give me time and maybe I'll remember them. Maybe I won't. But I'll tell you one thing, if you let your husband throw me out of this house, you'll never find out what I know because then I won't remember at all.'

# Chapter 31

'Have you done it?'

Trevor is standing in our living room, in front of the fireplace, with his arms folded like a Victorian father waiting to hear that his wayward daughter has cut all links with the cad who is ruining her reputation. In one hand, he's holding an object which seems to be wrapped in a towel.

'No.'

He's horrified. 'No!?'

'It's not that simple. He knows who killed Megan. If he leaves this house, we'll never find out who did it. We can't bury my sister, mourn her properly or let her rest in peace until we find out who murdered her.'

He crumbles. He holds his head with one hand and groans, 'Oh man . . .' He stumbles over to an armchair, sinks into it like a deflating balloon. He sits rubbing his forehead with the fingers of one hand and clutching his object with the other until he gathers himself again. He draws breath. 'OK. Let's see if this changes your mind.' He throws what he's holding in his hand at my feet.

'What is it?'

'Unfold it and see, only be careful, it's sharp.'

It's a knife, with a serrated blade, about eighteen inches long. The sort of knife you see the police recover from a stabbing on the street. For a few moments, in my mind, I try to reframe this weapon as an outsized penknife, the sort a boy of Sunny's age might carry. But it doesn't work. The cold steel of the blade on my fingers slashes to ribbons the veil of excuses I've draped around my nephew. I'm frightened now, the way I was warned to be by nearly everyone and I wouldn't listen. This knife is horrific. 'Where did you find this?'

'I searched his room while he was out with Kit. My thinking was there might be something in there that would help you come to an obvious conclusion and I think that weapon should be it. I'm not going to get into that bad acid trip that he's painted on his wall although if you wanted any more evidence, that's it.'

My hand is shivering holding this weapon. All of me is shivering. 'You think he's in a gang?'

'No, I don't. No self-respecting gang would have him as a member. He's his own one-man gang, the Sunny Boys. And he's got a beef with our family for whatever reason. I've been patient, Josie, but this is the end. I want him out of our house and I'm not putting up with any more of your stalling. He's got to go, otherwise we'll have to consider other options. I'm not letting my children share their house with him for a moment longer.'

'The thing is, Trevor, Sunny was in the flat the night Megan died. He knows what happened. He's as good as said if we don't throw him out, he'll tell me what happened, otherwise he won't.'

Trevor groans in despair. 'He was at his grandmother's. We know that and now he's telling you he was at the flat and saw it all happen, whatever it was, but he's not saying unless you let him, his knife and his mad paintings stay in our house? What's the matter with you? He's making it up. It's a carrot to dangle in front of you while he finishes his business here, whatever that may be.'

Trevor snatches the knife out of my hand and stabs it with extreme violence into the mantelpiece. I remember Kit's solicitor's snide suggestion at the meeting where Sunny's future was decided that perhaps Tova's injury was inflicted by someone in the family. 'This is Megan all over again. This is exactly the sort of stunt she would have pulled to grind more money out of you.'

'I know.'

He leaves the knife where it is and comes over to where I'm standing. He takes a deep breath and tenderly puts his arm around my shoulder before guiding me over to the sofa where we sit down together. 'Listen, Josie, we know you're soft-hearted, and we love you for it, but you're being played again. Wasn't it enough with your sister? You know, when Megan passed away I was very sorry about it but hoped at least it would give you a chance to move on. But you're not moving on. It's happening all over again, only in our house this time. Please see it for what it is.'

He's right but that's not helping. 'He was in the flat. I know he was. Sunny knows what happened to my sister. What can I do?'

'Who are you going to trust, Josie? Detective Constable Summers and his highly professional team of dedicated and experienced police officers who've concluded your sister's death was a tragic, if accidental, drug overdose? Or that evil little kid upstairs who wants, for reasons known only to himself, to destroy you and your family?'

He holds my hand and listens carefully as I explain what I've learned from Frieda's log and Rose's admission that Sunny was in the flat that evening, and I remind him about Megan's horror of needles. 'We're not religious, we don't believe in evil and my nephew is not evil. He's a traumatised child who needs support.'

Trevor is trying hard to keep it together but he spits, 'The kid is evil and I don't mean evil in the normal sense of a bit nasty or a little unkind. I mean he is actually evil, as in demonic. As for Sunny being in the flat, Kit or other people coming and going and who was arguing about what after all, who cares? She's not coming back, Josie.' He hesitates. 'Look, I didn't want to say this but I was actually a little relieved when Megan went. You know, the way some people are relieved when a relative dies after a long illness. Megan was your long illness.' He looks upwards bitterly. 'Now this. Please go upstairs and tell him he's got to go. It's time for all this to stop.'

'He wouldn't hurt anyone.' Who is this idiot telling her husband that Sunny wouldn't hurt anyone? How could I possibly know that? 'Let me speak to him. There might be a reasonable explanation.'

Trevor whispers curses under his breath before saying, 'OK.'

I don't believe Sunny would hurt my family. Perhaps I can't. Trevor is right to think he's here for a reason, it's just not clear what it is. I go upstairs again and into Sunny's room. I need to find out what kind of blackmailer he is. Through an emotional haze, I need to find out whether he's the kind that delivers or not. Sunny is still busy with his writing and doesn't appear surprised by my return. He's had time to prepare an answer on the knife because he knows Trevor has searched his room. He claims Rodney bought it and asked him to look after it. It's such a pathetic lie that I'm almost disappointed.

'I've just been talking to my husband. He doesn't want you living with us any more.'

Sunny nods. 'OK.'

'To be honest with you, Sunny, I'm not sure I do either.'

He's still unperturbed. 'OK.'

'I was hoping we could work something out for you but I can't see how. Now you admit you lied and you were in the flat with my sister on the evening she died but claim you can't remember anything about it. That's just heartless. If you can't remember anything and you just want to be cruel to me, there doesn't seem to be any further point in you staying here.'

His stalls for a moment and his pen hovers over his page. 'The thing is, I was wracking my brains trying to remember and you know something came back to me. It must have been about the time my mother got jabbed up. I was in my room reading a book but I heard her ring up a guy called Bill and she asked him to come over and help.'

Trevor might be right. Maybe he is evil. 'Who is Bill and what do you know about him?'

'Nothing really. He was one of her druggie friends probably. She used to call him up quite a lot. He helped her out with things.'

Sunny's an honest blackmailer. The kind who delivers. The kind who will return compromising photos to you if you pay up. 'Do you remember anything else about Bill, like where he could be found?'

Sunny's smirking to himself. 'Not at the moment but it might come back to me. I'll keep trying.'

He's the kind of blackmailer who delivers, but only some of the photographs at any one time. He wants more from you first. Sunny starts writing again.

'Is that all you can remember at the moment?'

He's busy writing and sounds hurt. 'You're making it sound like I'm misremembering on purpose.'

On the way out of his room, I decide to check on Sunny's pathetic lie about the knife, although it's a purely formal precaution. I knock on Rodney's door and ask him if he knows anything about Sunny's knife.

It turns out it wasn't a lie after all.

# Chapter 32

'You bought the knife that was in Sunny's room?'

Poor Rodney is nearly in tears. 'Sort of.'

I'm frozen. 'Why?'

'Sunny told me his dad needed one for work. He claimed his dad couldn't buy one because he's got convictions for violence and he couldn't buy one because he's too young. He asked if I could get one for him. I thought of Danny, the locksmith, where Dad bought the lock for Tova's room. I thought he might sell me one because he knows the family because we've been in there so many times. So, the pair of us went down there. Sunny stayed outside in the street and I went in and bought it. Danny didn't want to, but when I told him Dad needed it, he agreed as long as you or Dad came in later and confirmed my story was true.'

When I don't say anything, Rodney looks at my face and adds, 'I'm sorry, I don't know why I agreed. It's just Sunny was sort of so believable and I wanted to help even though I knew it was wrong. He asked me not to tell you because you'd get upset.'

'Did he tell you what the knife was really for?'

A tear falls down his cheek. 'He just said it was for his dad.'

What have I done to my family? I've assumed all along that we are all strong enough to take the weight of Sunny's troubles but it's all a delusion. I asked my family to do too much without thinking of the consequences. There was no excuse for inflicting this situation on my children. Actually, there was. I had to balance my responsibility for my nephew's welfare with that of my family and I've got it wrong. I can't put Sunny out of our house. It looks like I'll have to agree with Trevor's implied threat that if Sunny doesn't go, he and the children will have to. I'm staying though. Sunny has a story and I want to hear it whatever it costs me, but it's not going to cost my family. Not any more.

I spare Rodney the lecture and give him a hug and a kiss and tell him I understand. He's not to blame.

Next, I knock on Tova's door. She's lying on her bed with a book. She looks so sullen, she reminds me of her cousin. I cut straight to the chase. 'Tova, is there anything you want to tell me about Sunny? Have there been any incidents with him? Has he asked you to do things or asked you to keep any secrets? Anything you weren't comfortable with?'

She looks up at me. 'You bet there are.' I'm horrified at what might have happened until she adds. 'He creeps me out, he creeps everyone out, he's a creep.' She goes on in fury. 'And he's a cheat!'

If the worst that's happened to my daughter is a little sharp practice at a board game, I'll live with it. 'Yes, but anything in particular? You know, anything that you'd like to share with me?'

She's very firm about the particulars. 'Yes, he's a creep.' She thinks a little. 'I'm not talking to him so he's not going to creep me out, but I don't know why you brought him here anyway. Dad doesn't like him, Rodney doesn't likc him and I don't likc him. Even you don't like him, not really. So why is he here?'

I've spared Rodney the lecture about buying knives so I let Tova off the lecture about families and their responsibilities. She's far too young to understand about my relationship with her aunt so she's spared that as well. 'OK, look, this has been a difficult time for us but we'll work our way through it.'

'Unless you can think of a way to stop him being a creep, there's nothing to work through.'

With that, she picks up her book and my interview is over.

I don't bother to go and speak to Sunny a second time. He's not going to tell me what that knife was for and he's probably already got a story lined up about how it was Rodney's fault that he was persuaded to buy it.

I sit on the stairs after speaking with Sunny, Rodney and Tova. In their different ways, all three are paying the price for my obsession. All the more reason for it to be resolved. I'll be able to help my nephew a lot more when I know what happened. Perhaps Megan resting in peace will allow me to live in peace.

What do I know and who do I trust? I don't trust Summers, who chose to believe that my sister was another drugs death statistic that wasn't worth bothering over. Nor Kit, Rose and Dixie, who lied from the beginning and have their own reasons for not telling the truth. Not Megan, who lies and manipulates from the grave. And not Trevor either, who lied about his midnight summit meeting with Sunny in our back garden. There will be no questions about that because I don't trust him to tell me the truth. Oddly enough, the only person I do trust here is Sunny. He told me that Megan called 'Bill' around the time that she was 'jabbed up'. I know from Megan's phone that she did indeed call someone called Bill around the time she was injected. Sunny's told me the truth and he'll tell me more, I know it. But to do that, he has to stay here.

Trevor is right, what difference does it make if Dixie, Kit, Bill or anyone else killed my sister. She's still dead. What if Summers was right in inferring she might have killed herself? As soon as I walked into her hospital room on the night she died, I knew that moment had been coming all along. It was always how it was going to end. Perhaps the truth is that it was a relief.

It's true that what Sunny has told me doesn't help me very much unless I can track Bill down. But at least it shows Bill mattered and that he wasn't some random she called by chance, even if I don't know whether he actually did help her. He couldn't have done, by that stage she was already dying.

Trevor is back in the living room sitting in a chair staring into space, waiting for my return. When he sees me, he gets up. 'Well?'

'He wants to tell me who killed Megan. I know he does.'

He raises his hands and shows me his empty palms as if he has nothing left to offer. 'OK. You've got seven days. If he's not gone by then, I'm going to take the children to my parents until he is. You might be willing to play Russian roulette with their future but I'm not. At least that way, you'll have a chance to find out who he really wants to destroy. It'll narrow it down a little. Although what he'd have against me and the children is a bit of a mystery.'

I feel relief. There's no reason why my family should pay any price for my obsession. If anything, seven days is too long. But the mother in me makes me howl with outrage. 'You're not taking my children away!'

The howl comes out wrong. It sounds like a singer hitting the wrong notes to the wrong tune. My voice is mangled and unconvincing. I know why, it's because deep down I want my children and husband out of this house. The idiot who's pretending to herself that Sunny is no threat to anyone doesn't have to pretend any more. It's what I want, to have Sunny here on our own while I find out what happened to my sister.

Any risks when my family have gone will be on me.

# Chapter 33

Mercifully, I don't have to be in school today because it's an inset day. That means I don't have to play the illness card. Although in truth I really am ill, just not with anything a doctor could treat. At the same time, dodging my professional responsibilities makes me feel worse. It also means I can reassure my colleagues that I'm feeling better and am working at home. Trevor's at work. I'm at my desk with Frieda's log, Megan's phone and a not very helpful snippet of information from Sunny. The morning starts badly when I get a phone call from Tova's teacher. We know each other professionally. She beats about the bush a little before wondering aloud if perhaps Tova's experiencing any difficulties or problems at home. Eventually, she admits that my daughter is losing focus and is having difficulty concentrating in the classroom. Her marks in tests, which even a month ago were excellent, are starting to tail off. Her teacher suggests that it might be an idea if she, Tova and I got together after school one day and had a bit of a conflab about it.

It's humiliating for me to get a message like this from another teacher and she gets fobbed off. We don't need a conflab to find out what the matter is with Tova, we need to find out who murdered her aunt Megan. I ring 'Bill' from Megan's phone. It rings for a while before sounding the tone to leave a voicemail. I send Bill a text, telling him I'm Megan's sister and would it be possible for us to speak. That might not have been a good idea, he's forewarned now that I know about him. It's delivered but there's no reply. No doubt like Dixie, Kit, Frieda and Sunny himself, he doesn't want to 'get involved' with the authorities and thinks that might be what talking to me will involve. I send him another text from my own phone, telling him that anything he wants to tell me will be treated in strictest confidence. No doubt that was a mistake too. 'Strictest confidence' will sound a little official to Megan's druggie friends.

I call some of the other numbers on Megan's phone. People with names like Ringo, Taters and Mad Jimbo. They either don't answer or when they do, it's with a snarl, demanding to know who's calling them and who gave me their number. There is no time for an explanation or for me to appeal for help. They either ring off when they discover that it's Megan's sister calling or demand money out of me which they say Megan owed them. I ring Bill again, repeatedly. Eventually Bill is every other call in my phone log. Same pattern, the phone rings and rings until eventually it goes to answerphone. It's almost a relief when the front door goes and it turns out to be a delivery for a neighbour which I take in. On the way back upstairs, I call Bill for what must be the tenth time. I imagine him, anxiously sitting in a squat somewhere, looking at his phone every time it's called and wondering who it is that's ringing him incessantly. He probably thinks his name has been passed to the police in connection with Megan's death.

When I get to the top of the stairs, the phone goes to answerphone. But not before I realise that somewhere up here, very faint but unmistakeable, is the sound of a phone on silent, vibrating. I call Bill again and listen intently. My first thought is that it must be coming from Sunny's room, but when I burst in there, it isn't. It doesn't sound as if it's coming from anywhere at all and it crosses my mind that I'm imagining it. I ring it again. Standing under the trap door that opens into our attic, it finally registers where the vibration is coming from. It's up there, through the slightly ajar attic door.

When we moved into this house, we both agreed that a husband and wife need their own space, somewhere to call their own. My space is what can only be described as a roomy broom cupboard that looks out over the back garden. We agreed that Trevor would take the attic even though it can only be reached by a rickety foldaway ladder and you have to crouch down at the top when you get up there because of the eaves. I keep all my personal things in the broom cupboard and he keeps his in the attic. The pictures he doesn't like I hang on my walls, the mementos that I don't like sit on a shelf in his attic. Private papers are filed away in our respective spaces. I know some would sneer at our having luxuries like our own 'rooms' alongside the four bedrooms we use but I don't care, I've earned it.

We've always respected each other's spaces. We ask permission to enter them, admittedly in a rather jokey fashion. But that was then and this is now. The foldaway ladder comes down easily enough. Its steel is cold under my clammy hands and the steps rattle under my shaking legs. The trap door pushes open. Our spaces don't have locks on them because we trust each other. The only natural light comes from the small skylight above my head. At one end is Trevor's desk and chair. At the other end is an upright set of wooden drawers that we bought in a boot sale. It was sold to us as a Victorian antique, and while it may be Victorian it certainly isn't an antique. It's scuffed, badly varnished and some of the wood is starting to splinter. Two of the drawers hang slightly open. Inside them are bits of paper, takeaway leaflets and other junk that's never been thrown away. The drawer at the top though is firmly locked. I remember the key hanging out of the lock when we bought it. It was cast iron and twice the size of a normal one.

I stand by the drawers with my phone in my hand, unsure what to do next. Trevor posed the question of whether I want to drink this cup down to its last dregs. Do I really want to know whether Bill's phone is in this drawer? Do I want to know what else is in it? My fingers do the deciding for me and they call Bill. I jump slightly when the drawer echoes to the sound of a vibrating phone. It stops when Bill's phone goes to answerphone and the drawer, the attic and the rest of the house are silent now, never to be the same again.

The key must be in here somewhere but I don't need one anyway. We've just passed well beyond the trust stage. This isn't secret chats with Sunny in the back garden. It makes no difference to me if Trevor comes home to find his drawer has been broken into and it was me who did it. There are more important things for us to argue about. A cursory search for the cast iron key yields nothing, so I head back down the rickety ladder to find our tool box. In it is a hefty, hardened-steel crowbar which I take back up to Trevor's space. The crowbar fits neatly into the gap around the locked drawer but its wood is thick and solid and it's not going to come away easily, and that gives me time to falter. It's possible that Sunny had something to do with this. It's possible that Sunny got hold of Bill's phone somehow and Trevor caught him with it and took it from him. It's possible that's what they were discussing in the garden.

All possible, but it can't be true.

I lever the crowbar against the drawer. It bends alarmingly but stays fast. Perhaps my spirit is willing but my arms are weak. Do I really want that phone and to find out what's on it? I try harder this time and hear wood beginning to splinter. The splintering is caught up by another noise down below, someone is at the door. Only it's not someone at the door, it's someone coming through it. It's almost a relief not to be able to force the lock. When I scurry downstairs, Trevor looks surprised to see me.

'You're taking up burgling now?'

How does he know what I've been up to? Only when I look down do I realise that I've still got the crowbar clasped in my hand. When I can't think of a plausible explanation as to why it's there, he breaks the silence by asking, 'Are you alright?'

'Yes, I'm alright. You're home very early.'

'My boss took pity on me. He thinks I'm stressed and under too much pressure so he suggested taking the rest of the day off might be a good idea. I take it you haven't changed your mind about our lodger?'

'I only need a few days.'

He sighs. 'You've got seven. Actually, now you've got six. Anything else happening?'

He looks up the staircase with a puzzled expression and then at me again, then back up the staircase. He doesn't wait for an answer to find out if anything is happening. He merely drawls to himself in a whisper 'okaaay', walks up the stairs and climbs the ladder into his attic, closing the trap door behind him. On a side table in the hallway, under a mirror, he's put his keys. On the keyring, standing out because it's so much bigger and tarnished than the others, is the key to the drawer with Bill's phone in. It's then that I realise why 'Bill' is called Bill. It's another one of my sister's acronyms. 'Bill' stands for 'Brother-in-Law' with an extra L thrown in at the end.

# Chapter 34

'You'll never guess what he's done this time.'

I'm almost caught tracing the outline of the key to Trevor's drawer on paper when he reappears from his attic. I let the pen fall from my hand on to the side table as he comes down the stairs. 'Who are we talking about and what has he done?'

'Sunny. He's been up in my office. You know how I always put the foldaway ladder back up so the children can't get up there? Well, it's down again and that means someone has been up there and we can all guess who that was. He's rifled through my possessions.' He adds hurriedly, 'Not that I've got anything to hide of course.' His voice is laden with sarcasm as he adds, 'But I prefer my office to remain private, that's not unreasonable. What do you think he was looking for?'.

There's no danger of him connecting me, the attic and the crowbar. My husband would never believe it was me who was up there. We trust each other. 'You'd better put a lock on it like the one you put on Tova's door.'

'That's one solution. A better one would be to turn him out of the house today but of course we've already come to an agreement on that. You'd better put a lock on your door too. Honestly, a lock on Tova's door, a lock on my door, a lock on your door. The house is turning into a prison.'

Sunny's reputation has come to my rescue. As has Trevor's return. If I'd bust open the drawer, he'd soon realise what I was looking for and why. 'Has he taken anything?'

Trevor is reluctant to admit anything. 'I don't think so. But it doesn't matter, I don't want him poking his nose around in my things. I'm going to lock him out of there pending his departure.'

My phone rings. It's Mary, a colleague from school who wants to speak to me on a personal matter and it needs to be face to face rather than over the phone. She knows I'm ill but would it be possible to drag myself off my sickbed and meet her somewhere? She sounds embarrassed and I'm already worried what this means. We arrange to meet in a café after she's finished classes. As gently as possible, I grasp the paper outline of the key in my hand and drop it in my bag.

It's a ten-minute walk to a different local ironmongers than that of Danny who sold Rodney the knife. He's lucky he's not being reported to the police. This new guy's website proudly promises that problems are only there to be solved. It turns out that's wrong, some problems can't be solved. The locksmith furrows his brow at my outline of Trevor's key and isn't sure he can help. He takes a tin off a shelf and pours out the collection of ancient keys which it contains. We compare them to the outline. In the end he gives me half a dozen keys for free but he won't promise anything except that one might hit the jackpot, but not to get my hopes up.

Mary is sitting in the café waiting for me when I arrive. Given she's summoned me here she's very reluctant to get to the point. She asks me about Trevor. He's got a bit of a reputation in our staff room as the ideal husband and Mary is disappointed when I merely grunt about his welfare. She asks me if I'm feeling any better, which leaves me nonplussed for a moment until I remember I'm supposed to be ill. It's time to cut this short. 'You said you wanted to speak to me on a personal matter?'

Mary looks around the café furtively as if she's worried that we might be overheard. 'The thing is, Josie, you know your nephew Sunny has joined my "creative hour workshop"?'

'Yes.'

She tries hard to think of something to say and settles on, 'No doubt you're aware that Sunny is a very bright child with a wonderfully vivid imagination and we absolutely welcome that in class. At the end of the day, it's what we're all about. We want our students to express themselves in any way that feels appropriate to where they are on their journey through life and sometimes that can be quite challenging, of course.'

There's an enormous 'but' looming on the horizon here. 'There's an issue you want to raise with me?'

Mary nibbles her lip a little and slowly reaches into her bag. She pulls out a slim file and hands it over to me. It contains some loose sheets of paper with Sunny's handwriting on them. 'The thing is, Josie, some of the things Sunny is writing are raising concerns.' She adds hastily, 'Not everything, obviously, some of his work is brilliant, but some of it is a little more problematic. When he reads some of his stories out to the rest of his classmates, some have become rather upset at what they're hearing. One or two have spoken to their parents about it. As you can imagine this isn't the sort of feedback we really want to hear.'

I skim through the stories. It doesn't take long to get the gist. They're wracked with pain, cruelty, torment and death, all described in bright and sadistic colours. They're the verbal equivalents of the paintings in his room. I don't know why they should shock me by this stage but they do. I can only imagine what Trevor would make of them. 'Yes, Mary, I can see why you asked to speak to me and I'm grateful to you for doing so. I'll speak to him about this.'

'That would help, Josie, and for now we've decided that perhaps it's best if Sunny doesn't read his stories out in class. But the thing is that you know how paranoid the authorities are these days about violence and teenage boys, and really I should report this issue to the head teacher, or maybe the police, or perhaps a government agency like Prevent or something.'

I need her to dial this down. 'He's not a terrorist, Mary.'

'No, of course not, but you know how much trouble we would be in if we didn't take this further and then something happened. People would say we should have done something when we became aware of what Sunny was writing rather than turning a blind eye and ignoring it.'

It's too much to read any of Sunny's stories at length. Almost without exception they're stories of revenge where various antiheroes are pushed too far by all and sundry and then they exact an extremely violent and terrible payback. What anyone more senior would do with these tales is impossible to say but there are enough red flags here to make a parade of them. It's totally my responsibility to support Mary in reporting them.

But my sister was killed and Sunny knows who did it.

'Thank you for flagging this up for me, Mary, you totally did the right thing. I don't know how much you're aware of Sunny's background and what's currently going on in his life but these stories are evidently a reflection of that. As you probably know, he lost his mother recently and we're taking some time with that.' Without thinking about what I'm saying, I add, 'Megan was murdered, you see.' Mary looks bemused. The school thinks it was an accidental death. 'We just need some time to steady the boat and then we can move forward. I'm sure these stories are just a reflection of the pain and grief he feels at the moment. If you can hold fire on reporting this for a little while then we can discuss the matter again and see if it's really the right way forward. I'll take full responsibility, obviously.'

Mary's worried. My first thought is that she thinks she'll be in the frame if Sunny loses it and behaves like one of the characters in his stories. But that's not what it is.

'I'll trust your judgement, Josie. He's your nephew. But aren't you worried about yourself and your family? These stories are frightening. Shouldn't Sunny be getting professional support in a residential place?'

I know what the answer is and so does everyone else. No one's on my side because they don't understand my sister, Sunny and me, and our relationship which dates back to before he was born.

No one understands. Everyone thinks I'm putting others at risk by refusing to force Sunny out. They all think I'm going to be an accomplice in whatever happens with Sunny. Worse than an accomplice, an inciter, instigator and co-offender, along with my sister who created Sunny in the first place and who made me believe that I created the person she was. We're all guilty, Megan, Sunny and me.

When I get home, it's to see a step ladder by the door to the attic. Trevor has been installing a lock. The job is unfinished but it looks like it will be tomorrow. If I want Bill's phone I'll have to get it tonight.

# Chapter 35

As long as I can find a way to search the attic without being caught, by the morning I'll have hard evidence of some kind of relationship between my sister and my husband that was supposed never to have existed. At least that's what I was led to believe and there was good evidence to support it. Trevor never liked Megan who he thought was a sponging, narcissistic parasite who took advantage of me and who I allowed to exploit me for reasons he never understood. Only Megan and I understood why that was and it looks as if she shared it with her son. Or perhaps he found out for himself; he's more than capable of doing that.

Megan, meanwhile, preferred to sneer at Trevor as weak, boringly predictable and a straight suit of a man, the sort of husband who enjoys sex with the lights off and his socks on. It wasn't always clear though if she actively disliked him or whether she said these things as half-hearted revenge for his attitude towards her. At family functions, I always knew when Megan was nearby because Trevor would stiffen slightly and suddenly remember he needed to get a drink. As he sloped off to avoid her, Megan would ask me, 'Has your wet fish gone off to get himself some chips?' On another occasion though she admitted, 'At least you know your wet fish isn't going to do a flit with the company secretary along with the church funds before fleeing to South America. He's not that sort of husband. You could do a lot worse.' She added ruefully, 'Let's face it, I have.'

There has to be a simple explanation as to why Trevor would keep a burner phone locked away to speak to Megan with. There has to be a reason why she would have called him on it as she lay dying in her flat. There has to be. He's just not that sort of husband.

It seems only fair to give him a chance to 'fess up before being confronted with the evidence and being able to dismiss it on grounds I hadn't considered. Before that, I go up to see Sunny to have it out with him about the stories he's writing. When I get to his room, it's to find him writing more stories. He's a story machine. The computer we bought doesn't even appear to have been turned on yet.

'Sunny, we need to talk.'

He doesn't look up from his work. 'OK.'

'It's about these stories you've written and read out in the creative hour workshop.'

He's clearly needled and stops writing. Perhaps his pride is hurt by Mary's bad reviews.

'What about them?'

'Your teacher is worried about what they might say about you, and so am I.'

He's disgusted. 'You mean she thinks I'm a nutjob or something?'

Those aren't the words that professionals would choose to use but he's right, that is exactly what Mary means. 'No, it's just that they are rather disturbing.'

He shrugs. 'They're just stories, she's taking things too seriously.' He gets up from his chair, pulls a book from his collection and shows me the cover. 'You don't think this guy who writes about vampires actually wants to bite anyone's neck and drink their blood? They're just stories. If anyone's a nutjob in that classroom, it's her not me.'

'Your stories are upsetting your fellow students.'

He shakes his head with a smile. 'They've got fingers, why don't they use them and stick them in their ears?' He puts his fingers in his ears to show me how it works. 'Anyway, I'm banned from reading my stories in that class.' He adds in an undertone, 'What a bunch of pussies, honestly.'

He sits down, picks up his pen and begins writing again to signal that I'm dismissed. I can't fight this tonight and leave him to write his stories that shouldn't be taken seriously.

Downstairs, Trevor is putting his lock together at the dining room table. I devise a cover story to disguise my questions about Megan. It occurs to me that only a few weeks ago, devising a cover story to speak to my husband about something important would have been unimaginable. I'm holding a piece of paper and a pen as props. When he sees me, he smiles grimly. 'Joining your nephew in the story writing game? Is it about a family being wrecked by a lodger?'

'No, I'm making notes for a eulogy to give at Megan's funeral. I was wondering if you had any memories or stories about her that you could share. Unless you're planning to say something yourself?'

He puts down his lock. 'What's brought this on? You haven't even got a date for a funeral yet.'

'I know, but I want to have something ready and not leave it to the last minute.'

He pretends to have a think before saying in the most sarcastic way possible, 'Not really, no. I take the view you shouldn't speak ill of the dead, and if I can't speak ill of her, there's nothing really left for me to say.'

'You knew Megan, you must be able to think of something. Some moment you shared together, an amusing story about her, something that makes you smile when you think about her.'

He's disgusted. 'If you want me to contribute, you must be stuck for material. I hope she rests in peace and all that, and I know she's your sister, but that woman brought nothing but misery into my life.' He corrects himself. 'Our lives. You know I think what that cop Summers was insinuating was right. It's more than possible your sister took her own life and she did it to saddle us with that little hobgoblin upstairs. That's the kind of trick she would pull. She drove a wedge between us that's never been bridged.'

I hoped this conversation might help inform me but I didn't expect it to take this turn. 'How did she do that?'

'This whole thing between you and her that you never wanted to tell me about. This stranglehold she had over you, the leverage she used, the way she made a fool out of you and made you act not only not in your interests but your whole family's. And now this same trick she played means we're lumbered with him upstairs. She made you do that as well. Why? I've long since given up asking what it was, there's no point. That was the wedge she drove between us. I'll tell you one thing though.' He points upwards with his finger in Sunny's general direction. 'I bet he knows. You can be sure of that.'

That's very astute of Trevor. He's right as well, Sunny probably does know. Perhaps that's the reason why I slip up by saying, 'You must have something for me to include in my eulogy. Even something as simple as a phone conversation.'

He's horrified. 'What's that supposed to mean? A phone conversation? I didn't even have your sister's number, much less hold phone conversations with her.' He doesn't wait for an answer. Once again he points upwards. 'This is him, isn't it? What's he said to you this time? What nonsense has he filled your head up with?' He gets up from the table, leaving his lock behind. 'You know this is Megan again, doing you over from beyond the grave, using him upstairs as a catspaw. I wouldn't be surprised if she hadn't briefed him before she went about how to carry on her good work. And still you don't want to break free of her for whatever demented reason you have.' He's becoming very angry. 'Let me lay it on the line for you. I meant what I said about Megan dying because I thought it might loosen the grip that she had on you. Now she's gone but Sunny's taken up the slack, filling your head full of nonsense about phone calls.'

My voice is quiet. 'You're really glad Megan is dead?'

'Yes. And if you had any sense, you'd be glad she's dead too. But it won't make any difference now that your nephew is here continuing her good work. Maybe he'll do us all a favour and take an overdose too.'

I think about how the next conversation we have will be when I have Bill's phone in my hand, and that it will be very different.

He walks out of the room. He turns and repeats loudly and clearly so I'm in no doubt that this wasn't an off-the-cuff remark spoken in anger.

'Yes, I'm glad she's dead and so should you be.'

# Chapter 36

'And so should you be.'

I think about these words as I carefully mount the stepladder to Trevor's office in the attic. These words haunt me because I fear that they're just a bold statement of the facts: I should be glad that Megan is dead, and nothing that's happened since my sister passed would make me think it would be a mistake. In one hand I'm holding a key ring with the various ancient keys the locksmith gave me, in the other the crowbar I tried to use earlier. In my pocket I have a torch. Trevor is fast asleep on the sofa downstairs and the rest of the house is dark and quiet. It doesn't matter though. I'm having Bill's phone this time whatever happens.

I bump into a side table, which scatters whatever was on it over the floorboards in all directions, but I don't stop to pick anything up. Instead, I turn on my torch and shine its beam on Trevor's chest of drawers. But I'm too late. The top drawer which held the phone is hanging open. Whatever was in there, including Bill's phone, has gone. Now I'll never know what was on it. Perhaps there were other incriminating things in there but they're gone too. It's possible that Trevor was right about Sunny coming up here after all. Perhaps I wasn't the only person who paid this space a visit. At first, I was relieved that Trevor suspected Sunny of coming up here looking for whatever he could find, but it's plausible Sunny was indeed here for whatever reason. Maybe he too was looking for Bill's phone or for something else. Cheated, I run my fingers inside the dusty drawer from which the evidence has disappeared.

I run the torch over the attic and wonder what else my nephew might have been looking for, if indeed he was. One thing you can say for my husband, he's incredibly well organised. Everything has its place and everything gets put in the right one. I tap the keyboard of his computer and the screen comes to life but there's a password on it. Above, on one of the shelves is a line of files all neatly marked with labels that tell me what's inside. One is marked 'work correspondence'. To my disappointment, when I skim through it there is indeed only work correspondence to read. Another is marked 'private correspondence' but that too doesn't help much. The 'private correspondence' is letters to the council complaining about bin collections and street littering and so on and so forth, all the letters of a slightly prim middle-aged, middle class man. Another file is marked 'financial' and just in case prying eyes may be around, there's a second label on it marked 'private'. But nothing is private in this house any more.

It contains bank and credit statements and letters, and he's even neatly filed away various offers from the banks and credit card companies. It's all routine and most of the credits/debits in it are familiar to me, although I notice that he's a very generous giver to good causes. There's nothing suspicious in there that would suggest he's anything other than what he appears to be – a respectable, if slightly dull, family man. There are no direct debits to gambling casinos, no airline receipts that might suggest he's flown a lover to Paris or Venice and no subscriptions to websites offering pornography.

Next to the financial file is his phone company files. It's with some concern that this one is opened but that concern is misplaced. There's only one phone covered in there, the one he uses and I know that number by heart. From what I can see, there are no suspicious phone numbers on the statements. These papers are a wild goose chase. For a moment it occurs to me to wonder if Trevor is right. Has Sunny put this in my head and made me believe that Trevor is untrustworthy and unreliable? Is it possible that Bill's phone is something to do with my nephew and that he planted it up here for some reason? Except he couldn't have done that. Or is it also possible that I didn't hear what I thought I heard in that drawer or there's an innocent explanation for what I heard? Except that's not possible either.

Next to the financial file marked private there is another file marked 'financial sundry'. It's much thinner than the other one and consists of bank statements from a different account and there are far fewer entries in the credit and debit columns. In fact, there is only one transaction a month logged on the statement, a direct debit for a thousand pounds to a charity called DAA. A quick check on my phone shows this charity is logged as 'Direct Action for Animals' but it appears to be completely anonymous apart from that with no website or contact details. The first deposit in this account is from seven years previously and was initially funded by half a million pounds. This appears to have been Trevor's share of the sale of his eccentric grandmother's house, which was supposed to have been a prize asset and from which he was supposed to inherit a substantial sum when she died.

I remember when he returned from the solicitors after her will was read. There's no point in denying I was hopeful the family was going to be very comfortably off indeed once the grandmother passed. She promised me as much at a family function. 'Don't worry, Josie, when I go, your family will be looked after.' Except when Trevor returned from the reading of the will, it turned out that wasn't the case. Every penny of her inheritance went to Battersea Dogs Home. It's true she was an animal lover, but making no provision for anyone except our furry friends was a disappointment, although a furious Trevor's version was that she was 'a mad old bat'.

That though was a lie, or should I say another lie. He did get the money after all and put it in a separate account from which a thousand pounds a month was disappearing into another animal charity. Or perhaps it wasn't another lie. Perhaps there was a provision in the will that he could have the money but only on condition he couldn't spend it on human beings. That would be typical of the grandmother. Perhaps, perhaps—

'What on earth do you think you're doing?'

A ghostly hand comes from out of the darkness and seizes the file from my hand. When I turn it's to find Trevor standing behind me in the shadows. What on earth am I doing? My husband tucks the file under his arm. With no obvious story to tell, I resort to the truth. 'I've been ringing numbers on Megan's phone. The number she called after her overdose that night echoed up here. The phone was in the locked drawer in your cabinet over there. I came up here to recover it but it's already gone, so I was checking your files to see what else I could find.'

He seems disarmed by my frankness and sighs. 'Sunny's running rings around you. He sent you up here I suppose?'

'Not unless he put the phone Megan was ringing in your locked drawer, no.'

He shrugs. 'No, he didn't put it up here, I did. I took it off Sunny, he had it. Don't ask me where he got it from because I don't care.'

'Why didn't you give it to me?'

I can't see Trevor's face so I don't know how sincere it is.

'For two reasons. Firstly, because everything on it is deleted, secondly, because you're not well. This tag team Megan and Sunny are running to send you over the edge has gone far enough. You don't need to sit around theorising about any phones your sister might have been ringing because you're going to make yourself even more ill than you are already. Now, I want you to do two things for me instead. I want you to tell Sunny to go and I want you to go and see someone before this all gets out of hand. Do it quickly before your sister and her accomplice drag you down into madness or the grave.'

I lie in bed to the sound of chipping, sawing and the turning of metal. Trevor's decided he's not waiting for the morning to fit the lock. He's decided there's no further time to lose. He makes quite a racket as he does so but he obviously doesn't care. The rest of us have to put up with the noise. All except Sunny of course. I'm confident he's lying in bed fast asleep, oblivious to the noise around him as we're all locked out of the attic and away from Bill's phone.

# Chapter 37

The journey to school is even more funereal than usual. My tired hands are gripping the steering wheel too tightly. Tova and Rodney are sitting grim-faced in the back seat of the car, breaking occasionally to whisper things to each other. Only Sunny is happy, sitting in the front passenger seat, engrossed by another one of his books. He's not so engrossed though that he doesn't notice something after my children are dropped off at their school.

'This isn't the way we go.'

'We're not going to school yet, Sunny, we need to talk.'

I drive us both to a supermarket car park. I don't know why but it feels like a suitable place for a confrontation. I'm not playing any more but that mischievous grin playing on his lips shows that he is. He likes this. We both sit in the car.

'I've got some questions I want to ask you, Sunny.'

He's enthusiastic. 'I told you I'm trying to remember things.'

'No, it's not about what happened in your flat, it's this. Did my husband ever pay visits to your mother's flat?'

'You mean Trevor?'

I don't want to lose my temper but I'm not being messed around. 'Yes, Trevor's my husband, he's the only one I've got, I think we established that when you moved in.'

Sunny furrows his brow and thinks hard as if he has a problem to solve in a maths class. 'Let me see.' His eyebrows arch as if the answer is on the tip of his tongue before he finally admits. 'I can't remember.'

'You can't remember if Trevor ever paid visits to your flat?'

'Well, I wasn't in the flat most of the time, I was at my grandma's place.'

He pretends to be upset. What is so infuriating about his manner is that I'm not actually supposed to believe he's upset. It's all an act and he knows that I know it's an act.

This has gone on long enough. I take him by his jacket lapel and pull him across the passenger seat so our faces are close up. I can see into those steely grey eyes but I can't see what's behind them. 'You listen to me. Someone murdered my sister, who also happened to be your mother, and I'm going to find out who it was. Let's try again, did you ever see Trevor at home?'

He looks slightly alarmed and says nothing. I go on, 'I know you think I'm another kindly well-meaning teacher, social worker or counsellor who can be messed around with but you're wrong, I'm not. I'm from the block, just like your mother, and I know how to look after myself and get things done. Do you understand?'

He nods. 'I know what you're really like. My mother told me.'

We both know what he's referring too and he knows that his remark will be a stab to my guts. He gets a gentle shake to show I mean business. 'Let's try again. Was my husband ever in your flat?'

It's something that you notice with Sunny and other boys like him. He only respects people who are cruel and harsh with him. He respects and behaves himself with his father because Kit is a violent thug. For people like me who try and help and support him he has nothing but contempt. We stare into each other's eyes while he makes his mind up which kind of person he's actually dealing with here. He gets another shake to help him come to a decision.

Finally, he shrugs. 'Yeah, OK, Trevor came round the flat from time to time, big deal.'

We're still eyeballing each other. 'And how would you describe their relationship?'

He guffaws. 'What do you mean their *relationship*?' He spots another opportunity to stick the knife in by asking innocently, 'You mean, like were they having sex?' He waits for a few moments to see my reaction before saying, 'I don't know. I'm not a peeping Tom. Ask him, he's your husband. It takes two to have sex and now one of them is dead so he's the only one left who knows.'

He knows how to cheat at board games and in games like this too. My fingers loosen slightly. 'What happened in the flat that night, Sunny? You were there. You tell me.'

Now my grip is weakened, he's back to smiling but he's still wary. 'We've been through this. I was in my room all evening.'

'You didn't see or hear anything?'

He has another one of his thinking moments. He pays out some more details but they don't help. 'People came and went, there were arguments. But there were always people coming and going, there were always arguments. My dad showed up and had a row with her about something but my book was too good so I wasn't listening. It was *Lord of the Flies*. Really good book, have you read it? Let me tell you, Josie, schoolboys are bad people, you have to keep an eye on them. The guy got that totally right.'

'Why did you leave the flat then, if you had no idea what was going on while you were reading about bad schoolboys?'

His voice drops as if he's about to share a confidence. 'Well, I was on the last chapter and I went out of my room to get myself a drink, you know, there were loads of drinks lying around at mother's place. Anyway, when I came out, she was lying in an armchair, totally out of it, off her head on something or other.' He makes a face imitating Megan totally out of it. 'The flat was in total chaos and I thought, I don't need this tonight, so I got my book and walked over to my Grandma Rose's place.'

At last, we may be getting near the truth. I'm crushed. 'And you didn't think of calling an ambulance?'

Sunny appears to think this is a ridiculous question. 'Why? She was always out of it. The place was always wrecked. There were always people coming and going and they were always arguing. What do you want me to do? Call an ambulance every time it happens? I don't care, OK? I don't care. And of course, I didn't have a phone. She stole it from me and sold it, remember?'

He waits for me to respond. He doesn't get an answer because I'm fixated on the image of my sister dying on her own while her son, who doesn't care, heads off to stay with his grandmother. I look down and realise I still have my hands gripped on his jacket. I'm turning into his father, keeping a 'firm hand on the tiller'. I release him and mumble an apology for losing my temper while thinking it might be better if I was his father. To break the embarrassing silence afterwards, he goes on, 'Later, when the cops turned up, I told Grandma Rose to say I'd been there all evening. I'm not answering their questions. I don't like the police and it doesn't matter anyway, because, like everyone else, they don't care about a druggie who went too far.'

'I care.'

He laughs at me. 'Good for you. But I don't know why you do. She made a fool out of you like everyone else. She laughed at you behind your back. She did it to everyone.' He leans in to share another confidence. 'If you want my opinion, she did it deliberately, I mean the drugs thing. She'd had enough. She was talking about ending it all. Maybe she decided to close the door on all the people she made fools of, you know what I mean?' He sits back, satisfied with what he's said. 'Anyway, can we go to school now?'

I start the car engine. 'Was Trevor there that evening?'

'I don't know, I didn't hear him, he wasn't rowing with her if he was.'

I turn the engine off. I'm not in a fit state to drive anyway. 'Trevor said you were in his attic looking for the phone he took off you.'

Sunny is outraged. 'That's a barefaced lie!'

He's so outraged, it looks like he might be telling the truth. Like a lot of liars, he's very angry when someone tells lies to or about him. 'You'll have to walk to school from here, Sunny, I need some time on my own.'

'But it's miles!'

'You got in plenty of practice walking to your grandmother's, not caring about my sister. Now, please, go away, leave me in peace.'

He acts hurt and gets out of the car, slams the door and begins walking away across the car park.

It's only when my hands become wet and drops begin to fall into my lap that I realise I'm crying. What crushes my heart is that Sunny is right. I am the only one who cares, none of the others do. I can't even be sure I care for the right reasons either. A guilty conscience isn't the best motivation. He's still lying of course. Megan was murdered. Sunny's mixing in the truth with lies to punish and hurt me for whatever reason. He'll tell me in due course. I will just have to be a lot crueller to gain his respect and force the truth out of him. I'll have to out-cruel him. But I know too, though, that Sunny will choose the worst possible moment to finally tell me the truth. I know that.

# Chapter 38

'Hello, dear, you're back. Do you need a hand?'

Back at the police station, Summers was happy enough to let me have the key to Megan's flat when asked, his investigation is over. My story was that I needed to go through Megan's belongings and move them out of the flat, which is true. But I still felt guilty about telling him my cover story because of the increasing difficulty I'm having telling fact from fiction. Arriving at the flat though it was to find that not only was it locked but it was still boarded up to stop it being squatted. Frieda appeared from her door within seconds to offer assistance. Despite the fact that her unruly neighbour is dead, Frieda still seems to be hovering by her keyhole to see what's going on.

'Yes, I'm back, Frieda, but it looks like a wasted journey.'

She comes and views the boards. 'You mean these? Don't worry, dear, my late husband was a DIY person, we'll have something to fix that.'

She disappears for a few minutes and returns with a power tool and an extension lead which she expertly uses to remove the screws before taking the boards down so we can unlock the door. With the job done, Frieda lingers nearby. Her help was obviously just a ruse to get an invitation into Megan's flat, which of course she's never seen. I invite her in. It saves me the trouble of knocking on her door later to ask some questions that she may be able to answer. My visit is to search the flat for documentation that will show how my sister's lifestyle was funded, although deep down I think I already know. What I don't know is why, although deep down I suspect I already know that too. It was blackmail money.

Frieda is briefly disgusted by the state of the place and the musty smell that has already descended on it. Before long though she's opening windows to let the air in and tidying up for me. She's probably hoping to find something that will confirm all her worst fears about her neighbour. Meanwhile I begin the hunt for evidence. If Trevor is the model of efficient filing and precise organisation, his sister-in-law was the opposite. Letters from the authorities and statements from utility companies are randomly strewn around the flat. Down the back of an armchair are a batch of unopened red letters from various companies that provide services and loans. Marked urgent and confidential, they don't need to be opened to be seen for what they are. They're final demands and threats of legal action. For a woman with her resources, she wasn't in a hurry to settle accounts and invoices. None of this surprises me. She once told me that if you ignore problems, they usually end up going away.

In drawers, there are out-of-date-order bank statements from ten years ago but nothing recent. I wonder if she destroyed them and who might have suggested that. In the bedroom, Frieda has got to work stripping Megan's bed with a view to putting the sheets and pillow cases in the washing machine. I, on the other hand, open a cushion lining after noticing an unlikely bump where something is clearly concealed. Typical Megan, she always hid things where they could easily be found. Inside are her essential documents – her passport, various government cards and, bound up with an elastic band, her bank statements. The recent ones are in order. I know what I'm going to find when I unfold one. The list of debits is long but the list of credits is short and easily checked. Every month, she was receiving a thousand pounds from the fake DAA charity.

Megan was being paid off by Trevor.

'Excuse me, dear, you might be interested in this. I found it hidden under the mattress on your sister's bed.' Frieda hands me an official-looking file with a cover that suggests it's a religious tract. There are flowers, sunshine, huggable animals and a woman looking wistfully into the distance. In case I've missed it, Frieda points to the handwritten note in the top right-hand corner. 'In the event of my death, to be destroyed.'

'Thank you, Frieda.'

When Frieda doesn't take the hint and loiters nearby in order to see what's in the file, I say more firmly, 'Thank you, Frieda.'

Disappointed at missing out on what she was hoping might be some juicy gossip, Frieda goes back to the laundry. Inside the file are some booklets and advice sheets along with emails, notes and handwritten essays which an anonymous counsellor had encouraged her to write. They encouraged Megan to write down who she was, her journey through life, who she wanted to be, how she intended to get there and what mattered to her. But the essays clearly imply that she was through and done with who she was and where she wanted to be.

'Who am I? I'm a nobody. I've failed at everything. Everyone hates me, all my relationships have failed and I was to blame. My so-called friends and neighbours hate me, my parents hated me, my sister hates me, my boy hates me and he's right to do so. Let's face it, I'm a hateful person.'

It reads like something a self-conscious teenager with a martyr complex might write up as a poem but it still cuts me to the quick. There's a kind of pathetic sincerity to it which I never saw when she was scheming and grifting her way through my life.

'I don't want to go on. After all, what is life anyway? You look up and see a bird flying high across the sky and when you look up again a few moments later, your bird has gone. Probably caught by a cat. That's life.'

Her only concern is Sunny.

'If I check out, what becomes of Sunny? Josie will take care of him of course. She'll never let Kit get his hands on him and she's far too clever and conniving to let that happen. But Sunny hates Josie even more than he hates me. He gets upset when my sister shows up to take him out for the day or help him with his homework. I warn him to play nice because she's trying to help but he hates her. Trev says he knows why Sunny hates her, it's—'

This essay stops in mid-sentence and there are no further clues as to why Sunny hates me. The mention of 'Trev' should either fold me up or turn me into an avenging angel but instead it's almost incidental to what I'm reading. Trevor was right to warn me about the consequences of bringing Sunny into our house even if he wouldn't explain why. Although he did to Megan it seems. My nephew hates me. He's not trying to destroy me because he's troubled or traumatised, he's doing it deliberately. He's actually enjoying himself. This is why he won't tell me what happened in the flat when my sister died. It's because he's enjoying playing cat and mouse with me.

Meanwhile, it doesn't seem to matter what happened in the flat that night, it's already perfectly clear.

'I've told Kit that when I go, he can't have Sunny. My son will be living with Josie and Trevor, not him. He just laughed and asked me if this was the suicide thing again? He just shouted in return "good" and told me to make a decent job of it this time rather than taking a few harmless pills and a small glass of whisky. On Sunny, Kit says he'll take care of business, he's already on the case to get custody of Sunny and it doesn't matter what Josie does this time and there's no way his son is ending up with her. Kit says he's sorting things out, Sunny's in the picture and Trev agrees with them.'

*Trev agrees with them?*

When I look up again, it's to see an anxious-looking Frieda leaning over me, examining my face like a doctor. 'Are you all right there, dear? You seem to be having a bit of a funny turn. Do you want me to get you a glass of water? Or would you like something a bit stronger? There's plenty here if you fancy a drop of the hard stuff.'

'No, no, I'm fine.'

She's not convinced. 'You don't look it, dear, you look terrible.' Frieda gestures at the sheets of paper that are wilting in my hands. 'Is that the last will and testament, dear? Your sister sold you short, has she?'

Everyone hated Megan. Everyone's sold me short. It wasn't Megan that everyone hated it was me. 'No, it's nothing, really.'

Frieda is confident that I'm reading Megan's will and that I've been shafted. 'You can challenge it in the courts, you know, say she was pressured into leaving everything to someone else.' She scans the flat. 'Although to be honest, dear, it doesn't look like she had much to leave anyway.'

In my pocket is a photo of Trevor. My plan was to show it to Frieda after searching Megan's flat to see if she recognised him as one of the people who visited my sister. I don't need to do that any more.

I know what Summers would think if he saw the things that Megan wrote. He'd take it as proof that he was right all along and that Megan took her own life. It seems Sunny would agree with him. Thought through logically, I would too, all the evidence points that way. But no one else heard Megan's screams as a girl when she was confronted with a syringe and needle.

'Do you want this, dear? It obviously meant something to your sister. It was tucked into her pillowcase.'

Frieda hands me a photo. A note on the back shows it's from seven years ago, which means it was taken in the Caribbean village our father was from during Megan's famous journey 'back home' to 'discover' herself. That lasted twelve months, which was nearly twelve months longer than I expected. The picture is a family photo of our relatives back home with Megan centre stage. There are old people, adults, youngsters, children and babies all gathered together outside a cousin's house. Megan is looking happy, holding a small child with one hand and cradling a baby in another. Sunny was there too, but he's nowhere to be seen. Except he is, hiding behind one of the old folks, looking embarrassed.

Megan insisted the journey was to 'ground herself' but I didn't believe that at the time. In the end, though, I had to. There seemed no other plausible explanation.

# Chapter 39

## Seven Years Earlier

Josie felt she'd seen all the stunts and tricks that her sister could pull but she wasn't ready to hear the one Megan came out with one evening when Sunny was still only six years old.

'You should know this, sis, and you're the first to know, I'm leaving. I'm going back home.'

Josie was baffled. 'What do you mean, going back home? You mean Croydon?'

Megan was enjoying her sister's surprise. 'No, I mean going back to the Caribbean. I'm moving there for good.' When Megan didn't get an answer from her shocked sister, she went on. 'Yeah, I've been thinking about it for a while. My counsellor thinks it's difficult for a woman of colour to live an authentic life in England and she thinks that's why I have a chaotic lifestyle and why I'm self-medicating all the time with narcotics and alcohol. Back home, I'll be able to live my proper life and explore my roots, heritage and culture. You know, all that jazz.'

Coming from someone else this might be a prompt to an interesting conversation. Coming from her sister, Josie felt it had to be a joke. 'Right. And where exactly are you planning to live and what exactly is it that you're planning to do for a living when you go back home?'

'I've been in touch with our cousins and they'll put me up until I find a place of my own. As for work, there are plenty of options. I might think about renting a little farm and growing organic fruit to sell to rich Americans in New York. Apparently, our cousin Degsy does that and makes a good living out of it. He'll show me the ropes, and how hard can it be? You plant a few trees and help yourself to some ripe fruit, no problem.'

Josie was disorientated. 'You can't farm.'

Megan wasn't really listening. She was already dreaming the dream. 'Or maybe fishing. I think our grandad ran a little boat and sold fish on the beach and in the local market. Anyway, I'll find something.'

'Fishing?'

Megan finally realised that her sister wasn't buying it. 'You never cut me any slack, do you? You're the one who's always saying that I need to sort my life out. You're the one always saying that I need to find something and stick to it, to stop behaving like a teenager who's gone off the rails and start growing up. Now I'm actually doing it, you're sneering.'

These arguments always followed the same pattern. Megan would remind Josie that she was to blame for the accident that put her in hospital, that it was deliberate, that she lost twelve months of schooling and her education never recovered and that the trauma had permanently affected her development and personality. Josie would respond that the accident wasn't deliberate, that Megan lost two months of schooling not twelve and that the trauma she suffered had been an excuse for the chaos she chose to live in. Then the argument would be over. Until the next time when it would be repeated almost word for word.

'Take a look at these if you don't believe me.'

She passed Josie a collection of papers. They included an application for a foreign passport that Megan was entitled to because of their father's birthplace, applications for a bank account back home and some legal documents.

Megan was serious. But Josie still couldn't quite believe it. 'But what about Sunny?'

'What about him? He's well up for the idea, aren't you, boy?'

Sunny said nothing but looked up, smiled and nodded with enthusiasm. Josie still wasn't convinced. 'You know what I think, sis? I think you're planning on going on an extended holiday back home and you'll be expecting me to help you finance it. And I'll give it three months before you're back.'

Megan took her paperwork. 'We'll see about that, and for your information, I don't need your money. I've put together some cash from my savings and that'll keep me going until I'm growing avocados or whatever. You'll see, it'll be a whole new start in a different place and it's the right place for a woman of colour to find her life–work balance.' In a voice heavy with sarcasm as she looked her sister up and down, Megan said, 'Unless of course you're one of those women of colour who's sold out.'

Even when Megan sublet her flat and packed her bags, Josie couldn't quite believe it. Even when she took Megan and Sunny to the airport and waved them goodbye, she didn't really believe it. Only when they disappeared through departures did Josie finally accept that her sister was really going away to live her authentic life. When she was gone, Josie stood alone on the airport concourse and whispered to herself, 'I give it three months.' But the whisper was one of relief. Her relationship with Megan might be toxic but now at least it would be toxic at a distance of three thousand miles.

Josie was right, Megan and Sunny did return, it was only the timescale she got wrong. It was actually twelve months before they came back and picked up exactly where they'd left off, seemingly unchanged. Megan was evasive as to why things hadn't worked out. 'Life's too slow back home, sis, and I'm a fast girl, not a slow one.' On several occasions, a curious Josie asked Sunny how he'd found his stay 'back home'.

But Sunny was saying nothing.

# Chapter 40

'Hello, Trev.'

Trevor is sitting at the dining room table when I get home, working on his laptop. He looks askance when he's called by the nickname others use. 'Don't call me Trev please, I'm not a cab driver or a bookmaker.'

He taps away on his laptop. I don't know where to start so I don't. 'Kit's outside in his van waiting to pick Sunny up for this evening's visit.'

'That's nice.'

'Aren't you going out to say hello to him?'

He's distracted by his work. 'Sorry?' When I repeat the question, he's unfazed. 'Why would I do that? We don't need any roofing done and even if we did, he wouldn't be doing it.'

I sit down beside him, it's so much easier for me to deduce things now that I have some of the background facts. My teeth grind when I remember Kit and his solicitor's ambush at the meeting with social services to decide Sunny's future. How they implied that the injuries that Tova suffered after a fall from a swing might have been inflicted by someone in the family. I assumed at the time that it was Megan who told Kit about this. Now I know better. 'You told Kit about Tova's accident so he could use it against me at the meeting with social services to decide Sunny's future. You also told him to use the fact that you weren't going to the meeting as more evidence to use against me.'

His fingers slow slightly on the keys until they grind to a halt. 'Sunny told you that, did he? I'm surprised you're still indulging him in his various lies at this stage. You're supposed to be a clever woman and a fast learner.' His fingers pick up speed again.

'Oh, he's a liar alright, but then again, he's been taught by the best. And maybe he's not the only one.' The only noise is the sound of his fingers on the laptop. But they stop once again.

He snaps, 'All right, Josie, you're right, I did pass those suggestions on to Kit and how right I was to do that. Look at us. Our family's falling apart, you're going nuts and all because you wouldn't listen to me, all because of this debt you think you owe your sister, bringing that boy into our house.' He starts typing again. 'Damn straight I told Kit, and the only thing I regret is that I didn't give him more ammunition to fire at you and we wouldn't be in this situation.'

'Know him well then do you?'

His typing is now frantic. 'You know what I think of Kit but I'd help the devil himself if it saved my family from destruction.'

I hand him the bank statement that I recovered from Megan's flat.

'What's this?' he asks and begins to scan it. The line that shows Megan receiving a grand from the 'DAA' is highlighted with a marker pen. He closes his eyes for a moment but makes no attempt to claim it's nothing to do with him. 'Yeah, I supported Megan financially, big deal. Although it has to be said, it's probably only a fraction of the amount you spent on her.'

I wait for him to explain why he did it, as if we both don't know. I'm just hoping he doesn't use the catchphrase of the cheating husband, 'It's not what you think'. He sees me waiting for an explanation and carries on typing. Sadly, he's not a very imaginative person. 'It's not what you think.'

It seems only fair to give him a chance to be more creative. 'There must be an explanation as to why you chose to spend money from a family inheritance on my sister. Perhaps you'd like to share it with me?'

He sighs deeply but isn't rattled. He might even be quite convincing if he hadn't just admitted that he'd do a deal with the devil if it suited him.

He carries on typing. 'You may have heard of the saying, marry an alcoholic become an alcoholic. It happened to my cousin. Her husband was a soak, so she used to hide the booze in cupboards and the laundry basket to stop him drinking it. When that didn't work, she started drinking his supply herself so he couldn't. In the end, she became a bigger drunk than he was. Of course, it killed her in the long run when she was only thirty-eight. You might remember the funeral. They put pneumonia on the death certificate for appearance's sake but we all knew what it really was. You might recall her widower got pissed at the wake and made a scene.'

I do remember.

He goes on. 'Anyway, what happened to my cousin also happened to me, just in a different way. I married the victim of a selfish, narcissistic sponger and became the victim of a selfish, narcissistic sponger. You remember when Megan announced she was going off to live in the Caribbean for good to find herself, get in touch with her roots, to live a more natural lifestyle and to heal her wounds? She was going to rent a little farm and grow organic fruits and all the rest of it? She used to come round here to discuss her plans with you and you fell for all that ordure hook, line and sinker. You remember that? I knew you'd say you weren't paying for anything and I knew in the end you would. I thought to myself, Megan's taking things too far this time, getting you to pay for what was obviously going to be a luxury holiday, so I went round to the flat to have it out with her. Fair play to my sister-in-law, she as good as admitted this rootsy new life thing was all a con. That's when I made the fatal mistake that I've had to live with ever since.

'It was about the time my grandmother's house was sold, so I said to Megan I'd pay for her Caribbean getaway and send her money every month while she was away but on one condition, that she stopped sponging money off you in future. Megan agreed, but she had a condition of her own. She didn't want me to tell you what we were doing because she felt that would make her look bad. Like a fool, I agreed because there seemed no reason not to. There was no reason for me to worry about the money because it was obvious she'd soon get bored with her natural lifestyle and she'd be back. The only surprising thing is she lasted twelve months out there. When they returned, I stopped the money, but it soon became clear Megan wasn't having that. She threatened to tell you about the regular payments and imply there was a sinister motive for my doing it.'

He stops writing and stares out of the window. 'That was the only mistake I made in this whole grisly affair. Imagine me of all people watching while Megan dug me a gigantic bear trap filled with my inheritance, and then walking straight into it with my eyes open, knowing full well what she was like. Just imagine that.'

He looks as if he genuinely can't believe it.

The trouble is this cover story is horribly believable. 'OK, I don't know about any of this but I think it would be a good idea if we had some time apart while we work things through and perhaps it's best you leave for a while.'

He bursts out laughing. 'You think I should leave?' He spins the laptop round to show me the screen. 'What do you think I'm doing here? I'm making the arrangements to go now. My parents will take me in for a while and naturally I'm taking the children with me. You don't think I'm leaving them in this house with you, Sunny and Megan's ghost while the three of you go over a cliff together. I gave you seven days because I hoped you'd see sense. You haven't, so you'll have to take the consequences.'

I want the three of them out of the house so I can settle accounts with Sunny on my own with no danger to the others. The complaint I make now is merely formal but I feel I have to make it so I don't look like a bad mother. 'You can't take the children with you.'

'I'm not leaving them here with Sunny. If you don't like it, take me to court, I'm quite happy to explain the circumstances to a judge. You can come and see them whenever you like, just don't bring Sunny with you.'

I feel like I've gone from a wronged wife to the guilty party in the space of one conversation. Through the window, Kit is sitting at the wheel of his van waiting to pick Sunny up. I need to speak to him. When I get up from the table, Trevor grabs my wrist. 'Just remember this, Josie, I used to go round to see Megan using threats and blandishments in an effort to stop her blackmailing me. None of it worked, but while I was there I did get the measure of her son. Let me tell you this, if you stay in this house with Sunny, you're in serious danger, Josie, that boy is capable of anything.'

Outside, Sunny is getting into the van with Kit. I hurry out but they've gone and my chance to talk to Kit is gone too. Trevor comes out and stands with me. 'It's still not too late. Kick him out and, trust me, we can put the pieces back together.'

He still doesn't understand that if Sunny goes so does my only chance of finding out what happened to my sister.

# Chapter 41

We have our 'talk' with the children. We explain that they and Trevor are going to stay with his parents on a sort of extended holiday which will be quite exciting and I'll be paying frequent visits. I can't go because of work commitments. They don't believe us of course. They might be children but they're not stupid. Tova is frightened. 'Does this mean you'll be in the house with Sunny on your own?'

Only until he coughs up the whole truth, and I know he will when he's ready. I don't know why but I do. Then what? In my heart there will be some sort of resolution and my family will return, Megan will rest in peace and Sunny will be happier somewhere else with someone else while life will return to normal. That's what my heart says. But my head has given up on the whole business and is tired of its warnings being ignored. I'm on my own with only my heart for company.

'Sort of.'

She's horrified.

After the talk, Trevor begins to pack, and to reinforce the holiday theme he puts buckets and spades and flip flops in the cases as part of the ploy. He encourages the children to sing songs and includes lots of lines about how much fun it's going to be.

I'm surprised how good he is at pretending, but unless he's telling the truth about Megan and the money, he's had a lot of practice over the years. Too much information which both can and can't be believed has been stuffed down my throat since Megan passed. I don't believe his story about the money, but it fits so many facts at the same time. If he was being blackmailed by Megan, it's totally believable that he would use a burner phone to stay in touch with her, which explains why it was hidden in a locked drawer. It's easily explicable that Megan would call 'Bill' when she was dying and ask him for help, she was totally out of it on drugs and probably desperate to call anyone. It makes me feel better to believe this, and I want to believe it in the same way it makes me feel better to believe that my husband and children are really going on holiday to his parents.

Only when the front door opens and Sunny comes back from his few hours with Kit do I realise that the time for believing things is over and the illusion is shattered. My nephew knows what happened. What was it that he said to me in a briefly sincere moment with a briefly sincere smile? 'I know about a lot of things, Josie. You'd be surprised by the things I know about.'

Sunny is confused when he sees suitcases in the hall, as if this wasn't part of any scenario he'd planned on. 'Is someone moving out?'

'Trevor and your cousins are going on holiday to his parents. I'm not leaving until you tell me what happened in your mother's flat that night and anything else you know that might throw some light on it. You are going to tell me, I know you are.'

The penny drops. 'You already know what happened. What else do you want me to say? My mother got the dose wrong. She OD'd. You want me to say that Trevor or my dad did it? I'll tell you that if it makes you happy.'

All along, Sunny's tone of voice and manner veers wildly from a petulant child to a surly teenager to a world-weary adult and then back again between many various tones and manners. But he's had to grow up much too fast, he's seen too many things that a child shouldn't see and he's read far too many books.

'I don't want to be happy, Sunny. There's nothing left to know about my sister's death that could make me happy any more.'

Sunny throws a malevolent stare at the suitcases as if he's a cat who's let a bird escape through its paws.

'I know why you're here and what you're doing, Sunny. I know you want to punish me for something. I just don't know what. But I'm getting there.'

He turns his malevolent stare on me and sneers. 'No, you're not. You don't know anything.'

'I know more than you think.'

He doesn't answer, instead walking slowly past the suitcases, studying them as if he were the spouse whose partner was leaving rather than me.

He's left the door open and I can see Kit's van is still parked outside the house. On stepping on to the front path, one of a number of my enemies can be seen at the wheel fiddling with his phone. At least, he was supposed to be my enemy, now it's not so clear. When he sees me coming down the path, he throws the phone on the passenger seat and starts the engine. I'm too quick for him, running down the path and standing in front of his van. It's quite a risk really, there's no doubt he'd cheerfully run me over if he could. He leans out of the van window. 'Get out of the way, Josie, we've got nothing to talk about, you and me.'

'Yes, we have. Turn the engine off.'

He rolls the van forwards a few inches until it gently bumps into me. 'Get out of the way!'

'Turn the engine off!'

He gently bumps me again but I stand my ground. With a roll of his eyes, he finally turns off the ignition and dangles the keys from his hand in front of me to prove it. I hurry round to the driver's window and snatch the keys from him before going to the passenger door and getting into the van beside him.

'What do you want, Josie?' Before I can answer he looks over my shoulder and notices Trevor leaving suitcases on our doorstep. 'Are you going on holiday?'

'Trevor's leaving with the children and going to stay with his parents.'

Kit pulls up the handbrake and sighs. 'This is Sunny's doing I suppose? I'm afraid I've got no sympathy, Josie. You were warned what he was like, you were told he needed a firm hand on the tiller but you wouldn't listen. But that's typical of you, isn't it? You always know best, you with your smart suits and university degree and your 'contacts' and your determination to 'help' people. Josie always knows what's best for other people. That's why no one likes you.' He looks again out of the window at Trevor, who's assembling the children on the doorstep. He's amused. 'I guess Sunny told you about your sister and Trevor carrying on together and that's why you're throwing him out. Honestly, Josie, it's always the husbands you least suspect.'

I'm stung by his takedown of my character because it's partly true, but that doesn't matter to me right now. 'They were carrying on?'

He pulls a face. 'I don't know, but it looked like it. I was too busy rowing with your sister about my son to poke my nose into her private life. I do know he was a frequent visitor to the flat and she was lifting money off him so I assumed they were but who knows? She was grifting money off the pair of you. Listen, Josie, I know we don't get along but here's some free advice for you. Send Sunny to come and stay with me and my girlfriend. We're expecting a kid ourselves but we've got room. Then patch things up with your husband. He's not a bad bloke, just a bit soft.'

'Sunny's not going anywhere until he tells me what happened to my sister that night.'

Kit doesn't get it. 'How would he know what happened? He was at my mum's flat that evening. Let's face it, she killed herself, she was always talking about it, even when we were a couple.'

'Sunny was there at the flat. He says he was in his room reading a book and doesn't know what happened. But I know he does and he's stringing me along for reasons of his own.'

Kit is seriously alarmed. He begins drumming his fingers on the steering wheel and looking anxiously at the side- and rear-view mirrors as if he's being pursued. 'That's unfortunate, that's very unfortunate.' He peers over my shoulder at the house and comes to a decision. 'Alright, let me tell you what we're going to do now, you're going back to the house to pack Sunny's bags and then you're bringing him out here so that I can drive him home.'

He's actually frightened, which makes him vulnerable and might help me find out what he's frightened of. 'Don't be ridiculous. Why does the fact he was in the flat that evening mean you have to take him home?'

He loses control of himself. 'Just do it. Just do as you're told for once in your life!'

'No, you tell me why you're so angry. Were you in the flat when my sister was killed?'

There's a tap on the window. It's Trevor. 'Sorry to interrupt but we're leaving now. You might want to say goodbye to the children and promise them you'll ring them tomorrow.'

Kit's regained control of himself. 'Hello, Trev.'

Trevor turns to him. 'Hello, Kit.' He turns back to me. 'I'm sure the children would appreciate you saying goodbye.'

I'm torn between justice for my sister and justice for my children. The children win out and I turn to Kit, jabbing my finger at him. 'Wait here, we're not finished.'

Kit agrees. 'Yeah, you go and say goodbye.' Then he adds in a barely audible mutter, 'It might be your last chance.'

I've still got his keys. He's not going anywhere. On the door-step I perform a perfunctory hug with Trevor for the benefit of the children. The rest of us, the children and me, share a longer, more sincere and more profound moment together. I promise them that we'll all be together again soon and I sort of believe it. They get into his car and drive away, the two children looking out of the back window until I disappear.

I go back to have it out with Kit. His van is still there.

But he has gone.

# Chapter 42

'That's why no one likes you.'

That was a fair comment from Kit, no one does like me. My husband thinks I'm to blame because I wouldn't accept that Megan took her own life and because I wouldn't leave it alone. My children think I'm to blame because I put my nephew ahead of them even though I was warned by everyone, including my nephew himself, not to take him in. Kit thinks I'm to blame because I can't accept that not everyone wants or needs my help. Sunny hates me because, well, what? I interfered in his life when he just wanted to be left alone to read his books? Even I think I'm to blame. I've wrecked my family for nothing, collecting a lot of evidence that proves nothing.

What on earth have I done? I've gone off in pursuit of righting a wrong done to my sister when everyone's agreed that she wronged herself. And it's all rooted in the guilt I feel for injuring my sister in a silly argument when we were children. I've spent my whole life making it up to her and, in the end, all I've done is ruin the lives of those around me. But I won't give up. The only way I can justify my actions is by finding out the truth about how my sister died. Sunny knows and he will tell me. Then my sister can rest in peace and perhaps so can I.

I circle Kit's van waiting for him to return. Finally, I get his number from Megan's phone and call him but get no answer.

Sunny is in his room, writing. He's recovered from his disappointment at the rest of the family moving out and is aimable enough. 'What's up?'

'I just had a very interesting conversation with your father.'

'Yeah?'

I'm on the verge of losing my temper. 'He was very alarmed to hear that you were in your mother's flat the evening she died. He got very upset and wanted to take you away.'

Sunny is sniggering to himself. 'Yeah, I can see why. He's probably worried he's in trouble.'

'What did you hear that night?'

He stops writing for a moment to make me think he'll tell me and then resumes writing again. 'I told you, I can't remember.'

'Why can't you remember?'

He stops scribbling again. 'I don't know.'

'This is all a game to you, Sunny, isn't it? It's just like the Monopoly where other people obey the rules and you're allowed to cheat and then you blame the other players for not cheating themselves.'

He bursts out laughing. 'No one else is playing by the rules either, not my mother or my dad or Trevor, not even you, Josie. If you were playing by the rules, you'd never have given my mother any money and you'd never have taken me in after what happened to her. You'd never have treated me like a naughty puppy that needs house training all those years. Don't talk to me about cheating, everyone's cheating.'

'I'm sorry you feel that way about me.'

He gets up from his chair in fury. 'See? You can't even call me an ungrateful little bastard like a normal person would. You're not normal, you're weird.'

'What could I do to make you remember?'

He looks at his books as if they might help him decide. 'I'll tell you what, if I think of something, I'll tell you.'

He takes his seat and picks up his pen. I'm pleased. I'm nearly there and then all this can stop. The strange thing is I trust him on this. He's an honest cheat, unlike the rest of us.

When I'm leaving his room, he calls out to me. 'By the way, my father is lurking around outside, I thought you might want to know. He's probably not in a good mood, so be careful.' Sunny starts laughing. 'He's probably worried I'll tell you what I remember.'

I hurry over to the window. 'Where is he?'

'He was over the other side of the road.'

I call the police. They pretend to take me seriously but it's obvious that they don't. To be fair it's hard to blame them. I admit I haven't actually seen the man outside my house, nor is there any reason to explain why, at least in a phone call, he might pose a threat. They say they may send a car over 'if one's available'. I ring Summers, who's no more sympathetic, probably because he's finished for the day and is at home with his family. Once I admit that a call has been put in to his colleagues, he doesn't think there's much else he can do. Once again, he insists that Kit's not going to harm anyone unless there's evidence to suggest otherwise. Is there any hard evidence to suggest Kit's going to kidnap Sunny? When I tell him what the evidence might be, he asks me for 'hard' evidence rather than overheated 'suppositions'. He suggests that perhaps I'm being a little 'overwrought'.

I put the phone down on him.

Still stuck in the mantelpiece is the knife with the serrated edge that Trevor recovered from Sunny's room. It fits under my belt and I creep to our front door, leaving no time to wonder why a deputy head teacher, respectable member of the community and believer in peaceful resolution of conflicts is venturing on to the street armed with a knife. It's almost dark outside. I'm tired of sitting around waiting for people to do me harm, now I'm going to do someone else harm if I have to. The garden is clear. Out on the road, it occurs to me that Kit's empty van might be a good place to lie in wait for him if he tries anything. I've got his keys. I climb inside and leave the knife on the dashboard and sink low into the seat, keeping my eye on the road and using the mirrors to check behind me too.

It gets darker and a light comes on in Sunny's room. Occasionally, his face appears from behind the curtains. He's on his phone. It's possible he's checking the street to see if his father is lying in wait outside. More likely he's seen me in the van and is laughing at me, it's too dark to tell. The minutes tick by and it becomes more and more obvious that I don't need to see Sunny's face. There's no Kit on this street. Sunny really is laughing at me. It's another one of his little pranks. As I become less overwrought, I look for something to pass the time and rummage through Kit's glove compartment. Along with empty cigarette and sweet packets, parking tickets and screwed up receipts, there's evidence that suggests someone might be emigrating.

I find a brochure of apartments for sale in complexes in southern Spain. Apparently, they're ideal for retiring couples and young families who want all the advantages of living in England with none of the rain. Some of these apartments are circled. There are also information sheets explaining the process of setting up a business abroad and acquiring residency in foreign countries. They're not in any kind of order, nor is there anything to suggest Kit is actually planning to emigrate, but he's clearly been looking into it. It's a few moments before I remember that one of the subjects that Sunny is beginning to excel in at school is Spanish.

I gather the material together and get out of the van when my phone rings. It's Kit.

'Josie, it's me, I've got to come and collect Sunny.'

It's a trap, it's obvious. 'Where are you?'

'Listen to me. Things have moved on since we spoke earlier. I've just had a phone call from that cop, Summers. He wants to speak to Sunny tonight. Whatever he wants to talk to him about is obviously urgent.'

# Chapter 43

It has to be a lie. On the way in I ring Summers, expecting to be told off for calling so late and for being 'overwrought', but he confirms that he does indeed want to speak to Sunny and he would prefer to do it tonight. 'Otherwise, people might have time to get their story straight, if you know what I mean.' He also says no to my suggestion that I come with Sunny as his 'appropriate adult' rather than Kit. He prefers Kit to do the job. But he wants to speak to me tomorrow in light of what he calls very recent 'developments'.

It's nearly midnight but Sunny is still up. He's lying on his bed reading a book. He looks up when I come in and then looks down again. 'Did you find my dad?'

'He wasn't out there as you well know.'

He smirks. 'I'm sure he was.' Sunny suddenly stops smirking when he looks at my waist. It's only when I look down that I see the knife with the serrated edge is still under my belt. 'You weren't going to stab him with that, were you?'

What was I going to do with it? 'Who knows? I'm in a strange place.'

He pulls a face. 'That's a bit hardcore for you, Josie.'

'Who knows what I might do if you don't start remembering things. You haven't got long to do it either, your father's coming to collect you. He's taking you to see Summers. You remember him? He wants to talk to you again.'

He looks baffled. 'What does he want to talk to me about?'

'My sister's murder presumably.'

He glances at the clock on his bedside table. 'It's nearly midnight.' He sighs meaningfully. 'Someone must have said something to Summers. Yeah, someone must have said something, that's what's happened. Trevor probably.'

'What would Trevor say that would make Summers want to speak to you after midnight?' I mouth 'I can't remember' to myself to save him the trouble of saying it. He says nothing further. I'm silent for a few moments.

'You don't have a sister, Sunny, so you don't know what it means. I know because I did. We were different people, your mother and I, and we had a very complicated relationship, which is often what happens. She didn't like me very much and I didn't like her. We went off in different directions but despite everything she did to me over the years, and for whatever reason, if I died the way she had, she would have made it her business to find out what happened. She'd do that because I was her sister, she wouldn't have needed another reason. That's what sisters will do. I tried my best for your mother and it didn't work and it's too late to do anything for her now. But I can help her rest in peace and that can only happen when I know how she died. Do you understand that?'

He looks at me with a curious expression. It's as if he thinks I'm a character in one of his novels. He seems to understand. 'OK.'

He hesitates for a moment and leans over and begins patting me down.

'What on earth do you think you're doing?'

'You better not be wearing a wire.'

'Don't be ridiculous. We're not in a movie.'

When he's satisfied that he's not being taped, he rubs his chin with his fingertips. 'Alright, let me see. Ah yes, it's all coming back to me now. Earlier, that evening when my mother died, I came home from school and she was, as usual, stomping round the flat arguing with someone on the phone. I go to my room and that guy turns up, the boyfriend, Dixie. They have a massive row about something and she throws him out. Don't know what the argument was about, I tuned out. That's what I did when she argued with people, I just zoned out. Later Dixie comes back again to collect his stuff and get some money off her. Another massive bust-up, she throws him out again.

'Later my dad shows up. She was in a bad mood that night, probably the Dixie thing. My dad and her had another massive argument. Don't know what it was about, I was tuned out again. He goes. There's some more phone calls, think it was Dixie or my dad, I don't know which and it doesn't matter.'

He falls silent. There's nothing he's telling me so far that I don't know. 'Then what?'

'Hold on, I'm trying to remember.' There's more silence before he sparks back into life. 'Yeah, it's much later in the evening now. Someone else shows up at the flat but there's no argument this time. Actually, there is an argument but it's one of those arguments that respectable people have, you know, like you and your husband, lots of nastiness but at a low volume so the neighbours can't hear. I'm a bit curious, you know, so I go over to my door and open it a little, and that's when I see them, going at each other.'

'See who?'

He pauses for dramatic effect before continuing. 'My mother and your Trevor. They were finger jabbing, pushing and shoving. She wanted some more money out of him and he wasn't giving it up. She was threatening to tell you "things" and he said he'd make sure it wouldn't happen. All of a sudden, he gives in and says OK.

He disappears into the kitchen and comes back with a couple of drinks, everything's calmed down. Then – he pounces! Grabs my mother round her waist and holds his hand over her mouth so she can't scream, stabs her in the thigh with a knife. When she starts to slump a bit, he drops her on to an armchair and I can see it's not a knife he's stabbed her with, it's a syringe. He's drugged her up with smack. It's terrible, Josie, you know? He had the devil in his eyes. They were nearly red and totally mad.'

Sunny shrugs. 'Anyway, he starts looking round the flat and using a flannel to wipe things down, you know for fingerprints. That's when he realises I'm looking at him from behind my door. He comes over, throws the door open and grabs me up by the hair and drags me out. I think he wants to kill me too but he knows the law might believe my mother OD-ed but they'd never believe I did too. They don't care about some druggie taking it too far but her teenage son as well? So, I said to Trev – relax, I'm not saying anything to anyone. Take me over to my grandma's, she'll cover for me and no one's any the wiser. So that's what we did. To be honest with you, that's why Trev didn't want me in this house, he thought I might say something but he's worrying over nothing. I'm not saying anything.'

There's a clump as something falls to the floor and a pain on the side of my leg. When I look down, I see the knife on the floor, it nicked my leg as it fell. A trickle of blood rolls down to my foot. Outside, there's a knock at the door. When I look out of the window, it's to see Kit standing there. I take Sunny by the shoulders and choke up. 'When you see Summers, you tell him exactly what you just told me.'

Sunny is wide-eyed with both amazement and amusement. 'You must be joking! I'm not telling him anything!'

'My sister was murdered and you're going to cover it up? What's the matter with you?'

There's another knock at the door, louder this time.

'That's my dad.'

'I know who it is, we'll go and see him as soon as you promise to tell the police what you've just told me.'

'It's not happening.'

'If you don't, I will,' I insist.

He shakes his head. 'It's not happening. As long as Trev and me keep telling the same story, they can't prove anything. The police missed their chance, they should have done a proper job looking into it after my mother checked out. It's too late now. There's no reason why he should 'fess up and there's no reason why I should either.'

'There's no reason why the man you say murdered my sister should get away with it.'

Sunny explodes in fury. 'Trevor did me a favour killing her. He saved me having to do it myself! I owe Trev one because I don't have to live with that junkie and in that junkyard flat any more, and if it hadn't been for you, I'd be living in Spain with my dad by now! So yeah, I'm glad she's dead! Do you hear? Glad!'

# Chapter 44

'He's not coming back.'

I'm not really sure what Kit is saying to me when I hand Sunny over to him. I'm in another world now where everything is different and everything is dark, shattered, garish and surreal. Not only does my husband stand accused of murdering my sister, but my nephew's only problem with it seems to be that he was deprived of the chance to do it himself.

'Are you listening, Josie? Sunny is not coming back here. After Summers has finished with him, we're going to my place then we'll take things from there. If he shows up here again at any time in the future, don't let him in, call me before you do anything.'

After being asked to repeat what he's said to me because it's not going in, he's got more advice. 'You need to lock your house up and move to your in-laws.'

He doesn't wait for me to ask any questions, which is probably just as well. I'm not sure what they are or how to ask them. He snatches his keys from my hand and grabs his son by the scruff of the neck and takes him down the garden path. Before I have any time to think, the pair of them are gone. I hang on to the door with one hand like a sailor in a storm, inert and windswept, trying to understand what's just happened. When I begin to come to my senses, only one thought crosses my mind. My children.

I ring my mother-in-law and demand that she send the kids back to me in a cab. They can't stay under the same roof as a man accused of murder.

Her voice sounds like one long sigh. 'Josie, darling, let's leave the hour you've called to one side for the moment and let's be generous about your emotional state, which we all understand. It's not nice to lose a sibling at a young age, nor when a marriage runs into trouble. You have to remember that difficulties between couples will happen and can be resolved with some honesty, communication and goodwill on both sides. The way you don't resolve them is to call people up after midnight and to accuse your husband of murder. My suggestion is that you put the top back on the bottle, go to bed and sleep it off. Everything will look better in the morning.'

This is hopeless. 'Put Trevor on the line please.'

'He's not here. He had a phone call from the police, Summers I think his name was, and he's gone to the station for a chat. It's a lot of silly nonsense if you ask me but you know my son, he'll always make himself available to the police if it will help, even in the middle of the night. Don't ask me why it couldn't wait until the morning.'

At least he's out of her house and away from the children. 'Did he say what Summers wanted to talk about?'

'No, and I didn't ask. Something to do with your sister's sad demise would be my guess.'

I put the phone down on her.

The house is finally empty for the first time since we moved in, although not as empty as I am. There is no husband, no children and no nephew, only me. And my sister of course, Trevor's jibe that she haunts our house like a restless spirit is true. She's always been here, even when she was alive and even more so now. My strangled voice says aloud, 'You've finally taken your revenge on me this time, Megan. I hope you're satisfied.'

Megan says nothing. But then she doesn't need to, she can drift from room to room without making a sound, enjoying her moment. Meanwhile, I'm left to clear up her mess, the same as when she was alive. I pause for a moment. I'm missing something. Up to my neck in lies and the liars who tell them, something is wrong, something doesn't add up. Now I have some time to work things out. I sit on the stairs for a while and think. I'm smart and I've got plenty of leads to work with, there's a thread somewhere that will lead me to the truth. I gather the evidence – Frieda's log, Megan's phone and Trevor's bank statements – and take it to my little office. Trevor had to go out the evening Megan died, we know this because he disappeared after supposedly getting a phone call from work saying he had to go in to save the day for some spurious reason or other. It never occurred to me to think about that before because there was no possibility of connecting it to Megan's death. But I can't get everything to fit. Why did she call Bill's phone shortly before an ambulance was called and who called the ambulance anyway? She didn't call Trevor to come over and murder her, why do none of the timings match up?

I'm on the verge of a complete collapse. Trying to work things out is the only way to keep going. Only the motivations make sense. Trevor wanted Megan dead to stop her blackmailing him and I know what a blackmailer she was. But Sunny wanted her dead too, for imprisoning him in that flat. Megan wanted herself dead because she'd had enough. It crosses my mind that they conspired together to kill Megan and now they're trying to break me too. That makes sense, that fits.

Perhaps deep down, I wanted Megan dead too. Perhaps there were four of us in on it. Sometimes when we were young, on bad days, I wished that car I'd pushed her under had killed her. How much torment that would have saved me later when she wrung me out and guilt-tripped me. Thinking that made me even guiltier and even more of a sucker for whatever scheme she had going to exploit me. Small wonder that I reacted so badly when Trevor told me he was glad Megan was dead. Because I was glad too. Small wonder I was crushed when Sunny lost his temper and told me he was glad Megan was dead. Because I was glad too.

From deep within, my voice, or what sounds like my voice, calls out into the void, 'I'm glad you're dead, Megan.'

It feels so good that I do it again, only yelling this time, at the top of my voice so she can hear me wherever she is in the house. 'Megan! Do you hear me! I'm glad you're dead! Now leave me alone!'

I'm glad she's dead.

There's no point in trying to work out 'what happened' so I leave the room and haunt the house like my sister does. Up the rickety ladder to Trevor's office where he hid Bill's phone and kept the bank statements. Of course he paid her off. I'm in no position to criticise, she blackmailed us both, one way or another. I go into Sunny's room where he was able to keep books, a computer and his phone safe from his mother's thieving hands. She didn't steal my books, computer and phone, she stole my soul instead. She imprisoned him in her flat with men who poured vodka into his fish tank while she imprisoned me in my own life. Kit might be a violent criminal but he wouldn't have allowed that to happen.

I feel a stab in my guts though on remembering that it was me who helped her do it by making the case for her to the authorities. And it was me who brought Sunny into this house.

On his desk is the latest batch of stories that he's written. They're probably in the same vein as those from creative hour, stories full of red flags.

My legs are wobbling under me and it's easier to sink into Sunny's chair than continue standing. The story on top of Sunny's latest batch is called 'The Wolf Cub'. I read the first few sentences. It opens with a wolf cub called Lobo who lives deep in the forest with his mother. I skim it and flip the pages until its grisly finale. My colleague was right, there are plenty of warning signs here that the authorities might be interested in but never got to find out about because I preferred not to read his stories, afraid of what I might find.

It's pretty grim for Lobo where he lives in the forest with his mother and it's pretty clear whose side Sunny is on. I read the final paragraphs to myself and notice something about them. I don't feel quite so destroyed any more because things are starting to fit at last. Going back to the beginning of the story, the fog in my head starts to clear.

When I've finished it a second time, my hands are trembling under the weight of the pages.

Now everything makes sense.

# Chapter 45

******The Wolf Cub******

*Lobo's a wolf cub who lives in a den in the forest with his mother. The den is just a hole in the ground under a tree filled with bits of the old bones and snatches of fur of the animals they've eaten, which means the den honks like a rubbish bin. Lobo's fur is sticky and matted because it's never cleaned just like the den he lives in. The sun never shines into Lobo's den and the rain seeps in even when it's not raining. At night the other wolves in the forest howl to warn other wolves that they're there or just to talk to one another. Lobo howls in the forest too but not for the same reasons the others do.*

*Lobo and his mother live on their own but she's part of a pack. Other packs in the forest work together, they hunt, they look after each other and their young. When men come into the forest hunting wolves, these packs join up to stop each other being killed. They warn each other of danger. But the pack Lobo's mother is part of don't do that. They're lazy and greedy and attack each other, stealing and fighting, At night, when Lobo hears the other wolves out on patrol, doing what wolves do, Lobo becomes angry. But it's not because he wants to be in a pack himself. He just wants to be left alone to do his thing whatever that thing might be. But his mother and her dirty pack won't let him. They won't leave him be.*

*Lobo knows there are other forests out there. These are the forests where a wolf can live free and not be bothered by other animals whether they are wolves or not. That's what Lobo wants, to get out of this den and live free. He knows his mother can't keep him here; she's too busy fighting the other wolves. He could escape but Lobo has a problem. His mother has a relative called Jesse who works together with his mother to keep him in his den. She's smart, she knows the rules of the forest, she knows how to play the game. She knows all the boss wolves in the forest. That's bad. What really makes Lobo want to bite his own tail is that Jesse and the boss wolves say being in his mother's den is the right place for him. No amount of howling is going to change their mind so Lobo doesn't howl. He thinks instead.*

*He knows if he waits, he'll get his chance. His chance comes. There's another wolf called Carlos. Carlos is a bad wolf but he doesn't bother Lobo. He says he'll take Lobo to another forest in another country, far away from his den and all the other wolves. It all goes wrong though when Lobo's mother finds out. She says that she'll get Jesse to get the boss wolves and stop it happening. There won't be another forest in another country. Carlos will be put in a zoo and Lobo will be stuck in his den. When he finds out Lobo loses it.*

*In the forest the humans put down gin traps to catch wolves. These are metal jaws that snap shut around a wolf's leg. If the animal doesn't die of hunger or thirst, a human will come and kill it. They're horrible but they work. Lobo knows where the gin traps are in the forest and one day, he lures his mother out of the den and down a path. He circles round the gin trap but his mother doesn't. She walks on to it and the metal jaws snap shut round his mother's leg. Her broken leg bleeds and she cries. To escape, she has to chew through her own leg to get out of the trap. Her bloodied limb lies on the ground while his mother crawls towards him.*

*Lobo sits down on his hind legs and watches. He doesn't help. She didn't help him when he bled and cried so why would he help her? She is already weak and the loss of blood means she fades away, whimpering in pain before she reaches him. She dies, her jaws open, spattered with blood.*

*Afterwards, Lobo gets up and paws her body to make sure she's really gone. He walks up and down the forest paths to make sure no one has seen him kill his mother. But even if they did, it doesn't matter. After all, living in a zoo is better than living in his mum's den and he won't go back there.*

*No one blames Lobo. They think his mother is an idiot who stood on a gin trap by accident. In fact, everyone is sorry for Lobo, especially Jesse. She wants to help him but what she doesn't know is that Lobo hates her even more than his mother. He knows that he will end up in Jesse's den because she knows how to play the game with the boss wolves and fix it. That's what she does. That is great for Lobo, he's in the enemy's den. It's perfect. Lobo sets out to spoil Jesse's den. Wreck the whole place, spook Jesse and drive her mad. It's easy. In the same way that his mother walked on to a gin trap without realising, Jesse walks on to Lobo's little gin traps without a clue what's going on. When her den is destroyed, Lobo finishes the job. When Jesse least expects it, he sinks his teeth into her throat. He grips it tight, breaking her body the way his heart was broken. He makes her suffer the way she made him suffer but he doesn't feel bad while he tears her body apart with his angry jaws. After all, she didn't feel bad when it happened to him and it was all on her.*

*And after all, Jesse once tried to kill Lobo's mother. Lobo's mother told him about it. Jesse made her climb a tree in the forest and then pushed her out of it. The mother didn't die. She only broke her leg or something. The strange thing is his mother didn't hold it against Jesse. It meant Jesse owed her for the rest of her life. Jesse felt bad about it because she's stupid. What she should have felt bad about was not doing a better job. There are so many ways to kill someone.*

*When he's finished and Jesse is dead, Lobo sits on his hind legs and thinks about what's happened. If the other wolves find out, he may end up in the zoo. If they don't and Lobo is smart, which means they won't because he really is smart, he may finally be free. Free to do his thing, free to be Lobo the wolf.*

*In another forest, in another country.*

I skim through the other stories on Sunny's desk. They're varied but they all have a common theme. One after another there is a story of revenge and a villain and the final victim is always called Jesse, Janey, Joley or Julie and these names always meet a grim death after being tormented. In some of these tales he even forgets himself and calls me by my own name, 'Josie'. It's a thinly disguised version of real events, some of them not even so thinly disguised. It's a confession of sorts but it's not clear who he's confessing on behalf of, himself or Trevor, who doesn't seem to feature in these stories.

Whatever did I do to earn this hatred? Why didn't he say anything?

I take 'Lobo the Wolf' and put it in my bag to show Summers. Then I tour the house locking all the doors and windows but even that doesn't make me feel safe so I move some furniture to blockade the front and back doors. It's not clear to me who I need protecting from, maybe it's the world outside which now seems as dark as the night itself. Even random footsteps on the street or cars driving past carry a hint of menace. There's no real reason for me to worry about 'Lobo' coming home, he's safely away at a police station with Kit who promises me that Sunny won't be coming back. Nor do I need to worry about Trevor, he's with Summers and then he'll go back to his parents'. Megan's already in the house with me and there's nothing that can be done about that. I can't go to sleep until dawn breaks but sitting on a sofa, my head begins to swim and slowly it slithers down towards the cushions supporting me.

In my dreams, I'm pursued by a pack of wolves who chase me down and kill me. As one of the wolves grabs my throat in its jaws and digs its sharp claws into my arms, I hear Megan crying out to me. When I turn, it's to see my sister lying on the ground. She's missing a leg, which lies some distance away by a gin trap. In her mouth is bloodied flesh where she's eaten through her thigh to escape. Her hand is reaching down, clasping the reddened bloody stump of her thigh. She's begging me in a throttled wail, 'Josie! Can you lend me some money?'

# Chapter 46

I don't know where I am when I awake. Only that there's a knocking at the door. I tumble off the sofa and find to my surprise that an armchair is blocking the front door, but that makes no sense until I remember that it was me who did it.

'Who is it?'

'It's me, Trevor.'

For a few moments I struggle to remember why he can't come in the house. Then it comes back to me. 'Go away!'

'Don't be stupid, Josie! Let me in!'

In my current state, this does feel a little stupid. 'Go away! I'll call the police.'

The letterbox opens and Trevor's eyes appear behind it. 'Call them if you like. They've finished with me for now.'

'Go away!'

'Alright, I'll sit on the doorstep until you change your mind. Unless that is you want to hold a conversation through the letterbox?' He notices something. 'Why have you moved the furniture around?'

'Go away, enough is enough.'

The letterbox flaps shut. It opens again. 'What's Sunny told you this time?'

I crouch down and tell him. 'He says you killed Megan.'

There's an exhausted sigh on the other side. 'That's not what he's just told the police and there's an official record of that so you can trust it.'

I want him gone but my curiosity is aroused. 'What did he tell the police?'

'If you let me in, I'll tell you.'

It's clear from his tone of voice that he's had enough but that makes two of us. 'No.'

There's a long pause before he says as if to himself, 'Have it your way.'

The leaden steps of a man who's spent the night with the police fade away as he makes his way down the garden path. The front gate opens and closes. Without thinking about it I throw the door open. 'OK, you can tell me on the doorstep.'

He reopens the gate and carefully closes it again. Even at a time like this he's a model of suburban propriety. He walks up the path, pale, haggard and drawn, looking for all the world like a murderer. 'We're not talking business on the doorstep, Josie. I'm not a double-glazing salesman.'

He comes into the house and is allowed to pass. Flopping on to the sofa, he looks as if he's about to fall asleep. Neither of us says anything for a while and it begins to look as if he's just come here for a nap. His eyelids begin to droop but open again when I demand to know what's happened.

He draws a deep breath. 'The police got in touch with me last night. They had an anonymous tip-off by phone that I was to blame for Megan's overdose in some way. Summers' name was mentioned by the 'informant' and they passed this piece of misinformation on to him. The informant also told them that Sunny was in the flat when Megan overdosed. He didn't take it too seriously but he went to his office and checked back through his notes and realised they'd never properly interviewed Sunny because Rose told them he was at her flat. He also noticed other discrepancies. The anonymous tip-off also mentioned blackmail money I was supposed to be paying her and Summers checked that too. So, they brought me in for questioning. They also brought Sunny in to see what he had to say for himself.'

Trevor nods to himself as if this explains everything, but it doesn't even begin to.

'Where did this anonymous tip-off come from?'

Trevor looks at me as if I'm an idiot and sneers. 'Oh, let's go through the list of suspects.' He holds his finger to his lips and pretends to think. 'Let's see, yes of course, there's only one and it's your nephew, Sunny. Did you know what a good mimic he is along with his other talents?' He rubs his temples with his fingertips. 'Anyway, I decided it was time to 'fess up and tell them the truth. The police have got my statement now. You know those Westerns where the cowboy gets tired of running? That was me, tired of running, tired of playing Megan and Sunny's games, tired of everything really.'

There's been so much lying, I'm not sure I'd even believe the truth any more. 'What is the truth?'

'The truth? OK. I got the phone call from Megan late in the evening she died. She wasn't making any sense. She was in a dreadful state but she said she'd been attacked by Sunny and would I come over. She begged me not to call the police. I drove over to the flat to find Megan unconscious in an armchair. She was clearly in a very bad way and her pulse was faint. Sunny was in his room reading a book. When I asked him what had happened, he told me it was just Megan doing her thing with drugs as usual. No one had attacked anyone. I went into a blind panic. I just wanted to get out of that flat and away from everything again as fast as possible. I called an ambulance on Megan's phone and left the front door open so they could get in. Then I remembered about Sunny.'

Trevor pauses, obviously reliving that night. 'He was just standing there like he was wondering what all the fuss was about. I desperately wanted to tell him not to tell the paramedics or the police that I'd been there. The walls were closing in on me at that moment, Josie. Everything was coming down around my ears. Sunny seemed to feel sorry for me and offered to help by leaving; if he wasn't there then neither he nor I would have to explain what happened to Megan. Rose would back his story up. He threw me a lifebelt and I grabbed it. You have to understand, Josie, I was a desperate man.' Trevor's eyes are pleading with me. He desperately wants my compassion. I don't say anything but nod for him to continue.

'I took him to his grandmother's and then drove to a deserted car park, and waited. I knew you would call and tell me Megan was in hospital and I should come immediately. Once the story came out that Sunny was at his grandmother's and there was no way I could have been involved, I was stuck with it. I wanted to say something but I was afraid of Sunny's reaction, that he might blame me for attacking Megan. That would be a very Sunny thing to do. But as it's turned out he's just told the police a different story altogether.'

'I don't understand,' I say. 'What did Sunny tell them?'

Trevor breaks into a smile again but it's a bitter and acrid one. 'I met Kit outside while he was having a smoking break. Kit says Sunny told the police I wasn't there at all. He told them that he found Megan out of it in an armchair, didn't think anything of it and then walked off to his grandmother's flat to stay the night. Despite a browbeating from Summers, Sunny's sticking to his story no matter what and without his evidence, there's nothing Summers can do with me. But of course, Sunny might not stick to his story, in a month or six months or six years, he'll suddenly 'remember' I was in Megan's flat when she injected herself with the fatal dose and it was me who did it, just to get at you via me. It's just a game to him, he's enjoying himself, the same way he enjoyed destroying us. You know why he never expressed a view on where he was to live after Megan died? He told me he knew you'd win the fight with Rose and Kit. He didn't need to express a view. He knew he was coming here whatever happened.'

It all sounds very plausible but I'm beyond the truth and the plausible stage now. On the other hand, despite his experience in the matter, Trevor has never been able to lie very well. He just doesn't have it in him. He is what he appears, a nice random from the burbs who's made some very bad decisions because he's too weak to make the right ones. But then I can talk about making bad decisions.

'You're telling me you didn't kill Megan?'

He's outraged and his fury is completely convincing. 'Of course I didn't kill her. Your nephew did! He's never admitted it and I don't know whether he planned it or not but it was him! I know it was. Megan told me she was attacked by Sunny. What did that mean if he wasn't responsible for stabbing her with that syringe? Why do you think I didn't want him in the house in the first place! You have to remember that I was in Megan's flat and I know what he's like. He's contorted with hatred and he's sly and cunning with it. The only person he hated more than Megan is you, for whatever reason, perhaps because you're his mother's sister. I don't know what's going on in his head.'

His anger has exhausted him. 'If you don't believe my version of what happened, speak to Summers. He's coming to see you anyway.'

'I'll save him the trouble and go and see him himself.'

'Pack a bag and come with me. It's not safe for you to stay here on your own while Sunny's on the loose,' he pleads.

'He's not on the loose. Kit's got him on a lead now, he's staying with him.'

Trevor looks at me in despair but says no more. He gets up and goes to the door. Before he leaves, I ask him one final question. 'Is that everything? What other things about you and Megan have you kept secret?'

He avoids my eyes and whispers, 'I'm tired and I've done enough confessing for one day.'

He walks out, his weary legs carrying him down the garden path.

Trevor's right, Summers does want to speak to me. He sounds rather shamefaced when he calls and admits that Megan's death was rather more 'complicated' than had first appeared and that my suspicions on the matter might have been well founded. He'd like to clarify a few things before taking his investigation further. He's a nice guy and is obviously a bit reluctant to tell me that there are 'sensitive' matters in connection with 'inter-family relations' that I might find rather 'upsetting'.

'You mean that my husband was having sex with my sister?'

He's embarrassed. 'That's one avenue we need to explore, yes.'

He asks if he can snatch a few hours' sleep and then send a car over to fetch me. We agree that we'll meet at lunchtime. But our plans are disturbed. Just as I'm putting the phone down, there's a screech of tyres on the road outside my house. Looking out of the window, it's to see a high-end saloon pulling up. Out of it comes Kit, who leaves the keys in the ignition and engine running. He pushes the gate open and huffs and puffs his way up to the door, which he hammers on so that the whole house feels like it's vibrating. When I open up he grabs my arm and his thick fingers dig into my flesh so hard I yelp with pain.

'We've got a problem and you're coming with me.'

# Chapter 47

Kit barges his way in like a man possessed. He looks anxiously around the house before turning his eyes on me. 'Are you still standing here? Why aren't you putting a coat on?'

'Because I'm not going anywhere, that's why.'

He doesn't argue, just pushes me up against a wall so that my shoulders judder. 'You know what I'm like, Josie, so don't yank my chain, just get your coat and play nice.'

I've never seen Kit with his mask off before. I've heard about it from Megan but never experienced it first hand. He a frightening man, truly his son's father. My cheek is flecked with spittle where he's leaned into my face. 'We'll play nice here, Kit, by you getting your hands off me and leaving immediately. Summers is sending a car over and if you're still here when it arrives, I'll tell the cops to pick you up for assault.'

He turns his head and listens for a moment like an animal picking up a scent while stalking its prey. 'Is there anyone else in the house?'

It crosses my mind to say yes. 'It doesn't make any difference to you one way or the other, now get out.'

He shakes his head in anger. 'I haven't got time for this.'

He spins me round and clasps one hand over my mouth so I can't breathe, never mind shout or scream. He sweeps me off my feet like I'm a rag doll. He's slightly bowed, carrying me down the path like a werewolf with his victim while I make desperate but futile attempts to bite his hand and kick him. I'm shaken and bounced around until I realise where I'm going, it's into the back of the car. Before he throws me in, he whispers into my ear, 'Don't create on the back seat, don't shout, don't scream, don't kick, if you do, I'll pull over and punch you unconscious, you understand? Keep your head down, this is a borrowed car, if you know what I mean, the police might be looking for it.' He adds almost as an afterthought, 'You'll thank me later.'

He throws me on to the back seat, gets in the front, locks the doors, and takes off at speed.

I've read articles and seen documentaries about kidnappings. They say you always get one chance to escape and when that moment comes, you have to take it no matter what the cost because you won't get another. In the meantime, you play along to calm things down. You try to start a dialogue with your kidnapper. But Kit ignores my gentle, almost friendly, questions about what he's doing, why he's doing it and where we're going. Instead, he snaps occasionally, 'shut up' and 'keep your head down', and eventually my negotiation attempts are abandoned.

I can't fit what he's doing into what I know about Megan's death but I knew all along he must have had something to do with it. It might have been in concert with his friend 'Trev' or his 'boy' Sunny but he was bound to be involved. He's just the sort who would be. While I wait for my one chance to escape, it crosses my mind that deep down everything that has happened was foreseeable and the true colours of the people around me were flying all along. Both Megan and I knew she'd die with her boots on, that Kit would have something to do with it and that perhaps Trevor was too weak not to fall into the sort of traps that someone like Megan would dig for him. I always knew that Sunny resented me, only not how much, and my attempts to salve my conscience over my sister by taking him in were always doomed to disaster. In an acid moment as Kit throws the car around the road, it sinks in.

I'm as much to blame for this as anyone.

The car slows down to a crawl and finally to a stop. Kit isn't happy, leaning out of his window to shout at someone. 'Get out of the way! Or I'll make you!'

This is my chance. I turn round on the backseat, join both feet together and use them to hit one of the windows as hard as I can in an effort to break it. It doesn't even rattle. I pull myself up to the window and use my fists to hammer on it, screaming 'help' to attract the attention of passers-by. There are several of them walking by our stationary car. One is a mum pushing a pram who looks at me and then away again in embarrassment. An elderly man with a walking stick and a dog doesn't even seem to notice the woman screaming and hitting the car he's shuffling past. Two schoolboys look at me and look away again.

Kit is beyond angry now. His screaming at me to shut up and get down is louder than my own howling. He puts the car into reverse and shunts into the one behind, forward again to hit the one in front, back again for another shunt and finally, having found a space, the car lurches forward and takes off down the street, horn blaring so hard it shakes my body. His voice sounds calmer. 'You're a little spitfire, Josie, but that's enough please. Get back down and shut up. You've been warned.'

My one chance and it's gone and with the passing of that there's nothing left to do except to lie down and rest my head and wait for what comes next. Occasionally, I steal a look out of the window. We're on a main road but we're in the deep countryside, driving from nowhere to nowhere. I don't know how long it takes but eventually the car slows down and begins to twist and turn on a road before being parked up. Kit tells me to keep down for a minute and gets out of the car, walking around it as if looking for something. When he's done, he unlocks the door and climbs inside, sighing with relief. He lights a cigarette while I check the surroundings.

We're in a car park outside a nondescript block that appears to be a hotel, the sort used by travelling salesmen, delivery drivers and the cheaper sort of unfaithful husband. It looks like we're in the middle of nowhere. I turn to my kidnapper. 'What are you doing, Kit?'

'I'm booking you into this hotel for your own good. You have to give me a solemn promise that you'll stay here until I tell you it's safe to leave. You have to promise me not to call the police, not to start shouting and screaming and not to do anything else stupid. If you do that, we'll be alright.'

He nods to show that he agrees with himself, as if this is all perfectly reasonable behaviour.

'I'm not doing any of that. Now unlock the doors and let me go.'

His expression is one of hurt innocence tinged with anger. 'You really are an ungrateful bitch, do you know that? So up your own rear end, so pleased with yourself. Say what you like about Megan, she was never up her own rear end, never pleased with herself. I've stolen a car to drive you here and if the cops catch up with me, I'm in serious trouble. I've got a girlfriend and a kid on the way. I could go to jail. Show some gratitude for what I'm doing. We've got a big problem and I'm trying to help you out. You have to stay in this hotel. I know this place, you'll be safe here.'

'What is our big problem?'

He looks furtive again. 'If you promise on your honour to stay here, I'll tell you.'

I've got no problem with lying to a violent thug like Kit. 'OK, I promise.'

He relaxes. 'Good.'

He unlocks the doors and escorts me into the hotel and books a room for me for an indefinite period and pays for the first week in cash. The receptionist looks at me with suspicion because she notices I've got no luggage but she says nothing. She probably thinks I'm a prostitute. Kit helps himself to a piece of paper from the desk and takes me to the bar where he buys us two coffees. He doesn't appear to be in any hurry to tell me what our serious problem is so it's left to me to prompt him. 'I'm not staying here unless you tell me what all this is about.'

He sighs with what looks like a guilty face. 'I'll be honest with you, this is all my fault. The thing is I know Sunny killed Megan and I can prove it. The trouble is Sunny's on the loose and I think he's coming for you next.'

# Chapter 48

'It's all my fault.'

Poor Kit. It seems as if we have something in common after all. 'How do you know he killed Megan?'

He tells me the story. 'Last night I had to sit with Sunny while that cop Summers was interviewing him. Apparently, Summers had a tip-off from someone that Trevor was responsible for doing in Megan.' Kit starts laughing. 'I mean, would a soft prat like your Trevor actually kill anyone?' He adds in a hurry, 'No disrespect, obviously.'

'None taken.'

He goes on. 'Anyway, Sunny insisted that Trevor was never there, Megan did it herself, Sunny was used to her doing drugs, so he didn't call anyone while she was passed out, he just went to stay with my mum at her flat as usual. He wouldn't be moved on that version of what happened. But Summers had plenty of other questions for him like who sold Megan the heroin she used. Sunny said he had no idea. He thought it was whoever she normally bought her drugs from. And you know, I had a think about that afterwards because it's an interesting question. She didn't use heroin or needles, so where did they come from? The most likely explanation is that one of her druggie friends left them there. Trouble is, it's not like druggie people to leave their stuff with others because it'll probably end up purloined. So, I decided to look into that myself when Summers let me and Sunny go.'

No one else appeared to have asked that question at the time either and it was a good one. Summers had made his mind up from the start that Megan's death was self-inflicted and he told me he didn't press Sunny on the subject out of respect for the grieving son.

Kit's accused me of being pleased with myself and now it's his turn. 'I know where she usually bought her drugs from, it was that scrag-end boyfriend of hers who goes by the name of Dixie. I made a few phone calls to some old friends of mine who are still in the business to find out where he might be. He goes to this café before spending the day in the betting shop and juggling drugs by night. After Summers was finished with Sunny, I drove us both over in the van to the caff where Dixie has his breakfast. I left Sunny in the van and went inside to have a word with Dixie and asked him if he'd sold the gear to Megan. Of course he denied it but when you've been around as long as I have, you know when you're being lied to. So I took my guy out to the gents, which is in a little courtyard at the back of the place, and beat the truth out of him. Dixie says he didn't sell the smack to Megan. He gave it to Sunny instead because Sunny asked him for some but wouldn't say why. That puts a rather different spin on things.

'When I got back to the van and had a word with Sunny on the subject, there was no need to beat the truth out of him. He admitted taking the stuff from Dixie with a view to killing Megan with it. He was upset because Megan had found out about my little plan to take us all out to Spain together. He blamed you for that for some reason. He just waited for an evening when there were a number of different people in the flat and a number of different rows going on to give him cover. When the right evening came, he jabbed Megan with the needle. Sunny didn't seem to understand what the problem was. Megan's gone so we can all go to Spain together. As you can imagine that left me with a bit of a problem.'

It left Megan with a bit of a problem as well but that doesn't seem to be troubling Kit. Indeed, it's only me that seems to be troubled by it at all. 'What's the problem? Getting Sunny to confess to the police? He doesn't seem to have any problem confessing to others. Perhaps Summers can beat a confession out of him?'

My sarcasm goes over his head. 'No, I'm not worried about that. The thing is, Josie, the truth has to come out now, it's just a question of how that truth is presented, that's all. My plan was to go and see my solicitor and put a story together for my boy, you know, Megan was attacking him so it was self-defence or justifiable homicide or something. You have to remember the poor kid was traumatised by living in that flat with his mother, you can't really blame him for this. Unfortunately, I messed up by stopping to get us a burger on the way to my solicitor. While I was in the joint fetching our breakfast, the little bastard climbed into the driver's seat of my van and drove it off. I taught him to drive when he was ten. Now, he's out there on the loose. The thing is, I'm sure he wouldn't come after you but we can't take that chance. You stay here until I track him down. After that, I'll take him to my solicitor and then ship him over to see Summers with a story.'

Finally, something like the truth is emerging. I know why Sunny wanted Megan dead. What I don't know is why he wants me dead.

Kit fetches paper from reception and asks me to write a note that says I've gone away which he'll pin to my front door in case Sunny decides to come looking for me there. 'Are we agreed?'

Everyone else has a plan, so I have one of my own. It's to agree with Kit and then, when he's gone, to ring Summers and explain what's happened. I'll see what Summers says about my next move. 'Sure.'

Kit picks up the keys to his stolen vehicle and heads out to the car to hunt for the son who can't be blamed for any of this. Meanwhile, I ring Summers. There's no answer so I leave a message asking him to ring me back directly, it's urgent. I almost forget to add that Sunny killed Megan, although presumably he already knows if Trevor's told them the full story of his visit to the flat that evening. On the bed that's slightly damp and feels as if it's stuffed with hay I try to have a nap while waiting for Summers to return my call, but it won't come. When you finally get a diagnosis for a mystery illness it might not mean an end to the pain or discomfort but it does at least mean you know what you're suffering from and you can look forward to a recovery one day. Thanks to Kit, Trevor and Sunny himself, I know now more or less what happened to Megan and why. Perhaps if Kit were here he'd tell me that it wasn't my fault, that I was traumatised by my relationship with my sister.

But part of the diagnosis is still missing. Trevor told me that he'd done enough confessing for now, which leaves something unconfessed. I wake with a start from a half-sleep of stalled confessions when Summers calls me back. My finger moves across the screen of my phone but I don't take the call. He won't know what Trevor's not telling me, but there's someone out there who will. Nor do I listen to the message he leaves. I get off my bed and wash my face in the scummy sink before going down to reception and asking them to call me a cab.

The cab takes me back home through the countryside. We pass the spot where I blew my one and only chance to escape and where Kit rammed other cars in his own escape bid. There is still glass in the road. The streets slowly become familiar and eventually we pull up outside the house that I shared with my family what feels like a very long time ago.

When I get out of the cab, I stand outside my home and look at it for a long time. Twilight has fallen and the road is becoming dark. Kit has clearly been to pay a visit as the note I wrote for him saying I'd gone away is still flapping in a chilly breeze. All the curtains are drawn but then they were never opened this morning before Kit kidnapped me. It crosses my mind to ring Summers and get his assistance, but if I do that then I will probably never find out what is unconfessed and why Sunny hates me so much. He's still got things to tell me and I'm convinced he's in there. There's no evidence from the outside to suggest my nephew has returned, but I know he has. He's waiting for me. I put my phone back in my pocket and walk up to the front door.

# Chapter 49

'Sunny!'

The hallway, the stairs and the empty, gloomy rooms echo his name. 'Sunny! Where are you? I want to talk to you!'

The house stays silent. But he's in here all right. The armchair I used to barricade the front door to stop my husband gaining entry the night before is still sitting nearby. Its wheels scrape the floor as it's moved back into position to stop Sunny escaping, if that's what he decides to do. 'You said you knew all about Trevor, you said you knew a lot about a lot of things. Why don't you come out and share what you know with me? You must remember now, there's no point in not doing so. The police know it was you, Trevor's told them. I've told them.'

When he doesn't answer, I gingerly poke my head around the doors downstairs to see if he's lying in wait somewhere. He isn't. 'You want to blame me for something? That's OK, we can talk about that.'

Still silence. Sunny likes to play games, though, we all know that by now. I switch on a light in our dining room where the presents given by grateful parents and pupils sat on the table a few months ago, all saying how great I am. I didn't believe it then and I believe it even less now. The light doesn't come on. The lightbulb has been removed. In the other rooms, all the lightbulbs from the fittings and lamps have gone. There's still enough daylight to find my way around but it won't last much longer. I refuse to be scared of this scrawny little runt who murdered my sister and I refuse to join in with Kit, who's already thinking about how to get him off any charges. I have to stay angry because if I don't, I will become afraid and run away.

I've run away from his mother my whole life and I'm done with running away from her son as well. 'Sunny! Come out you little coward! Big tough guy who goes around killing people and wrecking families that have never done you any harm. Too scared to show your face?'

My attempts to start a dialogue with this sly and cunning child are proving no more successful than my attempts to start a dialogue with his father in the stolen car. The back door is also still barricaded along with the one at the front. In a cupboard under the stairs is a portable flashlamp that we keep along with other items for emergencies. We don't have emergencies in our house so it's never been used and it doesn't work any longer. I'm reduced to going back to the dining room and collecting a silver candlestick, an heirloom from Trevor's family which has spokes for five candles. We've got five candles in our emergency box which I light. I go to the foot of the stairs.

'Megan! Tell your kid to show himself!'

She doesn't answer either. I'm reluctant to go for the stairs for fear I'll be grabbed from behind. The candlelight flickers on the walls and banisters. Staying as angry as I can, I take a deep breath as my feet carry me up the stairs. Once again, after poking my head into empty rooms, I begin to wonder if he really is here after all. It would be classic Sunny to come to the house, remove all the lightbulbs and then leave again so I'm left spending all night searching for him. I pull down the ladder to the attic and the candlestick trembles in my hand as I go up into Trevor's office. There's no sign of him anywhere. But from the skylight it's possible to see out on to a neighbouring street. At the end of it, Kit's van is parked under a tree. Sunny drove himself here and he hasn't driven away again.

There's no point in repeatedly calling his name. When I come down the ladder from the attic, the candlelight shudders with each step and the shadows of my own body it throws on the wall make me think that Sunny is waiting for me on the landing. I raise my hand to defend myself, but once again I'm alone. 'Sunny!'

He could keep this up all night, this game.

It crosses my mind to threaten Sunny by warning him I'll call his father, so Sunny would face the sort of beating Dixie suffered if he didn't come out and tell me what I want to know. But I can't, even now I'm still me. There's been enough violence of one sort or another and there can't be any more.

I'm convinced I hear footsteps downstairs and hurry down, candlelight waving backwards and forwards, a garish lightshow. After another fruitless search, a way to flush him out finally occurs to me. In the living room the grate of the fireplace is filled with kindling and lumps of wood. Some firelighters are on the mantelpiece and with the help of a poker I start a fire that soon lights up the room and radiates heat. I throw what's in the emergency box out on to the dining room floor and carry it upstairs. He's listening somewhere, wondering what I'm doing and he's soon going to find out. In Sunny's room are his books and some of the ones that are most thumbed go into the box. On his desk are his stories and they go into the box too. On my desk are the stories that my colleague Mary gave me that raised the red flags. It adds fuel to my anger that I couldn't face reading them at the time. They join my collection of my nephew's reading and writing materials. When I go downstairs, box in one hand and candlestick in the other, I do so slowly, one step at a time.

Now it's him who's wondering rather than me. What's she up to?

I throw the box down by the blazing fireplace and take my candlestick out into the hall. 'Are you cold, Sunny? Do you want to come see what's on the fire? It's your books and your stories, come down and get warm, Sunny, as they go up in smoke.'

Back by the fireplace, I take a batch of his stories and throw them page by page into the flames. His precious books are torn to pieces and they join the bonfire. There is movement in the corner of my eye and with one movement the candles are blown out and a chilly hand reaches out of the darkness to grab my wrist. Now there's only the light of the fire. Sunny's face reflects the flames, flickering orange and black. His voice is petulant and whiny like a little child's. It's so easy to forget that he is a child. 'What are you doing that for? They're mine.'

His grip is icy on my arm and he won't let go. Occasionally the flames show what he's holding tight in his spare hand. It's the jagged knife Trevor recovered from his room.

'I thought we took that from you.'

Sunny looks at the knife. 'You dropped it on the floor when you cut your leg. I picked it up. It is mine after all.'

We both know why we're here. He wants to kill me and I want to know why he wants to kill me. I'm Jesse the wolf. There are other secrets that he might finally choose to 'remember' and share, particularly what Trevor was too tired to confess. But neither of us appears to know what to do now we're finally reunited in the house he tried to ruin. 'Your father tells me you admitted to killing your mother. Trevor says he's given the police a full statement on what happened. It's over now, Sunny.'

Is he shrugging or is that the fire playing on the shape of his body? 'I don't care. My dad's been put away, they can put me away somewhere, lock me up, it doesn't matter. I know what it's like. You get four walls, a roof and a bed. There are three meals a day, other people to talk to who are in the same boat as you and they have libraries. It's better than that rat hole I was locked up in at my mother's place.' He adds pointedly, 'And it's better than living here.'

I'm only here to find out his secrets, I'm not sure that it matters what happens after that. 'Do you want to tell me why you have this grudge against me? Why you've done these things to me and my family?'

He laughs. 'I told you, I can't remember.'

This is too much for me. I've risked my life to come here, only to find he still can't remember. I use my spare hand to cuff his head. He stumbles backwards, yelping with pain, dragging me with him on to the sofa. We're face to face now. He swings his arm round and holds the blade to my cheek. 'I told you I can't remember.'

I want to fight him for the knife and threaten him with it. But I can't. 'Please, remember.'

We're like two lovers by the firelight and he decides to share the secret like a lover would.

'Alright, alright, I suppose it doesn't matter now.'

But he doesn't get to say. There's a ferocious hammering on the door knocker, followed by more hammering on the woodwork as if an iron fist is being used. Before we're given any clue as to who this is, Sunny whispers in fear, 'I bet that's my dad.'

'Josie! Josie! Open the front door, I know you're in there! Open the front door or I'll kick it in!'

It is his father. Sunny's voice is tinged with dread and he loosens his grip on my arm. 'You better open it or he definitely will kick it in. That's what he's like.'

# Chapter 50

The door rattles in the frame as Kit kicks it. I had one chance to find out what Sunny wanted to tell me and I've wasted it and there won't be another one. He won't tell me now, I know he won't.

'Where is he? Is he here?' Kit flicks the light switches when he's let in. 'Why aren't these working?'

'Sunny took the lightbulbs. He's in the living room. Watch out, he's got a knife.'

Kit mutters, 'The lightbulb trick? He probably learned that off me.'

Kit's fury when he's let into the house is frightening but it's divided equally between me and Sunny. 'You never listen to people. You were told to stay where you were. It was obvious he'd come here and lie in wait for you but no, Miss Degrees has to come home again. Good job you were dumb enough to get the hotel to book a cab and give them your address otherwise you'd be dead by now.'

Sunny climbs over the sofa in an effort to escape his father's wrath but Kit's too quick for him, grabbing his leg, pulling him back and cuffing him around the head. 'You little bastard, you can give me that for a start.'

He seizes the knife from Sunny's hand and throws it on the floor. He takes his son by the scruff of his neck and jerks him straight and upright, displaying him to me. 'You don't get it, Josie.

There's only one way to deal with kids like this and that's to out-thug them. You understand? They don't want your help or support. This is what they want.' He shakes Sunny like a rag doll.

'While we're on the subject, you should have learned from Megan and out-thugged your sister as well. Feeling guilty all the time because of some silly accident when you were kids. This is how you should have treated her when she came round on the cadge.' Sunny gets another violent shake to show me how Megan should have been treated.

He turns to Sunny. 'Alright, son, you're coming with me. We'll go to my solicitor in the morning and we'll try and make sure we can limit courtroom damage on your mother's death. In the meantime, if you go AWOL again, I'll break your legs.'

He drags a sullen Sunny towards the front door but I stop him. 'He can't go yet. He wants to tell me things. If he leaves now, I might never find out.'

'What things?'

Even while he's being pulled around by his father, Sunny can't help an amused look. But it's over now for him and he'll tell me what he knows, I'm sure of it. 'Just give me five minutes with him.'

Kit gives him another shake. 'Tell your aunt what she wants to know.'

Sunny looks at me and then shrugs. Kit drags him backwards and shoves his son into the living room. 'I've got a better idea, let me have five minutes with him and I'll find out anything you want to know.'

Kit takes me firmly by the arm, drags me away and puts me out of the front door like a naughty cat. I struggle to get back in but he slams the door on me. I yell through the letterbox, 'Leave him alone! He's only a kid, don't hurt him!'

From behind the door Kit calls out, 'You're never going to learn, are you?'

Kit is hurting him. I hear Sunny's yelps, cries and appeals for help as he's knocked around inside our house. No amount of my hammering on the door or shouting through the letterbox makes it stop. I could bring this to a halt by summoning help from the neighbours or calling the police, but when the battering Sunny's taking stops and I hear him whimpering that he'll talk if his father stops hurting him, I pause for a moment. Ramming my ear up against the open letterbox, it's clear the violence has ended and this is a father and son talking to each other, but it's not clear what's being said. Words and names are used but they're not joined up. Sunny mentions my husband's name several times. Kit's voice is raised with a sneer. 'Trevor did that? You're kidding me? I didn't think he had it in him.'

The voices rise and fall until slowly they fade away and silence descends inside, broken only by my shock at hearing Sunny weeping, until that stops too.

'Kit! What's happening? Open the door!'

There's no answer, nor is there one when Sunny's name is called. It's as if there's no one in there any more. It crosses my mind that they may have escaped out the back, over the fence and back to where Kit's van is parked. I hurry down the side of the house, peering through windows to see what's happening until I reach the back door. It's still barricaded on the other side so there's been no escape. I can't see inside over the furniture and it's in darkness anyway but there's enough light from neighbours' houses to make me think that it might be possible to see. I fetch our step ladder and prop it up against the wall. Over the garden fence another step ladder is being erected and a neighbour's face appears at the top of it.

'I thought I heard something. Is everything all right, Josie? We're hearing a lot of noise. I texted a little while ago to see if you're OK and you didn't answer.'

Even now, in a situation like this, my desire for respectability and determination to avoid embarrassment get the better of me. 'Yes, everything's fine.'

'OK. Have you locked yourself out or something?'

I leap on this. 'Yes, that's right, I've locked myself out.'

'Do you want your spare key?'

We all keep each other's spare keys on this road, it's that kind of place. 'Do you have it?'

'Of course, wait one moment.'

The neighbour disappears and returns shortly and passes me the key over the fence. 'Are you sure you're all right? You don't look very well at all. Do you want me to call someone?'

I don't want this conversation now. What I want is to know what Sunny told Kit. 'No, it's fine.'

Hurrying along the side of the house, peering in through the windows again and seeing nothing, I get to the front door and try to put the key in the lock. But the door moves under the key. It's open and left ajar. That can only have happened from inside. Using my foot to open the door, I call Sunny and Kit's names but get no answer. For a brief moment, I remember my responsibilities to my family and myself. There's no need for me to go into this house. Even if the pair of them are still in there, it will serve no useful purpose. The right thing to do now is to call Summers and let him sort it out. But if Summers gets the answers that he wants that may mean that there will be no answers for me.

'Sunny! Kit!'

No answer. In the living room the fireplace is still the only light in the house. I open the door and step inside where the room is full of strangeness. The smell of burned paper and books hangs in the air like musk while the fire blazes in the grate. A crushed Sunny is sitting in an armchair. He's obviously been crying. The firelight is reflected on his wet cheeks and sunken eyes. Kit, meanwhile, is fast asleep on the sofa. Sunny doesn't seem to notice me enter the room. When he does, he says softly, 'I knew you'd come back. The open front door should have been a warning that I was waiting for you but my dad was right, you never learn.'

'What's the matter with your father?' Sunny says nothing, so I give Kit a gentle and then violent shake. He doesn't awaken. 'What have you done to him?'

Sunny sparks into life. He raises his hand and only then do I see he's holding the jagged knife in his palm. 'You did that! It's all your fault! You can't blame me for this. If you hadn't made him beat me up, it wouldn't have happened!'

There's blood on the knife he's holding. When I pull Kit's heavy body over the first thing I feel is a stickiness on my hands and fingers and only as my eyes adjust to the flickering darkness do I realise that Kit has a deep wound in his neck where he's been stabbed. He's dead.

'Don't look at me like that!' Sunny sounds like a cross between a petulant child and a professional assassin. 'I didn't come here to do my dad. It was to get you. You're to blame for all this. You're to blame for everything.'

# Chapter 51

'It's all your fault.'

These whimpered words appear to be Sunny's final words on the subject. He puts the knife down on the floor. Neither of us knows what to do next and for a half-minute I stand while he sits and we don't make a move or a noise.

'We need to call an ambulance, Sunny. Your father is badly wounded.'

He turns his sunken eyes on me. 'No, he's not. He's dead. It might be dark but you can see that. You might be evil but you're not stupid.'

The sensible thing to do is to tell him I'm leaving and that he has to stay where he is until the police and an ambulance arrive. But I left sensible behind a long time ago, the moment I realised my sister was murdered, or perhaps even further back when I pushed her under the wheels of that car. I'm not leaving, not until he tells me what I need to know.

'Sunny, is it OK for me to pick the knife up and then we can talk? Is that alright with you?'

His tear-stained face is orange, red and contorted with hatred. 'This is you negotiating again, isn't it? Even now, when you're about to join my parents on the other side, you still want to negotiate.

Why can't you be a human being for once in your life? Why can't you be real?'

He raises his hand to threaten me with the knife and is nonplussed to see it isn't there. He hurriedly reaches over and picks the weapon up from the floor. He climbs out of the armchair and comes face to face with me so his back is to the fireplace and his features are hidden. But I don't need to actually see the hate on his face, it passes through the air between us like a bitter wind. He presses the flat of the blade against my chest. 'If you were a real person, none of this would have happened.'

He doesn't need prompting any more, he's totally out of control. Finally, this is my chance. 'Why? What wouldn't have happened if I were a real person?'

He pushes the flat of the blade harder against me so I can feel its outline against my flesh. 'If you were a real person, you'd have let the social take me out of that hell hole of a flat we lived in, away from my mother and her sicko friends, away from all the muck and let me go and live with my dad or in a kid's home or a hostel or anything. Anywhere, anywhere, would have been better, a zoo would have been better. But no, instead of supporting me, you "supported" me by writing letters on her behalf, making excuses for her, turning up to meetings and using arguments with the social that she would never have thought of for herself, so that I was kept in that prison where she stole my books and phones and let her friends treat me like a dog. You were calling in favours from all your friends who worked in the business and it worked because you speak their language and know how to stroke their fur. You know what really sticks in my throat? You weren't even doing it for me nor even for my mother, you were only doing it for yourself because you felt bad about shoving her under a car when you were kids. But that's about the only real thing you've ever done, it's just a shame you didn't make a better job of it and save us all this trouble. You're a fake, you're a phoney.'

Lobo's spelt it out for me. 'You should have said something before now, Sunny.'

'Said something? Did I have to say I didn't like it there? Does a homeless person have to say he doesn't like sleeping in shop doorways? How stupid are you, Mrs Teacher?'

Deep down, I know he's right. Perhaps not in the way he thinks he is or for the reasons he thinks he is. But he is right. 'You should have said something after your mother died. You didn't need to come here and do what you did. You could have taken your revenge on me alone.'

He has a think about that. 'I feel bad about Tova and Rodney.' He has another think. 'But not about Trevor. He was in on my misery as well. He was giving her blood money to keep her going. You didn't know why he was doing that though and I'll bet he's not going to tell you either.'

I think I already know why Trevor was giving Megan money, but Sunny knows for sure so he can confirm it. 'No, he hasn't told me yet.'

Sunny bursts out laughing and his voice turns back into that of a mischievous child. 'Because Trevor and my mother had a kid together, a girl. My mother even had the nerve to call her Sunette, so it was Sunny and Sunette. I bet Trevor and my mother didn't tell you that.'

He's finally remembered.

I slap his face very hard. Sunny feels his cheek with his free hand but doesn't seem to mind. 'That's more like it. You're acting human now.'

I slap his face again, even harder. 'You're a liar.'

'Yeah, ring your cousins back home, they'll tell you about it. You can go and see Sunette if you want. You remember when we went off to the Caribbean for a year, mother and me? That's why she went, to have Sunette out there so you wouldn't know. Trevor paid for it all. Of course, she didn't care about you knowing, but Trevor did. He said he wasn't going to pay for Sunette and the rest of it unless it was all kept quiet. So my mum farmed Sunette out to one of your cousins. It's all true, ask Trevor, he'll probably admit it now, he's got nothing to lose. Of course Mum kept the money Trev gave her for Sunette. Because of course she kept it.'

I shove him violently with both hands. He doesn't expect this and stumbles backwards on to Kit's dead body. He lunges at me with the knife, which slices my arm. The blood streams and bubbles, running down on to my hands and my poor limb begins to grow stiff almost immediately. I don't care though. All the violence and anger that's been stoppered up in me since my violent and angry attack on Megan that ended with her in the road wells up, and Sunny, Megan and Trevor are my targets. With my good arm, I take another swing at him and this one catches him on the side of his face. He tumbles, mewling, but I don't wait until he gets up, delivering two of the heaviest kicks I can muster to his body. He's lost his grip on the knife. He's had his revenge, now I must have mine for myself and my children and perhaps even for my husband. He crawls around the side of the sofa out of my reach and rises again on the other side with the knife back in his hands. He shouts but with what sounds like a note of regret and apology, 'This is all your fault.'

No, it's not my fault.

I climb over Kit's dead body and even though Sunny punches me again, I deliver one final kick, which catches him on the chin and he falls, groaning, in front of the roaring fire while I fall back over the sofa on to the floor below. Stunned, I realise he's got the chance to finish me off. But he doesn't come. He's lying prone in front of the fire, clutching his face and sobbing again. Struggling to my feet, I hold my side with my good arm and see that it wasn't a punch that hit me, it's a stab wound, but it doesn't look that deep. I find the knife where Sunny dropped it and stand over him with it. My sliced arm is stiffening now but even so I manage to fasten both hands around the knife handle. I raise it over my head to plunge it into Sunny.

He looks up at me, still choking with tears. 'Yeah, go on, do it, stab me up. You'll be doing me a favour.'

Still stunned, shocked, in pain and uncertain what I'm doing, stabbing him seems to be the right thing to do. Why is everyone else in this world allowed to be angry and take their revenge? Why am I not allowed? For a brief moment, it seems that rather than Sunny's life flashing before him as he's about to die, it's mine flashing before me. In those moments, rather than Sunny lying before me, it seems it's my sister Megan lying in the road, screaming 'Look what you've done! Look what you've done!'

Look at what I did. While Sunny lies before me, it feels like Megan has joined us both and is standing on my shoulder, whispering 'Look at what you're doing. Do you want to get angry again like last time?'

Still gripping my knife, I turn and slash at the thin air where Megan's standing.

When Sunny sees my exhausted arm drop to my side after knifing at nothing and that I'm not going to kill him, he's disgusted.

'You're pathetic.'

# Chapter 52

It's been a month since Kit was murdered and Sunny tried to murder me. It's only a couple of months since Megan was murdered, although that already feels like a lifetime ago. I use the words 'murdered' but there appears to be some doubt about that. It's my understanding that Kit's solicitor is already trying to argue that 'manslaughter' might be a better way of describing what happened to Megan and Kit. Certainly, in the case of Megan, she's arguing that the balance of Sunny's mind was disturbed after years of abuse when the killing happened. As for Kit, the solicitor is suggesting that a better way of looking at things might be that Sunny was acting in self-defence because his father was beating him. On the slicing of my arm and the jab to my chest, the solicitor thinks 'wounding with intent' might be a better charge than attempted murder. That's if I want to press charges at all, and the solicitor is floating the idea that there's no point when Sunny is already on the hook for a couple of killings anyway. My nephew, meanwhile, has freely admitted his role in everything. Now it's over, he doesn't seem to care about what happens next, nor that I survived his attempt to finish the job.

Perhaps Kit's solicitor is right. Others aren't so sure. Summers for one doesn't think so. As he grimly said when he visited me in hospital after I'd spared Sunny's life and the battered boy was arrested in our house while I was wheeled off to A&E, 'That kid was only one more death away from being a serial killer.'

Before my visits to see Sunny, I have to keep reminding myself that he's a thirteen-year-old child, a deeply disturbed boy who's been through things no child should have to endure. Before going into the unit where he's being held, I walk up and down outside the gates, trying to keep this in mind and using it as the background context for what happened to all my nephew's victims, dead or alive. Context is everything and I try to leave my personal feelings out of it. He's not a stranger. He's still my nephew. I still want to support him, however hard that may be.

Others think this is a bad idea. Summers isn't sentimental, telling me that Sunny is a devious, manipulative gaslighter who will soon have me believing that it was me who murdered Megan and Kit. On my first visit to see him, Sunny was emotionally lifeless after what had happened. On later visits, his personality once again veered from that of a child to a teenager to an adult and back again, as if he was no longer sure who he even was any more. Sometimes I hear him say he's the real victim here, on other occasions he takes full responsibility for what he did, at others he seems to be suggesting that he and I are co-collaborators in the death and chaos that started with Megan's death. Us two get it he claims, no one else does.

Today he's repeating, probably verbatim, sentences that he's picked up from counsellors. 'I'm talking to some people while I'm in here. They think I'm suffering from PTSD and borderline personality disorder. They're working it through with me at the moment. Things are clearer now.'

Sunny is sitting on the other side of a table in the visiting room in a secure unit. It's a very civilised place with only a few guards and locks to suggest that anyone is being held here against their will. I'm glad of it. On the table in front of us is the latest book he's reading, interviews from Vietnam war veterans about their experiences. He's been explaining what's happened since he was arrested and today hasn't stopped apologising since I sat down. Presumably, his counsellors have taught him the importance of taking responsibility for your actions. But he sounds sincere enough and I'm not arguing with him about what happened. He still bears the wounds from our fight. There's still an ugly, if fading, bruise on the side of his face where he was punched, but he insists I was totally right to take him down.

'You were angry, it was totally legit. I didn't have to stick the knife in with the thing about Sunette either. I don't know why I told you that, that was just mean.'

'Trevor was going to tell me anyway. Or so he says.'

Sunny rushes to Trevor's defence. 'Be fair, he was probably trying to let you down gently. I mean, I hope you're not going to dump him over this. He's a good guy. A bit soft but still a good guy.'

I tell him not to worry, we're talking and a way forward might always be possible.

'I feel bad about Rodney and Tova.' For the first time he genuinely sounds guilty. 'It was nothing to do with them.'

'No, it wasn't.'

He sees my face and realises that mentioning what my children went through was a bad idea. But he still asks tentatively, 'Are they OK?'

OK? OK after having their home and family wrecked by an intruder with a grudge against their mother and aunt? Once again I have to draw breath and think about context. 'They're resilient children and their parents are supporting them.'

He avoids my eyes. 'Yeah, resilience, that's an important word.'

His voice trails off while I try to remember this is a traumatised kid with a history. My words are genuine. 'And how are you managing, Sunny?'

'Managing what?'

I look around the unit, which is still an institution however civilised. 'Being in here.'

Sunny doesn't seem to understand the question. 'It's OK. The staff are nice enough and they do creative writing and guitar lessons, which passes the time.' He taps his latest book. 'They've got a good library, there's lots to read.' Sunny gestures with his thumb at the outside world beyond the walls. 'Anyway, there's nothing going on for me out there. Let's face it, Josie, I was probably always going to end up in a place like this sooner or later. It was bound to happen.' For a moment, there's a brief flash of the other Sunny's eyes, the one who came to my house to destroy it. 'Be honest, I'm better off in here than I was at my mother's, no one can argue with that. And no disrespect but I'm better off in here than I was at your place. Better off for everyone.'

An officer appears to escort me out but Sunny has a piece of advice for me before I leave, no doubt culled from his reading and sessions with his counsellors. 'You've got to forgive yourself, Josie.'

Is he trying to wind me up? 'Forgive myself? I didn't do anything wrong, Sunny, except to try and support you and my sister.'

He's not trying to wind me up. 'Nah, I'm not talking about that, I mean shoving my mother in front of the car that time. Put your hands up if you like but you can't keep feeling bad about it. It was more of an accident really. You need to move on.'

He's very sure about that. He's not the ideal person to be taking lectures on self-help from but I nod and say I'm trying. 'What about you, Sunny? With the right help, are you going to move on in time?'

He looks forlorn. 'I don't know. Everything just sort of happened. It was like playing Monopoly with Tova and Rodney. By the time they realised I was cheating, it was too late to go back and start the game again. How could things have happened differently? I feel bad about everything but I don't know what I could have done about it with the way things were playing out.'

When I leave, Sunny is still sitting at the table where we talked. His face is confused, unhappy and drawn as if he were a small child on the street who'd just lost his parents.

# Chapter 53

There's a lot to be said for living in a collection of cliches. In front of the terrace where I'm sitting is an expanse of sand which doesn't really count as a 'golden' beach. Rather it's so white that it almost vibrates on your eyes and you need a pair of sunglasses to view it properly. Beyond that is a sea so blue that the word 'blue' doesn't even begin to do it justice. Above me, palm trees are waving in the breeze and occasionally a coconut falls from one to remind us what these trees did before becoming scenery in a Caribbean holiday. There is sun, of course, so much sun that it almost becomes boring. All this picture really needs is a crew from an advertising agency shouting 'cut' after I've delivered some copy for a travel company.

Paddling in the sea are Rodney, Tova and their half-cousin/half-sister Sunette. Nearby, Sunette's father Trevor is trying to join in the fun but he seems to be surplus to requirements, as he should be to me too. Over the past few months we've done some negotiating. It was suggested to him by someone that he should write me a letter explaining how he and my sister became an item behind my back and how everything unfolded from there. It was long and I only read half of it. It was such a wearily predictable story. Apparently it all started when Trevor was round her flat on one occasion and Megan was upset so he gave her a comforting cuddle. One thing led to another and before either of them were aware, well, you know the drill. Although I doubt if my late sister was unaware, that wouldn't be like her at all. I don't have her version of events, of course, but no doubt she worked out the easiest thing to do was to finish her pregnancy here and then farm out Sunette on the family while collecting child allowance/blackmail money from my dopey and appallingly soft husband.

When I reassembled my family in our new rented home, Trevor was excluded from it. Tova and Rodney weren't happy that their father was being turned into a bedsit/contact-visit dad and in the end neither was I. It was pointless continuing to be angry with him. Sunny was right about that. Trevor's a good person just a weak one, and ultimately it's not his fault he's like that. Trevor did some sincere Sunny-style apologising about what happened. He obviously meant it and in the end I relented. It even amused me a little that Sunny was sticking up for our marriage after he did so much to wreck it. Perhaps that's not his fault either. I can't make my mind up about that.

On my laptop is a newspaper account of Sunny's trial, which finished yesterday. Obviously, he was anonymous because of his age, but he put on a bravura performance for the judge and was sentenced to indefinite detention in a secure mental health unit. Summers warned me to get ready for Sunny being back on the streets much, much sooner than I would expect. Sunny himself, meanwhile, has assured me on one of my regular visits that he's 'processed' his trauma and is no longer any threat to me or my family. He's also asking if Tova and Rodney might like to pay him a visit but he can whistle for that.

We came to the Caribbean for three reasons. One was to scatter Megan's ashes as far away as possible from anywhere that might remind me of her. A second was to be out of the country for Sunny's court case. The third was to introduce the family to Sunette, who lives comfortably with one of my distant cousins, who's a doctor. It's ironic really that I took Sunny in on the 'Caribbean' principle that children are taken in by family if necessary, and now the same thing has happened to my stepdaughter/niece Sunette. I was dreading meeting her. My fear was she would look like, and have the same features and tropes as, my sister or Sunny or even my errant husband. In certain ways she does. She's pretty like my sister and clever like Sunny and she loves her books. I soon forget the genetic connection though. Sunette is slightly serious for a little girl but there's no sign she'll be causing any problems later in life, rather the reverse. She gets on well with my children, explaining local things to them while taking the appearance of her father after all these years completely in her stride.

'Sunette!'

When she's summoned, Sunette runs up the beach to where I'm sitting. I don't know why I've called her, perhaps it's the needless worry that there might be something about her that I've missed even though it's clear there isn't. I settle on, 'Are you enjoying playing with Tova and Rodney?'

She doesn't answer at once, maybe she thinks it's a silly question. 'Yes.'

'OK! Just checking!'

She turns to leave but turns back again. 'Aunt Josie, no one calls me Sunette, everyone here calls me Sunny, for short.'

Within reach of my hand is the laptop with the account of my nephew's trial. 'Do you mind if I don't call you Sunny and call you Sunette instead?'

She's perfectly charming about it, nor does she ask me why I prefer it. 'No, I don't mind at all.'

With that she turns and runs down the beach to the sea that's too blue to be called blue.

# ACKNOWLEDGEMENTS

No book is ever written by the author(s) alone and every author owes a big debt to all those who've helped it in their various ways, both great and small, along the way. *Watching You Fall* is no different in that respect to any other. It was our brilliant senior editor at T&M, Sammia Hamer, who first picked up on our idea and helped develop it in its earliest stages and put it on its feet. It was the amazing Arzu Tahsin who helped with the structural work and contributed so much in terms of plot, characters and development. Finally, it was our highly professional and diligent editors Jill Sawyer and Caroline McArthur who flagged the obvious mistakes, holes and ruts in the story. No thanks are too much for the work they did. Then there are the cover designers and everyone else at T&M who have helped and we're truly grateful.

Meanwhile, there are a number of people who've helped without realising over the years – friends, colleagues, acquaintances and professionals who've added to our knowledge and discussed issues with us. To them, too, we owe a debt of gratitude. Finally, readers of our previous books always have input. Their feedback has helped immeasurably to hone our writing and we always welcome it. Many thanks to them too.

# LETTER FROM THE AUTHORS

There's a quote out there somewhere that suggests that guilty people who have something to feel guilty about should actually feel really guilty. There's obviously some truth in that. Accepting responsibility is part of the reparation process. Those who do prison work often say that one of the hardest parts of their job is getting prisoners to accept they've done anything wrong in the first place. The burglar will tell you his victims were insured so what's the problem? The bank robber will claim that banks are robbing people's money themselves. The murderer will maintain that the victim deserved it. If not guilt then certainly some responsibility is in order in such cases. There are, however, different kinds of guilt and Josie's tragedy in our story is that the guilt she feels isn't justified and leaves her wide open to exploitation by her sister.

Her 'crime' is to lose her temper and push her little sister over in the street. In almost all such cases the worst that will happen is a grazed knee and some tears, followed by a stern word from a parent. It's the two sisters' complicity in covering up what happened that lays the ground for their relationship later in life. Josie feels she owes Megan and in a way she does, but she doesn't realise what the consequences of her debt will be. Josie has accepted her sister's 'offer' to cover the incident up and afterwards is trapped within a story that she can't get out of. She could of course get out of it by telling the truth, but feels she can't.

If that was Josie's only issue, it might be manageable, but the first leads onto the second. How much responsibility do we have to take for helping a close family member whose problems are at least partly their own fault but who we love despite everything? Where is the line drawn, so far and no further? How much guilt can we accept when that line is drawn and our loved one spirals downwards, perhaps to death itself? Josie never draws the line until near the end of her sister's life and then blames herself afterwards for having drawn it. Finally, guilt makes her insist on taking in Sunny, even though she quickly comes to realise she'll wreck her own family by doing so. This is where her misdirected guilt ends up. Trevor is no one's idea of the perfect husband but he's proved right all along about his wife's guilt and what it will lead to. Although perhaps that's because he has more facts at his disposal than Josie does.

When author's say goodbye to characters at the end of a story, they often wonder what will happen to them next. Already, some of those involved in the development of the story have been unimpressed by Josie's decision to take Trevor back in the epilogue and we're already worried about what might happen when Sunny is back on the streets. As Dixie suggested, that boy is meant for the gallows. We like to think, though, that with Megan now resting in peace after the truth of her death is revealed that Josie will find some peace herself and be able to move on. We hope so anyway.

# ABOUT THE AUTHORS

Her Majesty Queen Elizabeth II appointed Dreda an MBE in her New Year's Honours' List 2020.

She scooped the CWA's John Creasey Dagger (New Blood) Award for best first-time crime novel in 2005, the first time a Black British author has received this honour.

Ryan and Dreda write across the crime and mystery genre – psychological thrillers, gritty gangland crime and fast-paced action books. *Spare Room*, their first psychological thriller, was a #1 UK and US Amazon Bestseller.

Dreda is a passionate campaigner and speaker on social issues and the arts. She has appeared on television, including *Celebrity Pointless, Celebrity Eggheads, Alan Carr's Adventures with Agatha Christie*, BBC *Breakfast, Sunday Morning Live, Newsnight, The Review Show* and *Front Row Late* on BBC2. Ryan and Dreda performed a specially commissioned monologue for the groundbreaking Sky Arts' *Art 50* on Sky TV.

Dreda is one of twelve international bestselling women writers who have written a reimagined Miss Marple short story for the thrilling bestselling anthology, *Marple*. She talked about this on The Queen's Reading Room.

Dreda has been a guest on many radio shows and presented BBC Radio 4's flagship books programme, *Open Book*. She has written in a number of leading newspapers including the *Guardian* and was thrilled to be named one of Britain's 50 Remarkable Women by Lady Geek in association with Nokia. She is a trustee of the Royal Literary Fund and an ambassador for The Reading Agency.

Some of their books are currently in development as TV and film adaptations.

Dreda's parents are from the beautiful Caribbean island of Grenada. Her name, Dreda, is Irish and pronounced with a long vowel ee sound in the middle.

# Follow the Authors on Amazon

If you enjoyed this book, follow Dreda Say Mitchell and Ryan Carter on Amazon to be notified when the authors release a new book!

To do this, please follow these instructions:

## Desktop:

1) Search for the authors' names on Amazon or in the Amazon App.
2) Click on the authors' names to arrive on their Amazon page.
3) Click the 'Follow' button.

## Mobile and Tablet:

1) Search for the authors' names on Amazon or in the Amazon App.
2) Click on one of their books.
3) Click on the authors' names to arrive on their Amazon page.
4) Click the 'Follow' button.

## Kindle eReader and Kindle App:

If you enjoyed this book on a Kindle eReader or in the Kindle App, you will find the authors' 'Follow' button after the last page.

# PRAISE FOR DREDA SAY MITCHELL & RYAN CARTER

'As good as it gets.'

—Lee Child

'A fast-paced thriller that will keep you guessing until the very last page.'

—Paula Hawkins

'A truly original voice.'

—Peter James

'Thrilling.'

—*Sunday Express* Books of the Year

'Awesome tale from a talented writer.'

—*The Sun*

'Fast-paced and full of twists and turns.'

—*Crime Scene Magazine*